I0544564

Louis L'Amour on Film and Television

ALSO BY ED ANDREYCHUK
AND FROM MCFARLAND

American Frontiersmen on Film and Television: Boone, Crockett, Bowie, Houston, Bridger and Carson (2005)

Burt Lancaster: A Filmography and Biography (2000; softcover 2005)

The Golden Corral: A Roundup of Magnificent Western Films (1997)

Louis L'Amour on Film and Television

Ed Andreychuk

McFarland & Company, Inc., Publishers
Jefferson, North Carolina, and London

LIBRARY OF CONGRESS CATALOGUING-IN-PUBLICATION DATA

Andreychuk, Ed.
Louis L'Amour on film and television / Ed Andreychuk.
p. cm.
Includes bibliographical references and index.

ISBN 978-0-7864-3336-0
softcover : 50# alkaline paper ∞

1. L'Amour, Louis, 1908–1988 — Film and video adaptations — Catalogs.
2. Western stories — Film and video adaptations — Catalogs. 3. Television
adaptations — Catalogs. 4. Film adaptations — Catalogs. I. Title.
PS3523.A446Z52 2010 791.43'65878 — dc22 2009044022

British Library cataloguing data are available

©2010 Ed Andreychuk. All rights reserved

No part of this book may be reproduced or transmitted in any form or by any means, electronic or mechanical, including photocopying or recording, or by any information storage and retrieval system, without permission in writing from the publisher.

Front cover: John Wayne, Lee Aaker, and Geraldine Page
in *Hondo*, 1953; background ©2010 Shutterstock

Manufactured in the United States of America

McFarland & Company, Inc., Publishers
Box 611, Jefferson, North Carolina 28640
www.mcfarlandpub.com

To the family and fans
of Louis L'Amour

Acknowledgments

Many sources were helpful in preparing this book.
They include Bantam Books' invaluable input of the works of Louis L'Amour; the Central Branch of the Enoch Pratt Library; the Library of Congress; Eddie Brandt's Saturday Matinee; Jerry Ohlinger's Movie Material Store; and the Larry Edmunds Bookshop.

Table of Contents

Preface

"Usually I am characterized as a Western writer. I do not mind the term, but it is not strictly correct. To me and to many others, I am a writer of the frontier, not only in the West but elsewhere."

These words were written by Louis L'Amour. They are from his memoir *Education of a Wandering Man* and reflect his feelings on the many short stories and novels he wrote in over 50 years as an author.

This book covers motion pictures and television shows based on L'Amour's writings. There is also a short biography included, but it is not intended to be a definitive one. That is left up to other writers. The intention here is only to capture his essence, the spirit of a man truly revered by his readers.

At 6'2", and with his own Western heritage, L'Amour was the perfect embodiment of the westerners he wrote about. They were strong, fearless men, whether good or bad, with a tenacity that only injury or death could stop.

Perhaps even more important in L'Amour's work was his attention to authenticity and to details. Every one of his admirers knew that *he* had been where his characters had.

For the most part, however, his work is fiction. *Frontier,* a 1984 tribute to the American wilderness beautifully photographed by David Muench, was an exception, as was his memoir. Despite being fictional, the novels and short stories were clearly drawn not only from L'Amour's creativity but on his past experiences working throughout the West and as a merchant seaman traveling all over the world.

A passage from Louis in *Frontier* sizes it up splendidly: "The greatest stories ever told are around campfires, in bunkhouses, or in ship's fo'c'stles with a bunch of wandering men.... [T]he best of their stories are always for each other, for the ones who have not known the life will not believe what they are hearing." Louis L'Amour always made us believe.

Biography and Overview

During August 1862, the Sioux Indians in Minnesota revolted. In their drive to oust the white population, the Indians killed a few hundred soldiers and settlers.

The troubles began over a decade earlier with the signing of a treaty which promised payment in gold to the Indians for land bought by the United States. Tensions arose when the U.S. reneged on the payment because of a later treaty and costly involvement in the American Civil War.

Even though 38 Sioux were hanged for the uprising, further retaliation was sought by the U.S. Army. Generals Henry Hastings Sibley and Alfred Sully were sent with troops into the Dakota Territory to find the Indians who escaped.

One of the confrontations between the Sibley Expedition and the Sioux occurred on July 24, 1863, between what is now Tappen and Pettibone, North Dakota. Sibley's group included a settler from St. Cloud, Minnesota. Scalped by the Indians, his name was Ambrose Freeman. He was the great-grandfather of Louis L'Amour.

Before his death, Ambrose crossed trails in 1862 with another man, Abraham Truman Dearborn, also fighting the Indians. Earlier that year, Dearborn even fought in the Civil War; he was sent home to Minnesota after his unit surrendered in Tennessee.

Abraham fought again in the Civil War after meeting Ambrose's oldest daughter Elizabeth, whom everyone called Betty. Wounded in battle the same year as Freeman was killed, Abraham convalesced at home; he and Betty married in 1864 at her aunt's Illinois home. Five children were born to them on their Minnesota farm including Louis L'Amour's mother, Emily Lavisa Dearborn, in 1870.

Another grandfather of L'Amour's saw action in the Civil War. He was from Ontario and his name was Robert L'Moore. He married a woman from Montreal, Angeline LeDoux, and they lived in Michigan.

In 1868, twins were born to Angeline and Robert — a son and a daughter. The boy, Louis Charles, would grow up and use the last name LaMoore. His sister and mother died while he was still young. Louis Charles married Emily Dearborn in 1892 and they lived in Jamestown, North Dakota. The Dakota Territory was awarded statehood just three years earlier.

Seven children came out of the LaMoore union. The first six were Edna May (1893), Parker (1897), Yale (1899), Emmy Lou (1901), and twins Clara and Clarice (1903). Emmy Lou died when she was a teenager and the twin girls as babies. The last born was another son, Louis Dearborn LaMoore. He would grow up to become the famous writer of the West and the frontier.

The birth date was allegedly March 22, 1908. When he was a boy, Louis wanted people to think he was actually older. But getting older made him secretive about his age. The year before he died, he reflected, "I conscientiously object to anyone telling his age. You can't judge people by age."

Having a prodigious love for books and reading most of his life, L'Amour (who changed his last name when he became a professional writer) took great pride in his heritage and French-Irish ancestry, and in the knowledge that he was not the only writer in the family. He said that over 30 other family members were writers at various times.

Louis L'Amour looking every bit the Western man. His own physical appearance fit the mold for the strong and heroic men he wrote about.

Especially notable was his oldest sister, Edna May. In the 1920s, she began reviewing Western books and writing a number of her own books.

Louis and Edna's grandmother was the subject of a 1931 memoir. Written by Edna and titled *Yet She Follows: The Story of Betty Freeman*, it and another book she wrote in 1932, *Dakota*, focused on the Sibley Expedition. After he became an author, Louis expressed an interest in writing about the expedition. A bit of rivalry even developed between Louis and Edna, who always claimed the story as her own.

It was as a child that Louis first became fascinated by the fact that he had family who had fought Indians and were in the Civil War. In later years, he also pointed out that his ancestral roots could be traced back to the 1600s, and that an army doctor in the American Revolution, Levi Dearborn, was the grandfather of Abraham Truman Dearborn.

Louis's own father was a veterinarian by trade. Doc LaMoore's other pursuits included being a deputy sheriff in Jamestown. He also taught Louis and his other sons the skills of boxing.

Another boy, John Otto, also lived with the LaMoore family. About a year older than Louis, he was an orphan from New York. Louis considered John another brother.

Doc and Emily LaMoore had a hundred or so books at home for their children to enjoy. Between having parents who were good storytellers, and reading at the local library, Louis found countless hours of enjoyment.

In his very first autobiographical profile as a writer (for the *Thrilling* magazine chain in 1940), Louis shared his boyhood love of literature: "Somewhere along there I stumbled across stories of Stevenson and that led me to those of Jack London, Herman Melville, and Rudyard Kipling." Louis was particularly captivated with Robert Louis Stevenson's *Treasure Island* as a boy. Another author who held young Louis spellbound was Zane Grey, the most prolific writer of Western adventures in the first half of the 20th century. (Louis L'Amour would achieve that status in its second half.)

At age 12, Louis discovered pulp magazines (printed on wood pulp paper) and the science fiction adventures of Edgar Rice Burroughs. This was when Louis was working as a messenger boy for Western Union.

In his 1989 memoir, L'Amour stated, "The idea of education has been so tied to schools, universities, and professors that many assume there is no other way, but education is available to anyone within reach of a library, a post office, or even a newsstand."

Self-education was a concept that L'Amour applied faithfully throughout his life. It was one of the reasons he dropped out of school in the tenth grade at 15 and set out on his own. This, and a strong sense of wanderlust.

Another reason, according to Louis, was the setback which his parents faced once tractors began replacing horses on neighboring farms. While Doc LaMoore's veterinary business may have suffered for it, he found part-time work repairing the machinery needed on the farms. Edna May claimed that her parents sold all their interests in Jamestown to simply seek out better living conditions elsewhere.

In 1926 when his high school classmates were graduating back in Jamestown, 18-year-old Louis was in Singapore as a merchant seaman. Prior to going to sea, however, he worked at a variety of jobs including as a roustabout for the Hagenbeck-Wallace Circus, and skinning over 900 dead cattle on a Texas ranch alongside a white man who once lived with Apache Indians.

He even hoboed in Texas, searching for work. Traveling aboard freight trains from El Paso to Galveston, Louis was introduced by another hobo to the series of pocket-sized *Little Blue Books* which featured stories from Kipling, London, Edgar Allan Poe, and many other authors.

In his memoir, L'Amour mentioned that on his initial voyage on a merchant vessel he weathered a hurricane in the West Indies. Not mentioned was an earlier claim that he was shipwrecked after the boat struck a reef. A voyage to England was made aboard a ship called the *Steadfast*. Louis maintained that during the trip he suffered his worst case of seasickness in the rough waters near Cape Hatteras.

Returning to the Southwest, Louis found himself hitchhiking along a lonely stretch of road in New Mexico. (As a teenager, Louis hitchhiked many times.) A motorist gave him a ride to Arizona; along the way they had breakfast and shared stories about the past.

Louis told the man of an earlier episode when he had visited brother Parker in Oklahoma and they met Bill Tilghman, a notable Old West lawman. Tilghman taught the two brothers how to shoot a six-gun. The man in the car had also been a lawman of distinction named Jeff Milton. When Louis met Tilghman and Milton they were old men, but each had left a mark which became Western lore. In 1877, Tilghman was a deputy sheriff in Dodge City, Kansas, and seven years later the town's city marshal. During the 1880s, Jeff Milton was a Texas Ranger and then deputy sheriff of Socorro, New Mexico.

A pair of jobs for Louis at small, isolated mines soon followed. Except for some animals to keep him company, and an old Indian man who occasionally wandered by, Louis was left alone as caretaker at that first mine in Arizona. However, he did find an abundance of reading material there, including some Hopalong Cassidy stories.

At the other mine, again alone, Louis's job was to dig it out a bit and remove rocks from the road. After a car breakdown, he had to walk through seventy miles of the Mojave Desert with only a can of pears to eat. Whenever he found water along the way, he filled the can.

In San Pedro, California, L'Amour spent a little time as a beachcomber as he waited for a merchant ship bound for the Far East, a part of the world he'd wanted to see ever since reading the *Arabian Nights* when he was younger. This was the sea voyage which eventually took him to Singapore. In Shanghai he met another beachcomber, Russian Joe Smith, who came aboard and shared his books with L'Amour. One was Joseph Conrad's *Lord Jim*, which he reread a number of times.

Although not mentioned in his memoir, other biographical profiles added exciting details to L'Amour's Far East adventures, including winning an $1800 purse as a prizefighter in Singapore, salvaging $50,000 in sunken treasure off Macao, and fighting in China with Chiang Kai-shek, then-commander of the Nationalist Army.

According to the L'Amour legend, he used the $50,000 to live the Bohemian lifestyle in Paris, France. Another part of the legend had Louis in India bicycling across the same terrain described in the Kipling story *Kim*.

"Wandering men have always had a love for poetry," L'Amour wrote in his memoir, "perhaps in part because it can be easily memorized and provide company on many a cold and lonely night." During what he called the "knockabout years" of his youth, Louis often found solace in reciting poetry he liked. One of his favorite poets was Stephen Vincent Benet, who also wrote stories he enjoyed.

L'Amour's very first book, a collection of poetry, was *Smoke from This Altar*, published in 1939 by Lusk Publishing, an Oklahoma City company, and supposedly financed by L'Amour. At the time, Louis was living with his father and mother in Choctaw, Oklahoma. To concentrate on his writing, he had ended his seafaring days.

His initial sales as a writer were magazine stories. *True Gang Life*'s gangster yarn "Anything for a Pal" was long considered the first one. But *10 Story Book*'s "Death, Westbound," about hoboes, actually came first.

In the early 1930s, L'Amour submitted stories and poetry to various publishers. Along with a small number of unpaid acceptances, L'Amour received some 200 rejection slips before his writing began selling.

Having been in more than his share of fistfights during his knockabout years, L'Amour seemed the right choice to coach a Choctaw team of Golden Gloves boxers. Three of the fighters went on to earn championships. L'Amour also boxed for a time, as a light-heavyweight, and allegedly won 51 out of 59 matches prior to becoming a coach.

In the 1930s, some of the writers whose work he enjoyed were Eugene O'Neill, H.G. Wells, George Bernard Shaw, and William Shakespeare. As a novice professional in the writing market, L'Amour was able to review some of the books he read for the *Sunday Oklahoman* newspaper (under the editorship of Dr. Kenneth Kaufman). At this stage, Louis's own short stories were exclusively for the pulp magazines. L'Amour studied the short stories of O. Henry and others. He reasoned, "A pulp story had to start fast and it had to move, and above all, you had to have a story to tell."

Over 100 short stories followed before L'Amour's first novel about the West appeared in 1950: *Westward the Tide* from World's Work Publishing in England. Ten years earlier, in March 1940, there was an initial Western story from L'Amour: a novella called "The Town No Gun Could Tame." Published in *New Western* magazine, its original title was "The Marshal of Basin City."

Between these two L'Amour Westerns, he saw military service during World War II. He was 34 years old when he was inducted into the United States Army; he was concerned that it would hurt his budding writing career.

Following his basic training in 1942 L'Amour graduated from the Tank Destroyers at the Officers Candidate School in Camp Hood, Texas. Two years of his four-year wartime service were then spent as a survival instructor in Michigan and as a cargo control officer in San Francisco.

Sent overseas to the European Theater of the war, Louis was assigned to the Tank Destroyers and Transportation Corps. Among his duties was commanding a platoon of gas tankers supplying fuel to tanks and planes. When he was honorably discharged, Louis held the rank of first lieutenant. He also was awarded four Bronze Stars.

Back in New York City during 1946, Louis contacted Leo Margulies, the editor of Standard Magazines, a major publisher of pulp magazine titles. A series of stories L'Amour wrote in the early 1940s were for Standard's *Thrilling Adventures* magazine and revolved around a heroic adventurer named Ponga Jim Mayo. This title had gone under during the war years as adventure stories were losing their popularity. Western tales were popular so Margulies convinced L'Amour to write more stories about the West.

However, there was a catch. Although L'Amour could use his own name on some of the stories, Margulies wanted to use a more "he-man"–sounding name for others. L'Amour chose Jim Mayo, after his earlier fictional character.

The first story with the Jim Mayo byline was "Jackson of Horntown," published in the magazine *Texas Rangers* in March 1947. Some 50 Western tales followed for L'Amour-as-Mayo in various magazines until 1953.

In 1950, L'Amour wrote four Hopalong Cassidy novels for the Double D Western imprint at Doubleday. They were initially published between 1950 and 1952. The first pair, *The Rustlers of West Fork* and *Trail to Seven Pines,* were printed in *Hopalong Cassidy's Western Magazine* before they were seen in book form. The magazine soon folded and so the other two, *The Riders of High Rock* and *Trouble Shooter,* came out in book form only.

Clarence E. Mulford originally created Cassidy three years before Louis was born and wrote stories about him until 1941. Mulford's character chewed tobacco, cursed and walked with a limp. The film series which began in 1935 made Hopalong Cassidy into an enormously popular hero, especially for children. As embodied by William Boyd, who became a millionaire from all the success, Hoppy was an upright, dashing figure in black who rode a magnificent white horse called Topper.

When Mulford could not be coaxed into writing further adventures about his famed character, the torch was passed to L'Amour, who wrote his stories under the pen name Tex Burns. But Doubleday changed L'Amour's conception of Cassidy from the original characterization to Boyd's hero. L'Amour therefore disavowed the four books in his lifetime but they can now be found under his own name from Bantam Books (as can the Jim Mayo material). Beau L'Amour, Louis's son, in an afterword for the new printings wrote, "Mulford chose my father. Now that I have read some of the original Cassidy stories, I am not in the least surprised, for they were soul mates. Although the sound and flow of their writing was different, both wrote with boiling energy."

Louis was living in a small apartment in Los Angeles when Hollywood beckoned. An original L'Amour story was the source for a 1953 adventure film, *East of Sumatra,* released by Universal-International. He also had a few stories filmed by television's *Fireside Theatre, Climax, Cowboy G-Men* and *City Detective.*

L'Amour had a short story, "The Gift of Cochise," published in *Collier's* magazine in 1952. It became the source for James Edward Grant's *Hondo* screenplay. L'Amour was able to turn the screenplay into a novel for Fawcett–Gold Medal Books. The Warner Brothers motion picture and the book both came out in 1953.

The following year, another L'Amour story was turned into a Western movie. *Giant Western* magazine's 1949 yarn "In Victorio's Country" was the probable source (although uncredited as such) for the 1954 Universal-International release *Four Guns to the Border.* In 1962, Louis expanded his initial story into the novel *High Lonesome* for Bantam Books. Two Hollywood Western films based on L'Amour's writings were released in 1955: United Artists' *Stranger on Horseback* and Allied Artists' *Treasure of Ruby Hills.* The latter was based on "The Rider of the Ruby Hills," a novella Louis wrote as Jim Mayo in 1949 for

West magazine. He rewrote it for Bantam in 1976, as the novel *Where the Long Grass Blows.*

A collaboration began in the mid-fifties between L'Amour and Bantam Books which has lasted past his death and into the 21st century. Beginning with an original frontier novel, *Radigan,* in 1958, Louis wrote two books a year for them. Later it became three.

Louis was once engaged to actress Julie Newmar. It didn't last, but she introduced him to her actress-friend Katherine Elizabeth Adams. This relationship did last. On February 19, 1956, Louis and Katherine were married. The groom was 48 years old, the bride 22, and their marriage lasted the rest of his life. Two children were born to the L'Amours, son Beau Dearborn in 1961 and daughter Angelique Gabrielle in 1964.

Katherine and Louis raised their children in a large, Spanish-style home in Bel-Air, California. The family also acquired other property both in California and Colorado. Louis's fame as a writer made him a wealthy man. In their California home, Katherine built for Louis a massive double row of bookcases. In later years he claimed their shelves held some 17,000 books.

Although a fiction writer, Louis was always the historian, utilizing material which proved useful for his own books. The diverse materials he collected reflected aspects of history, science and geography. His love for reading was passed on to his son and daughter as they grew.

Daughter Angelique reminisced in her 1988 tribute to her father, *A Trail of Memories,* about his reading to the whole family some of his own books. She said, "This didn't happen too often, maybe six or seven times as I grew up. There was magic when he read his own words, for I believe he wrote to be read aloud."

In the early 1950s, Louis lost both his parents and brothers Parker and Yale (John, his adopted brother, had been killed years before in an automobile accident). Louis's father died in 1952, while his mother and other brothers all died in 1954.

In the years 1956 and 1957, L'Amour's work became the source for four Western films and four television programs. First in '56 was the Columbia release *Blackjack Ketchum, Desperado,* which was based on his novel *Kilkenny* (Ace Books, 1954).

Warner Brothers' *The Burning Hills* was the second 1956 film. L'Amour's novel of the same title had initially been serialized during 1955 in *The Saturday Evening Post.* Book publications of the novel came in '56 from both Jason Press and Bantam Books.

The 1957 Western films began with Columbia's release of *Utah Blaine.* As Jim Mayo, L'Amour wrote the same-name novel for Ace Books in 1954. The next movie, the Allied Artists release *The Tall Stranger,* was based on a 1948 *Giant Western* magazine tale, "Showdown Trail." Louis rewrote the short story in '57 as the novel *The Tall Stranger* for Fawcett–Gold Medal. The four TV entries were for *Chevron Hall of Stars, Schlitz Playhouse of Stars, Sugarfoot* and *Maverick.* He was involved too on *The Texan* series.

Apache Territory was the final Western film of the 1950s to use L'Amour as a source. Released by Columbia in 1958, it was based on L'Amour's 1957 Fawcett–Gold Medal novel *Last Stand at Papago Wells.*

His writings took a most remarkable turn in 1960 when his very first novel about the Sacketts was published by Bantam. *The Daybreakers* began the landmark series of frontier adventures (17 books over the next quarter century).

The year 1960 also saw a pair of Western films based on earlier L'Amour works. Ten years before, as Jim Mayo, he wrote for *West* magazine the story "Guns of the Timberlands"; under Louis's own name, it then became a 1955 novel for Jason Press. The Warner Brothers release was called *Guns of the Timberland* (singular). The other '60 entry was *Heller in Pink Tights,* released by Paramount. It was based on the 1955 Fawcett–Gold Medal novel *Heller with a Gun.*

By the early 1960s, L'Amour frontier tales were becoming distinctive in their regard for familial characterizations. Not only was this realized with the Sacketts but with his 1963 Bantam novelization of the motion picture *How the West Was Won.* This epic Western was released by MGM in Cinerama the year before. James R. Webb's original screenplay focused on the Prescott and Rawlings families over a 50-year period.

Four additional Western movies and a television series used L'Amour works as sources to round out the decade. First was the 1964 Universal release *Taggart.* Louis had written the source novel in 1959 for Bantam. However, a prior (1951) magazine story he wrote for *Argosy,* "Trap of Gold," was also worked into the novel.

Kid Rodelo was released by Paramount in 1966. A then-unpublished L'Amour short story, "Desperate Men," was the original source. Louis expanded the story into novel form and it was published by Bantam shortly after the film's release. Both had the same title.

Seen on ABC-TV in 1967, *Hondo* was a series based on L'Amour's story "The Gift of Cochise" and the *Hondo* screenplay by James Edward Grant. Two of the 17 episodes were edited into *Hondo and the Apaches,* a film released by MGM overseas.

The last film entry of the decade was based on a 1962 L'Amour novel for Bantam Books. It was distributed in 1968 by Cinerama Releasing Corp. Both the novel and film were called *Shalako.*

L'Amour made a number of television appearances during the 1970s. They included CBS's *Merv Griffin Show* in 1971 and NBC's *Today Show* in 1975. Perhaps his most notable TV appearance was on the CBS program, *60 Minutes,* which initially aired on November 14, 1976. He was interviewed on the latter telecast by correspondent Morley Safer, who praised Louis as "our professor emeritus of how the West was won." Safer was very observant in pointing out that L'Amour's storylines, while fictional, contained historically accurate details.

By the mid-seventies, Louis had surpassed John Steinbeck as Bantam's number one author in book sales. In 1977, the Western Writers of America named two Louis L'Amour novels among the best 25 Western novels of all time. *Hondo* was number 14 on the list. A 1960 Bantam publication, *Flint,* was number 22. The top three novels chosen were *The Virginian* by Owen Wister, *The Ox Bow Incident* by Walter Van Tilburg Clark, and *Shane* by Jack Schaefer.

This famous shot of John Wayne is from ***Hondo.*** **The Duke had the heroic title role.**

Between 1971 and 1979, two western movies, a comedy film, and a TV miniseries all drew their inspiration from L'Amour's novels published by Bantam. MGM's release of *Catlow* in '71 was based on a 1963 novel of the same title. The comedy *Cancel My Reservation* was released by Warner Brothers in 1972; its source was a modern-day Western novel, *The Broken Gun,* published in 1966. National General Pictures distributed *The Man Called Noon* (1973), based on a 1970 L'Amour novel with the same title.

Perhaps the most exciting treatment of L'Amour's work since 1953's *Hondo* was an NBC-TV miniseries seen over two nights in 1979. *The Sacketts* took its storyline from a pair of L'Amour novels for Bantam Books, 1960's *The Daybreakers* and 1961's *Sackett.*

In the 1980s, three Walt Disney television entries used L'Amour's frontier adventures as their source material. First up was a 1981 prospective series pilot for CBS, *The Cherokee Trail.* L'Amour's novel of the same title was not published by Bantam until the following year. Although not picked up by CBS-TV, the pilot was reworked and became a series for the Disney Channel. It was televised between 1983 and 1985 under the title *Five Mile Creek.*

Airing on the Disney Channel in 1986 was the film version of *Down the Long Hills.* The L'Amour novel of the same title was published in 1968 by Bantam.

Between these Disney productions was another CBS entry, a 1982 Western called *The Shadow Riders.* It was based on an outline L'Amour wrote; he turned the story into a novel which Bantam published around the same time as the telecast.

The Quick and the Dead was the last Western film of the 1980s made from the work of Louis L'Amour. Televised by HBO in 1987, it was based on the 1973 Bantam Books publication. This latter title proved to be the final one made before Louis died of lung cancer. He was 80 years old when he passed away on June 10, 1988. Louis was a nonsmoker; it was speculated that the cancer may have had its origins in his early years working in various mines in different parts of the country. But Louis believed otherwise since he had not worked in any coal mines.

Louis L'Amour undoubtedly enjoyed the many awards and accolades that he received during his lifetime. Among them was a 1972 honorary doctorate in literature from Jamestown College, in his own North Dakota hometown. His greatest honors, however, were the two presented by President Ronald Reagan on separate occasions at the White House. The president was an admirer of L'Amour's work.

On September 24, 1983, Louis received from the president the Congressional Gold Medal in recognition of his distinguished writing career and depiction of the West and its settlement. On March 26, 1984, for his reflection of the American pioneer spirit in his work, Louis was bestowed by President Reagan with the highest civilian award that the government could give, the Presidential Medal of Freedom.

These accomplishments were no small feat for an author whose work was often ignored by the book critics. And sometimes when the critics were not ignoring Louis, he was judged too repetitious and hasty with his writing. But Louis knew that he wrote for the people who loved his books and could not wait for each and every one. Courage against adversity amidst landscapes rich in detail were among the things appreciated by his readers. Even after he was gone, Louis's family continued to have his early short stories, novels, and his book of poetry reprinted.

And it was not just the American people who read Louis L'Amour's work. By 2007, over 120 books, including collections of short stories, had sold 300 million copies worldwide. They have been translated into at least 20 different languages.

While the literary success of Louis L'Amour continued beyond his life, interest in Western films based on his work has diminished. Therefore the only entries during the 1990s to use Louis as a source were a couple for television. Both were based on novels for Bantam Books. *Conagher,* televised on the TNT network in 1991, was based on Louis's 1969 novel of the same title. Another prospective series for CBS, *Shaughnessy: The Iron Marshal,* aired in 1996; the L'Amour novel was published in 1979.

The new century got underway with a pair of television films using L'Amour as their source. Louis's 1954 frontier novel for Ace Books, *Crossfire Trail,* was the source for a same-name TNT network film in 2001. (The same L'Amour story appeared as "The Trail to Crazy Man" in *West* magazine during 1948.) *The Diamond of Jeru* (also 2001) was televised on the USA Network; it was based on an early adventure story Louis wrote with this title. Bantam Books published it in 2000 as part of a collection of L'Amour stories in a book called *Off the Mangrove Coast.*

A bit of irony lies in the fact that the first and last feature-length films listed in this book are based on two of Louis's stories in exotic, faraway lands. Yet the majority of the films, like Louis L'Amour's books, are Western or frontier tales.

In our lifetimes, we can read over and over his vast body of work and view a good selection of films based on it. By doing so, we all make sure that the spirit of Louis L'Amour lives on.

We all share in riding along the many trails with him this way. It helps to make our own pathways through life a little less lonely.

THE 1950s

Fireside Theatre

1953. A Frank Wisbar Production.
NBC Television.
30 Minutes/Black and White.

Episode: "Let the Cards Decide"

Credits: Frank Wisbar (Producer, Director), Sam Rolfe (Teleplay), Benjamin Kline (Photography), Holbrook Todd (Editor). Based on a story by Louis L'Amour.

Cast: Paula Raymond, Craig Stevens, Jeff York, Dabbs Greer, John Close, Lee Phelps, Hank Patterson, Kid Chissel.

Synopsis: In the Old West, an unusual poker game takes place, and the stakes ultimately include a young bride. She is rescued by a gambler from marriage to an unsavory character.

Commentary: *Fireside Theatre* began airing in the spring of 1949 on NBC-TV; shown both live and on film were dramas, comedies and musicals. However, the series soon switched to mostly filmed dramatic stories and many of the guest stars would become better known in later years. This anthology series was regarded as the first hit filmed series on television. In the 1952–53 season, Frank Wisbar became its host, with Gene Raymond taking over this function during the 1953–55 seasons.

Raymond also performed in some of the episodes, as did actresses Jane Wyman when she replaced him from 1955 to 1958. She became so recognized with the series that it was even known as *The Jane Wyman Show* and drew name players.

Episode 14 in the fifth season, "Let the Cards Decide," was directed and produced by Frank Wisbar. Its airdate was on January 6, 1953. Sam Rolfe's teleplay was supposedly derived from an original story by Louis L'Amour.

Paula Raymond and Craig Stevens starred as the distressed bride and heroic gambler. *Variety* opined that she made "a handsome prize" and that he "displayed enough restraint to temper the heroics."

A number of television Westerns were highlighted by having Miss Raymond as a guest star. They included *Cheyenne* in 1960 and *Maverick* in 1961. She also co-starred with Dennis Morgan in the 1955 feature film *The Gun That Won the West.*

An earlier TV appearance for Craig Stevens was a 1950 episode of *The Lone Ranger.* The bigger roles which followed included the 1958 Western film *Buchanan Rides Alone.* But he will probably be best remembered for his great private eye in the *Peter Gunn* TV series (1958–61).

Writer Sam Rolfe was involved in other Westerns for both TV and the movies. One was the 1953 feature film *The Naked Spur* starring James Stewart.

East of Sumatra

1953. An Albert J. Cohen Production.
Released by Universal-International.
81 Minutes/Technicolor.

Credits: Albert J. Cohen (Producer), Budd Boetticher (Director), Frank Gill, Jr. (Screenplay), Virgil Vogel (Editor), Bernard Herzbrun, Robert Boyle (Art Directors), Russell A. Gausman, Joseph Kish (Set Decorators), Rosemary Odell (Costumes), Bill Thomas (Gowns), Bud Westmore (Makeup), Joseph Gershenson (Music Director). Adapted by Jack Natteford from a story by Natteford and Louis L'Amour.

Cast: Jeff Chandler (Duke Mullane), Marilyn Maxwell (Lory Hale), Anthony Quinn (Kiang), Suzan Ball (Minyora), John Sutton (Daniel Catlin), Jay C. Flippen (Mac), Scatman Crothers (Baltimore), Aram Katcher (Atib), Anthony Eustrel (Clyde), Eugene Iglesias (Pablo), Peter Graves (Cowboy), Earl Holliman (Cupid), Michael Dale (Co-pilot), Gilchrist Stuart (Mr. Vickers), Charles Horvath (Corcoran).

Synopsis: In Malaya, mine supervisor Duke Mullane comes under scrutiny by his new employer, Daniel Catlin, after manhandling a drunken employee. Mine owner Craig Keith gives Duke a new assignment digging for tin on the island of Tungga.

On Tungga, Duke dines with the island's ruler, Kiang. Duke is able to make a deal with him to use natives to help in the mine in exchange for supplies. During a ceremony where Kiang's fiancée, Minyora, is dancing, he becomes jealous over Duke's interest in her.

While the natives prove to be hard workers, a setback occurs when the plane arrives without the expected supplies. Further friction develops because of a troublesome native, Atib, who spies on others. Made aware of an innocent encounter between Duke and Minyora, Kiang becomes upset.

A rich vein of tin is found in the mine, but when another plane lands on the island with only Lory and Catlin, Kiang prevents his natives from working until they get their supplies. Catlin blames Duke for the problem, but Minyora defends him. This infuriates Kiang to the point that he refuses to have the natives help at all.

Having earlier stolen Duke's lighter, Atib accidently causes a fire in the natives' supply hut. When Kiang finds the lighter in the ruins, he burns the plane with the intention to trap and then starve the white people on the island.

Minyora tries to help Duke and the others find refuge in a mountain temple but Kiang prevents this from happening. Feeling helpless, Duke gets drunk and tries to kiss Lory since he still has feelings for her. After Minyora is seen again with Duke, Kiang believes she has been unfaithful and goes on a bloody rampage with his natives.

Duke is disturbed when Kiang has two of his men killed and a third is wounded. To stop the bloodshed, Duke is willing to sacrifice himself. Seeing this, Lory reveals her love for him.

Challenged by Kiang, Duke and the island ruler fight to the death with fire and machetes. In the struggle, Kiang is impaled on a machete. Before he dies, Kiang makes Minyora queen and the island's new ruler. Her first command is to allow the natives to help the mining crew. Resigned to the fact that Lory's heart belongs to Duke, Catlin leaves the island.

Commentary: *East of Sumatra* was released in October 1953. It was shot the year before, from November 20 to December 29. Louis L'Amour wrote the original story with Jack Natteford. An adaptation of their story was then developed by Natteford and it became a screenplay written by Frank Gill, Jr.

Jack Natteford, due to his large body of work, could be regarded as the Louis L'Amour of motion picture writers. Prior to *East of Sumatra*, well over 100 Western and adventure film credits going back to the 1920s attest to Natteford's abilities.

In *East of Sumatra* the romantic attraction between Marilyn Maxwell's heroine and Jeff Chandler's hero is obvious as a somewhat disgruntled John Sutton looks on.

While this particular adventure film moved with a quick pace under Budd Boetticher's direction, it was deemed by *Variety* as "pot-boiler escapism of the type acceptable to the non-discriminating and gets a standard presentation...."

"When technological West (embodied in a mining engineer) meets stereotyped and melodramatic East in an exotic locale," reflected *National Parent-Teacher* magazine, "you can expect a routine adventure yarn."

But a solid cast helped to give the film's action and romantic entanglements a much needed boost. Jeff Chandler was the epitome of a L'Amour hero — tall, handsome, brave and noble. As the villain of the piece, Anthony Quinn was nonetheless seen in a somewhat sympathetic light. And as their respective love interests, Marilyn Maxwell and Suzan Ball also provided elements of conflict for the two men.

The movie's core conflict developed into the climactic duel between the male leads. The story ended in a typical Hollywood fashion with the good guy winning the fight and the girl, and the bad guy losing the girl, the fight and his life.

Quinn won a Best Supporting Actor Oscar for 1952's *Viva Zapata!* He also co-starred in two other films in '53 for director Boetticher, *City Beneath the Sea* and *Seminole.* A fourth Quinn-Boetticher teaming, *The Magnificent Matador*, reached the big screen in 1955.

Boetticher is perhaps best known for his seven Westerns with Randolph Scott. Released between 1956 and 1960, they were *Seven Men from Now, The Tall T, Decision at Sundown, Buchanan Rides Alone, Ride Lonesome, Westbound,* and *Comanche Station.*

Champion (1949) with Kirk Douglas was among the films in which Marilyn Maxwell was the leading lady. She was also a popular entertainer with the troops during both World War II and the Korean War.

Suzan Ball was only 22 years old when she died in 1955 from cancer; it supposedly developed from an injury on her knee while making *East of Sumatra.* Her last film, with Victor Mature in the title role, was 1955's *Chief Crazy Horse.* At 6' 4", Jeff Chandler did seem the perfect Hollywood leading man. He became a star with the 1949 adventure *Sword in the Desert.* With his mature good looks and a quiet nobility, he was most persuasive playing ethnic roles. His most memorable was as the Apache leader Cochise (alongside James Stewart) in the 1950 Western classic *Broken Arrow*, for which he received an Oscar nomination in the Best Supporting Actor category.

In two other Westerns—1953's *The Battle of Apache Pass* and 1954's *Taza, Son of Cochise*—Chandler again portrayed Cochise. His movie career was cut short by death at the age of 42 in 1961. The cause was blood poisoning after surgery for a slipped disc; the injury was sustained while making his last film, *Merrill's Marauders* (1962).

The year before *East of Sumatra,* Chandler starred in another Universal-International release, *Red Ball Express* (also directed by Budd Boetticher). It was based on an actual World War II event: supplies, including fuel, were trucked to the armies of General George Patton and others in the massive Allied drive to Paris, France. Louis L'Amour was one of the 23,000 men who actually made up the Red Ball Express. L'Amour's outfit

Jeff Chandler readies for action as Eugene Iglesias (left) and Earl Holliman look on in *East of Sumatra*. Holliman also co-starred in the film version of L'Amour's novel *The Burning Hills*.

helped to transport the fuel. Some 132 companies utilized 5,958 trucks in the 81-day operation (August 24 to November 16, 1944).

L'Amour was no stranger to the part of the world that provided the setting for *East of Sumatra*. Louis not only traveled to the island of Sumatra in Indonesia as a young merchant seaman, he wrote short stories set in many of the distant lands he visited.

Prior to his wartime service, Louis wrote nine short stories featuring the bold sea captain Ponga Jim Mayo. Between January 1940 and November 1943, they were all published in the magazine *Thrilling Adventures*; the titles were "East of Gorontalo," "From Here to Banggai," "On the Road to Amurang," "The House of Qasavara," "Well of the Unholy Light," "South of Suez," "West from Singapore," "Voyage to Tobalai" and "Wings Over Brazil." The initial seven were published in book form in 1987 under the title *West from Singapore*. "Voyage to Tobalai" was published in the 2003 book collection *With These Hands* and the novella "Wings Over Brazil" was part of the 2001 collection *May There Be a Road*. All these collections were published by Bantam Books.

The Ponga Jim Mayo adventures took place in exotic locations such as Indonesia. Although the rugged hero battled against the Nazis and Japanese to reflect the wartime fighting at the time, he could have fit the heroic mold for Jeff Chandler's Duke Mullane in *East of Sumatra* without missing a beat.

Hondo

1953. A Wayne-Fellows Production.
Distributed by Warner Brothers.
84 Minutes/WarnerColor/3-D.

Credits: Robert Fellows (Producer), John Farrow (Director), James Edward Grant (Screenplay), Robert Burks, Archie Stout (Photography), Ralph Dawson (Editor), Alfred Ybarra (Art Director), Al Gonzalez (Special Effects), Carl Walker (Wardrobe), Web Overlander (Makeup), Emil Newman, Hugo Friedhofer (Music). Based on a story by Louis L'Amour.

Cast: John Wayne (Hondo Lane), Geraldine Page (Angie Lowe), Ward Bond (Buffalo Baker), Michael Pate (Vittorio), James Arness (Lennie), Rodolfo Acosta (Silva), Leo Gordon (Ed Lowe), Tom Irish (Lt. McKay), Lee Aaker (Johnny Lowe), Paul Fix (Maj. Sherry), Rayford Barnes (Pete).

Synopsis: In the American Southwest of 1874, cavalry dispatch rider Hondo Lane walks onto the small, isolated ranch of Angie Lowe and her son, Johnny. With Hondo is his dog, Sam. Having lost his horse in a fight with Apache Indians, Hondo is given one of Angie's unbroken horses to tame.

Partly because of fear of his intentions, Angie lies to Hondo about her husband returning soon. Her husband, Ed Lowe, has abandoned his family. Hondo realizes all this after seeing how much work the ranch needs. For Angie's hospitality, Hondo helps out tending to the horses and cutting firewood.

There is an attraction between Angie and Hondo. He tells Angie that she reminds him of his dead Indian wife. Hondo kisses her before riding out. Although he wanted her and the boy to leave with him for their safety, Angie refused because of a belief that the Indians, while angry about a broken treaty, will still not harm them.

After Hondo leaves, Apache leader Vittorio arrives at Angie's ranch with his men. One of them, Silva, starts trouble and little Johnny fires a pistol at him. Impressed by his courage, Vittorio treats the boy well. He later demands that Angie must decide on a new husband from one of his men.

Back at the cavalry outpost, Hondo is reacquainted with scout Buffalo Baker. Hondo gets into an argument with a settler; later, after beating the man in a fistfight, Hondo learns that he is none other than Ed Lowe.

Lowe and another man trail Hondo when he leaves the outpost, intending to kill him. When Indians strike first, killing Ed's companion, Hondo and his dog, Sam, fight them together. Although Hondo saves his life, Ed goes for his gun against him and is killed in self-defense.

Trying to return to Angie's place, Hondo is chased down, captured and tortured by the Apaches. Having earlier found a tintype of Johnny with Ed, Hondo's torturing is stopped when Vittorio sees it among his belongings. Nonetheless, Hondo is challenged by Silva to a knife fight. Although injured in the struggle, Hondo defeats him and spares his life.

The Indians take Hondo to Angie; to save his life, she pretends they are married. Hondo is told by Vittorio to teach Johnny the ways of the Apaches. Before the Indians ride off, Silva kills Sam.

Johnny is taught different things by Hondo including how to swim like an Indian boy. Meanwhile, Angie declares her love to Hondo. He tries to tell her the truth about Ed's death when Vittorio appears. Hondo gives his word not to join the approaching cavalry against the Apaches, but he refuses to promise to lie to the soldiers about where the Indians have gone. This greatly impresses Vittorio.

Cavalrymen soon ride in and are rounding up all the settlers in the area for protection against the Indian danger. With the soldiers are Buffalo Baker and another scout, Lennie, who is knocked down by Hondo for trying to blackmail him for his rifle. Angie witnesses this and hears Lennie's accusation that Hondo bushwhacked and killed her husband. She is taken aback but soon realizes that Hondo was only defending himself.

When the soldiers return from a fight with the Apaches, word arrives of Vittorio's

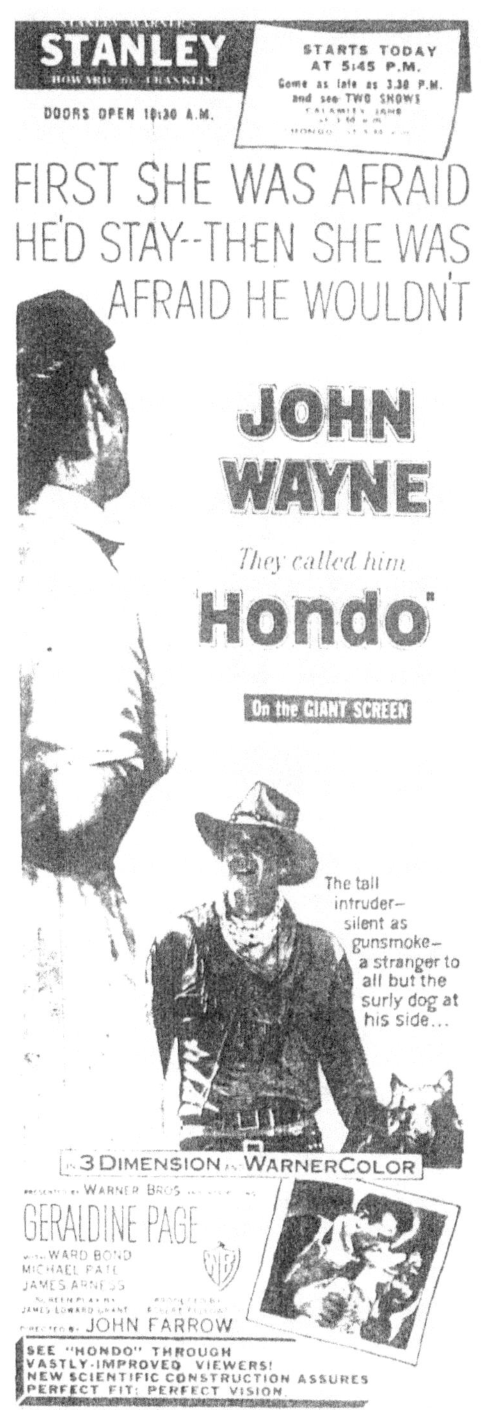

***Hondo* was originally shown in 3-D, a popular fad at the time in films.**

In *Hondo*, John Wayne's frontier scout meets the pioneer family played by Lee Aaker and Geraldine Page.

death. Silva, the new leader, is determined to kill all the soldiers and settlers. With the cavalry commander, Lt. McKay, wounded, Hondo leads everyone in an effort to get back to the outpost as quickly as possible. With him, of course, are Johnny and Angie, who are planning to begin a life with Hondo on his own ranch in California.

In the fighting between the Indians and the soldiers, casualties mount on both sides until Hondo is able to kill Silva. Now temporarily without a leader, the Apaches ride away. This gives the cavalry unit and wagon train settlers the opportunity to move on.

Original Source: The short story "The Gift of Cochise."

Plotline: In Apache country, young mother Angie Lowe lives with her children, Jimmy, seven, and Jane, five. After trouble with the Apaches, the family is befriended by their leader Cochise. Angie's husband Ed meets a tragic end helping a stranger named Chez Lane in a gunfight in El Paso. Chez then attempts to go and help Ed's family and runs afoul of Cochise and the Indians.

Commentary: Louis L'Amour's story "The Gift of Cochise" first appeared in the

July 5, 1952, issue of *Collier's* magazine. *Collier's* was certainly a step up from the pulp magazines which L'Amour was submitting his short stories to at the time.

Over the years, this famous short story would be reprinted. In 1975, Bantam published it as part of the collection of L'Amour frontier tales titled *War Party*.

Wayne-Fellows Productions bought the screen rights to "The Gift of Cochise" for just $4,000. James Edward Grant was given the assignment to write the script. Actual film production took place between June and August of 1953, and included location work in Camargo, Mexico.

When the motion picture premiered in November 1953, it was called *Hondo*. To coincide with the release by Warner Brothers, a novel was published by Fawcett–Gold Medal. It was written by Louis L'Amour and derived from the screenplay. There were many reprints, including Bantam's 30th anniversary edition in 1983.

While Grant's screenplay drew its inspiration from the original tale of Apache conflict and a man trying to help a frontier family, he greatly expanded on it. And Louis's novel added details not visualized in the filmed scenario.

"He was a big man, wide-shouldered, with the lean, hard-boned face of the desert rider." This description of Hondo Lane was included in the opening paragraphs of the L'Amour novel. They reflected admirably the character in the film as well.

Whereas the film opens with Hondo on foot after losing his horse to Indians, the novel depicts the earlier fight with them. When his horse is killed by an Apache arrow, Hondo is forced to shoot down two Indians trying to kill him.

After helping Angie and Johnny around the ranch, Hondo beds down for the night on the floor of their home. A misunderstanding develops when she recognizes his full name and recalls his reputation as a noted gunman. Both accounts address this tense situation which culminates to Angie actually firing a gun at Hondo, although it is unloaded. In the film, Angie reads his name printed on his rifle; in the book, she sees it on his saddle.

Both book and film share the story's most eloquent passage: Hondo speaking to Angie about his departed Indian wife, Destarte. It is a moving moment and conveys the new feeling developing between the man and woman.

The biggest omission from the film, yet depicted in the novel, is the confrontation of the army's Company C by the Apaches. Forty-seven seasoned men, led by Lt. Davis, are overwhelmed and meet their destinies. Both versions, however, have Hondo bringing word back about the outcome.

In L'Amour's account, Hondo, while returning to his post from Angie's ranch, kills two Apaches who were part of the battle against the soldiers. He sees the actual aftermath of the destruction across the battlefield. In the novel, when a storm creates flash flooding, Hondo finds refuge in an abandoned stone cabin. His thoughts at this point show deep concern for the fallen soldiers as well as for Angie and Johnny.

The film's Vittorio is called Vittoro in the novel. He substitutes for Cochise in L'Amour's short story. Unlike the episode in the movie where Johnny shoots Silva, knocking him down, in the book the Indian momentarily loses consciousness.

At the army post, Hondo is accused of horse stealing by Ed Lowe when he recognizes the horse Angie had let Hondo break. This is part of both versions. Ed's partner-in-crime is unnamed in the film. In the book, the man is called Phalinger.

During the course of the novel, Silva makes a number of threatening gestures towards Angie. Included is a sign of scalping her; he also taunts her that she will become his new squaw. Fearful that she might become an Apache squaw, Angie plans to leave the ranch with Johnny.

The Apaches' pursuit of Hondo is more elaborate in the film. A massive body of riders surrounds him on the screen whereas in the book, Hondo must deal with fewer warriors.

In both accounts, Hondo's dog Sam is killed by a lance thrown by Silva. Hondo is powerless to act at this point as he lies injured in Angie's home from his earlier knife fight with the Apache. In the book, Hondo quietly shares his grief over Sam's death with Angie. In the novel we see more of Hondo honoring the Apache leader's request to teach Johnny the Indian ways of life. Hondo does this by showing the boy how to extract medicine from certain plants and how to distinguish animal tracks.

Their relationship a bit uneasy at first, Duke Wayne and Geraldine Page share a tense moment involving a gun in *Hondo.*

Also in the book, four Mountain Apaches come upon Hondo and Johnny. These Indians are not part of Vittoro's band and Hondo is forced to kill one; the other three respect the headband Johnny wears as Vittoro's blood brother. Vittoro has Johnny count coup on the slain Indian by touching the body. Overwhelmed by the entire situation, the boy cries in Hondo's arms.

In L'Amour's novel, Angie and Hondo spend the night together outside as Johnny sleeps in the cabin. In both versions she confesses her love to Hondo. And while he also told Angie that Ed is dead, she still doesn't know how he was killed. To Hondo's credit, he does try to tell her.

But Angie does learn in both accounts, through scout Lennie's remark that Ed died by Hondo's hand. During the climactic fighting with the Apaches, Lennie gets the chance to redeem himself in the film. The scout Buffalo Baker tells Hondo that Lennie saved his life with the very rifle he had earlier tried to blackmail Hondo over. As a token of appreciation, Hondo gives the rifle to Lennie.

Both novel and motion picture conclude with Silva's death and the Apache threat dissipated. Angie and Johnny will go with Hondo to California and begin their new life as a family.

"As a Western with more human pulse than is common to the genre, this picture bears some resemblance to the popular *Shane*," the *Hondo* review in *Newsweek* began. A number of similarities were evident in these 1953 Westerns. A lone gunman in buckskin comes upon a small ranch and helps a struggling family in each. The strongest component shared is the bonding by the two title heroes with the frontier families.

But there is a more powerful resonance between Shane and the little boy, Joey, than that realized by Hondo and Johnny. Unlike the no-good Ed Lowe in *Hondo*, *Shane*'s Joe Starrett is a good father. Ed's only redeeming quality is that he carries a tintype of his son.

With Shane's respect for the father being so high, his code of honor prevents him from going beyond the subtle romantic attraction felt with Marion, the mother. Although Hondo is clearly upset that he has to shoot Ed, this frees him to pursue Angie, so there is a more forceful romantic development in *Hondo* between our hero and his frontier lady than the one between Marion and Shane. In fact, Angie and Hondo's romance is so touching that *America* magazine called it "several cuts above the usual Hollywood fiction."

John Wayne and Geraldine Page gave two of the strongest performances in their respective careers. She received her first Academy Award nomination as Best Supporting Actress for *Hondo*. Wayne's acting was regarded as his most "powerful" in the 1950s until *The Searchers* came along three years later.

Having been in the film business for over two decades prior to *Hondo*, Duke Wayne had scored in a large number of earlier films. In 1949, he received his first Best Actor Oscar nomination as Sgt. Stryker in *Sands of Iwo Jima*. Ten years before that, Wayne found major stardom as the Ringo Kid in *Stagecoach*. In the interim, he also showed tremendous acting ability, playing men older than he was at the time, in *Red River* (1948) and

She Wore a Yellow Ribbon (1949). The year before *Hondo*, Wayne was seen in yet another distinguished motion picture, *The Quiet Man.*

Geraldine Page had her first starring role in a major film with *Hondo*. (She had made her film debut in a 1947 movie called *Out of the Night.*) Fresh from the Broadway stage success of *Summer and Smoke* in the early 1950s, she proved a dynamic actress in all her performances in the years ahead.

Wayne and Page both eventually won the coveted Oscar award: the Duke in 1969 for *True Grit*, she for 1985's *The Trip to Bountiful.* Between *Hondo* and her Oscar win, Page received six additional nominations — three as Best Actress and three more as Best Supporting Actress.

After Wayne, Michael Pate had the next strongest male role in *Hondo*. Pate gave fine support in many films in his career. In *Hondo*, he was on an equal par with Wayne in bonding with the little boy played by Lee Aaker.

While young Aaker's acting career wasn't extensive, he gave a very natural performance as Johnny. He is perhaps best remembered as Cpl. Rusty on the 1954–1959 TV series *The Adventures of Rin Tin Tin.*

Although Ward Bond and James Arness had relatively small roles as frontier scouts, they were seen to good advantage. Both were friends of Wayne and had appeared with him in earlier films. Arness and Bond enjoyed particular success on television in two long-running Western series (respectively, *Gunsmoke* and *Wagon Train*). Unfortunately for Bond, he only had a few years as *Wagon Train*'s Major Adams because he died of a heart attack in 1960. But Jim was seen for 20 years as *Gunsmoke*'s Matt Dillon.

Another friend of the Duke was writer James Edward Grant. He not only wrote the screenplay for a 1947 Western with Wayne, *Angel and the Badman*, but directed it as well. Among Grant's other screenplays for the Duke was their biggest one together, 1960's *The Alamo*.

A second Academy Award nomination was received by *Hondo*. The category was Writing (Motion Picture Story), and Louis L'Amour was the recipient. However, this particular category stressed original work written for the screen. L'Amour was thereby deemed as ineligible after informing the Academy of Motion Picture Arts and Sciences that the film was based on his short story "The Gift of Cochise."

Wayne and Robert Fellows, whose production company made *Hondo*, first set up their outfit in 1950. *The Bullfighter and the Lady* in '51, directed by Budd Boetticher and starring Robert Stack, was their initial feature. Another film, released the same year as *Hondo*, was *Plunder in the Sun*. It starred Glenn Ford and was directed by John Farrow. When *Hondo* was being readied, Ford and Farrow were pegged to work together again. However, disliking the director, Ford refused. So Wayne, who really liked the role of Hondo Lane, stood by Farrow and took over the part.

To compete with the growing television market, Wayne and Fellows opted to make *Hondo* using the 3-D process then in vogue in motion pictures. Just the year before, *Bwana Devil* had scored a big success in 3-D. The three-dimensional imaging added

The Duke beat his adversary (Rodolfo Acosta) in their exciting fight in *Hondo*. Looking on is the noble Apache leader played by Michael Pate.

depth to any film which used it. It was especially striking in action scenes, most notably the fight between Wayne's Hondo and Rodolfo Acosta's Silva; their knife thrusts seemed to come out of the screen to impale audiences.

Only a week or so following *Hondo*'s release, the two projectors needed in theaters to show the film proved so troublesome that standard prints of the film were shown instead. Although a number of Hollywood films used 3-D, the fad passed in the face of more lucrative options such as CinemaScope.

Hondo did not completely measure up to *Shane*'s artistic and commercial success, but it was a box office winner. It grossed over $4,000,000, which was a handsome sum at the time. The novel version also gave Louis L'Amour his very first best seller.

With the harsh desert landscapes from both the novel and film, and a protagonist from which any true Western figure could be drawn, the film and novel are indelibly identified with Wayne and L'Amour. This does not disparage the contribution to *Hondo* by James Edward Grant by any means. But never did two better embodiments of the great American frontier spirit exist over the years — one as a filmmaker, the other as a storyteller.

Four Guns to the Border

1954. A William Alland Production.
Released by Universal-International.
82 Minutes/Technicolor.

Credits: William Alland (Producer), Richard Carlson (Director), George Van Marter, Franklin Coen (Screenplay), Alexander Golitzen, Eric Orbom (Art Directors), Russell A. Gausman, Julia Heron (Set Decorators), Jay A. Morley, Jr. (Costumes), Bud Westmore (Makeup), Joseph Gershenson (Music Supervisor). Based on a story by Louis L'Amour.

Cast: Rory Calhoun (Ray Cully), Colleen Miller (Lolly Bhumer), George Nader (Bronco), Walter Brennan (Simon Bhumer), Nina Foch (Maggie Flannery), John McIntire (Dutch), Charles Drake (Jim Flannery), Jay Silverheels (Yaqui), Nestor Paiva (Greasy), Mary Field (Mrs. Pritchard), Robert F. Hoy (Smitty), Bob Herron (Evans), Reg Parton (Bank Cashier), Marshall Bradford (Banker).

Synopsis: Ray Cully is the leader of an outlaw gang in 1881 New Mexico. The other gang members are Bronco, Dutch, and Yaqui. After fouling up a robbery, the outlaws ride out of town past Simon Bhumer and his daughter Lolly. Simon and Dutch once rode together as gunmen.

Despite the threat of marauding Apaches and some hard ground to cover, the Bhumers are determined to travel on to their ranch in Shadow Valley. Inadvertently attacked by the outlaws along the trail when they are not recognized, Simon isn't hurt but Lolly is knocked unconscious by Cully.

Planning to rob the bank in Cully's hometown of Cholla, the outlaws have stopped en route at the store of Greasy, a friend. In short order, Simon and Lolly stop by as well. During a storm that night, Cully kisses Lolly. After Simon intervenes with his shotgun, the Bhumers move on.

Riding along with her father, Lolly is upset with him for making her leave. Having taken a fancy to Cully, she makes an attempt to return to him. Her horse breaks a leg and Simon must shoot the animal to put it out of its misery.

When Cully enters Cholla, he picks a fight with Sheriff Jim Flannery. Cully was once a friend of the sheriff and his wife Maggie until he was forced to leave town. The fistfight between the two men is a trick by Cully to attract a large crowd while his gang robs the bank. Maggie stops the fighting and Cully rides out to rejoin his gang. The sheriff does not know yet that the bank has been robbed.

After their last horse breaks a shoe, Lolly and Simon have to walk. Meanwhile, the outlaws find that the Apaches have killed Greasy and burned down his store.

Back in town, Flannery rounds up a posse and sets out after the bank robbers. Nearing Shadow Valley, the Bhumers are attacked by the Indians. When they hear the gunplay, first Cully and then each one of his comrades gives up their chance to escape to the border, riding to the aid of Lolly and her father.

During the fighting, Yaqui, Dutch and Bronco are killed. While Bronco's dying

On horseback is the outlaw leader played by Rory Calhoun in *Four Guns to the Border.* Looking up at him is John McIntire.

words to Simon are about Cully being a good man, Simon discerns that the four men are thieves. Cully is shot in the stomach by the Indians as they are driven off by the advancing posse.

Lolly convinces Simon to take Cully to the ranch. Although Cully tries to make a stand against the sheriff, when he comes for him after recovering the stolen money, the outlaw's injury makes it hard. The love Lolly and Cully feel for each other finally does bring him to surrender. Cully will be able to return to her after serving a short jail sentence.

Uncredited Source: The short story "In Victorio's Country."

Plotline: In the Apache country of southern Arizona, Red Clanahan leads three other desperadoes, Bronco Smith, the Dutchman and Yaqui Joe. When they commit a crime in Cholla, Sheriff Bill Gleason and a posse give pursuit. Tragedy awaits the outlaws when they help a brother and sister against marauding Indians.

Commentary: "In Victorio's Country" was not the official source for *Four Guns to the Border.* L'Amour first wrote this short story for the June 1949 issue of *Giant Western* magazine (and it was one of nine L'Amour short stories in the 1995 Bantam Books publication *Valley of the Sun*). Yet Louis definitely contributed a story for the November 1954 film release by Universal-International. It is therefore not implausible to believe that "In Victorio's Country" was the uncredited source because of the similarities between story and film.

Both have four men, three with the same names, robbing a Cholla bank and then trying to escape through hostile Indian country. In both accounts, the gang leader and town sheriff were once pals. In the short story, the outlaws risk their opportunity to escape by aiding two sibling children. An old gunman and his daughter are the recipients of their help in the movie.

L'Amour did use the daughter and her father in his novel *High Lonesome*, which was published by Bantam in 1962. Their names, however, were changed to Dave and Lennie Spanyner. Still, the novel was clearly drawn from the earlier Western film.

Except for Dutch in both accounts, the outlaw names are also different. In the novel, the others are Considine, Hardy and Kiowa. But Dutch is physically a bigger and brawnier man in the L'Amour novel. Dave Spanyer and Dutch did know each other in the past. Obaro, not Cholla, is the town robbed in the book. Pete Runyon is the sheriff and his wife is Mary.

The fistfight between the sheriff and the outlaw leader is one of the major action sequences of novel and film. Storeowner Greasy in the movie becomes Chavez in the book. And Lennie and Considine share a passionate kiss like Lolly and Cully do in the motion picture.

In L'Amour's novel, the place where the s and the outlaws battle the marauding Indians is called High Lonesome. The climactic action sequence is the highlight of both film and novel.

Hardy, Dutch and the Kiowa face the same fate in the novel as do their counterparts both in the short story and film. Unlike the movie's final passage where Sheriff Flannery marks Cully for arrest, each lawman in L'Amour's accounts seem to turn the other cheek in favor of the outlaw leader's sooner-than-later freedom. (Hollywood Westerns would allow an outlaw's escape sometimes and none was better than 1939's *Stagecoach*.)

George Van Marter and Franklin Coen took the story Louis L'Amour wrote for the film back in the 1950s and turned it into a screenplay. The *Variety* review of the film claimed their writing "makes good use of the plot framework and the succession of action events have been well-staged by Richard Carlson."

The working title of *Four Guns to the Border* was *Shadow Valley*. The William Alland production was made between April and May 1954, and included location filming in Apple Valley, California.

Coen and Van Marter's writing credits over the years included both film and television work. A 1960 TV episode of *Dick Powell's Zane Grey Theater* and the script for *Alvarez Kelly*, a 1966 Western, were written by Coen. In 1955, Van Marter wrote a couple of episodes for TV's *The Lone Ranger.*

Director Richard Carlson is perhaps best remembered as an actor during the 1950s. This included science fiction films like *It Came from Outer Space* (1953) and *Creature from the Black Lagoon* (1954).

Rory Calhoun's youthful experiences (including car thief) might have helped him play the good guy–bad guy in some of his films, including *Four Guns to the Border*. Being tall and ruggedly handsome certainly didn't hurt. He was a formidable presence in a good many Westerns during this same period, 1952's *Way of a Gaucho* and 1953's *Powder River* attesting to that fact. The same year he made *Four Guns,* Calhoun co-starred with Robert Mitchum and Marilyn Monroe in *River of No Return.*

The steamy kiss shared by Calhoun and actress Colleen Miller in their film was considered a bit daring for its day. Whether or not L'Amour originally wrote it that way is not known, although he did include it in the later novel. While Miller made for a most attractive heroine, her acting credits were relatively few. She did co-star with Tony Cur-

In true Hollywood fashion, the noble bad man (Rory Calhoun) from *Four Guns to the Border* will be given a chance to return to his sweetheart (Colleen Miller) by the understanding lawman (Charles Drake).

tis in two other Universal films—*The Purple Mask* in 1955 and *The Rawhide Years* in 1956.

Walter Brennan, who played her father, is one of the greatest character actors of all time. Three Academy Awards as Best Supporting Actor reflect that with certainty. One was for his colorful portrayal of Judge Roy Bean in 1940's *The Westerner.*

In *Four Guns to the Border,* John McIntire, George Nader and Jay Silverheels were Rory Calhoun's partners. All were fine actors who worked extensively in television and the movies. Silverheels is remembered fondly as Tonto in TV's *The Lone Ranger* (1949–57). Later work for Nader included guest roles on the TV series *Laramie* in 1960 and *The Andy Griffith Show* in 1961.

Many a Western film in the 1950s benefited from the expertise of John McIntire. In '54 and '55 respectively, he appeared with Burt Lancaster—as scout Al Sieber in *Apache* and as Burt's big brother in *The Kentuckian.*

"The Western action in *Four Guns to the Border* is brought off satisfactorily," opened the review in *Variety.* The *New York Times,* however, called it a "commonplace Western film."

Treasure of Ruby Hills

1955. A William F. Broidy Production.
An Allied Artists Release.
71 Minutes/Black and White.

Credits: William F. Broidy (Producer), Frank McDonald (Director), Tom Hubbard, Fred Eggers (Screenplay), John Martin (Photography), Ace Herman (Editor), George Troast (Art Director), Oscar Rodriguez (Wardrobe), Charles Taylor (Makeup), Edward J. Kay (Music). Based on a story by Louis L'Amour.

Cast: Zachary Scott (Ross Haney), Carole Mathews (Sherry Vernon), Barton MacLane (Chalk Reynolds), Dick Foran (Allan Doran), Lola Albright (May), Gordon Jones (Voyle), Raymond Hatton (Westbrook "Scotty" Scott), Lee Van Cleef (Frank Emmett), Steve Darrell (Tom Hull), Charles Fredericks (Walt Payne), Stanley Andrews (Marshal Garvey), James Alexander (Rolly Burt), Rick Vallin (Bob Vernon).

Synopsis: The year is 1877. In the western town of Arlington, Vin Carter is mortally wounded by backshooter Frank Emmett, after Carter filed a water rights claim on Thousand Springs in the Ruby Hills. The claim was shared with Ross Haney.

Accompanied by old gunslinger Tom Hull, Haney goes to Marshal Garvey about the shooting. Being the son of an outlaw, Haney is warned to stay away from gunmen like Tom. But it is Tom, not Haney, who ends things so the young man can begin a new life as a rancher.

Along the trail, Haney meets Sherry Vernon and after making a bet they race their horses into the nearby town of Soledad. Upset when she loses, Sherry refuses to pay up. Sherry and her brother, Bob, run a ranch in the Ruby Hills valley.

Haney receives a job offer from rancher Walt Payne. There is an ongoing feud between Payne and another rancher, Chalk Reynolds, and *both* ranchers have run roughshod over the smaller ranchers in the area. Haney refuses Payne's offer even as he clarifies his resentment of Frank Emmett, who works for Reynolds.

Haney gets a room at the hotel run by Westbrook "Scotty" Scott. Vin Carter and Scotty were also friends. In an effort to help Haney against Payne and Reynolds, Scotty sells him the only other water rights in the Ruby Hills.

At the saloon, Haney meets ranch hand Rolly Burt. Rolly works for Reynolds yet feels no partiality in the feud between his boss and Payne. Bob Vernon enters the saloon and starts trouble with Haney for not going outside to see his sister. After apologizing to Haney about her earlier conduct and paying the bet, Sherry is kissed by him as payment for the trouble her brother started.

The foreman of the Vernon ranch, Allan Doran, is Sherry's fiancé. He turns out to be the biggest obstacle all the ranchers must face: Doran is the secret leader of a gang

In *Treasure of Ruby Hills,* Zachary Scott and Carole Mathews are the hero and heroine whose love wins out.

comprised of riders from the various ranches. Included are Frank Emmett and a Payne rider named Voyle. Doran has also enflamed the rivalry between Payne and Reynolds. To make matters worse, Doran has taken over the Vernon ranch by blackmailing Bob for a murder and thus forcing Sherry into a forthcoming marriage.

Like Walt Payne, Chalk Reynolds offers Haney a job. Refusing again, Haney reveals that Reynolds killed Vin's father to take over the Carter ranch.

Using two of his gang, Doran tries to kill Rolly Burt. Although injured, Rolly kills one of his assailants. Scotty and May, a waitress, hide Rolly until Haney can safely get him out of town.

Haney is a witness to the murders of both Reynolds and Payne by gunman Voyle. Further gunplay breaks out between their various ranch hands until Doran offers them work.

Rolly informs Haney that Bob Vernon is also working for Doran. Despite her love for Ross, Sherry is too afraid to reveal to him the extent of her brother's involvement. In one more step in his plan to take control of the Ruby Hills, Doran intends to frame Haney on a murder charge. But Bob reveals that the Doran gang is hiding in the ghost town of Silvertown.

A posse formed by Haney includes Marshal Garvey, Rolly, Scotty and Tom Hull. In the big gunfight which follows, the posse defeats the gang. Doran is killed by Haney, but Tom also dies after getting hit with a bullet during the fighting. Waiting to join Ross is Sherry and they ride off together.

Original Source: The novella "The Rider of the Ruby Hills."

Plotline: Lone rider Ross Haney enters country where range warfare is brewing. An attraction develops between Haney and ranch owner Sherry Vernon although she is engaged to entrepreneur Star Levitt. May, Allan Kinney and Westbrook Scott are among the townsfolk of Soledad who befriend Ross, even selling him land in the nearby Ruby Hills. Behind the struggle for the range is Levitt and his secret gang of gunmen like Emmett Chubb, Sydney Berdue, Kerb Dahl, and Voyle. When violence is used against the other ranchers, including Walt Pogue and Chalk Reynolds, Haney is in for the fight of his life. Aiding him are cowboys Bill Mabry and Rolly Burt.

Commentary: "The Rider of the Ruby Hills" first appeared as a novella in the September 1949 issue of *West* magazine, written by L'Amour using the pseudonym Jim Mayo. It was retitled *Treasure of Ruby Hills* when it became a film, produced by William F. Broidy in less than two weeks between October and November 1954. A few California ranches were used for location filming, including the Placeritas Ranch in Placerita Canyon. In January 1955, the film was released by Allied Artists.

Louis rewrote the story as an actual book novel, under his own name, for publication in 1976 by Bantam. It was called *Where the Long Grass Blows* and followed the initial story's plotline very closely. Details, however, were added to expand story into novel. An example is in Chapter 13 with a descriptive layout of the town of Soledad.

A number of names were changed for the novel from the novella. Ross Haney was changed to Bill Canavan, Sherry and Bob Vernon to Dixie and Tom Venable, Chalk Reynolds and his RR brand to Charlie Reynolds and the CR, and Kinney's first name Allan to Allen. Kinney was not used as a character in the film nor were Bill Mabry, Sydney Berdue and Kerb Dahl.

The biggest name difference was that of the head villain. While he is Star Levitt in each of the L'Amour stories, he is called Allan Doran in the movie. Also in the film, Walt Payne is the name used for Walt Pogue from the stories, and Frank Emmett for Emmett Chubb. The character of Tom Hull in the film was not in either of L'Amour's stories.

As the film was based on the novella, rather than the novel, the original leading character names of Ross Haney and Sherry Vernon were carried over, as were Bob Vernon and Chalk Reynolds. Other supporting characters from both stories who made it into the film were May, Voyle, Westbrook Scott and Rolly Burt.

Known for sometimes failing to recheck his writing, Louis could then certainly make mistakes. An error does occur in Chapter 7 of the novel when Canavan says that one of Dixie's riders uses a brand which actually belongs to rancher Pogue in both the novella and novel.

There seems to be an error in continuity as well. During the novel's Chapter 14, Dixie Venable turns in for the night after talking with Levitt in her dining room. Yet in the next chapter, it is still the same night and they are in the dining room together as Bill Canavan watches from outside.

There is at least one instance that is more detailed in the novella than in the novel. This too is in Chapter 7 and reflects the hero's interest in reading. Unlike the novel, actually mentioned are Plutarch's *Lives* and Shakespeare's sonnets and plays as reading material. In a good many of his stories, Louis's protagonists were intelligent readers.

In both of the L'Amour tales, and the film, the hero and heroine's first encounter is a horse race into town. Later, following his rough exchange with her brother in the saloon, she does make amends for being a sore loser. Boldly entering the saloon in the stories, she remains outside in the film. Some Westerns, like *Treasure of Ruby Hills*, held to the notion that decent women didn't go into saloons.

It is the gunman Voyle who shoots down the two rival ranchers, Payne and Reynolds, in the movie. While Voyle participates in their murders in the stories, Sydney Berdue and others join in as well.

Prior to their demise, both ranchers offer the hero work in each of the three versions. It is Reynolds in the film, but Pogue in the stories, who has the hero's friend Vin Carter killed for his ranch land. In the film, Carter and Ross Haney actually started as business partners in the Ruby Hills.

The single greatest difference between L'Amour's stories and the motion picture is its climax. The hidden valley of cattle and the cavern with the geyser, spectacular in the stories, were replaced in the film with a standard gun battle in a ghost town. Undoubtedly the restraints of a low budget kept such settings from being realized.

Following its release, *Treasure of Ruby Hills* did receive harsh criticism. "A jerky, talky script attempts feebly to explain the childish goings-on," griped *National Parent-Teacher. Variety* added, "A complicated story line brought on by over-plottage reduces this Zachary Scott Western to the also-ran category, a waste of good talent." Scott, not considered as "believable" in the role of Ross Haney by *Variety*, was perhaps not a strong enough presence to fill the boots of L'Amour's tall, rugged hero.

Still, the actor had a number of creditable Western film roles under his belt, which included 1949's *South of St. Louis* and 1950's *Colt .45.* Scott made an impressive film debut as a villain in 1944's *The Mask of Dimitrios,* and was somewhat more effective in that mode.

His leading lady, Carole Mathews, appeared in a good many television shows during the 1950s and 1960s. Her Western TV assignments included *The Adventures of Jim Bowie* in 1957 and *The Texan* in 1958. In 1961, she played Belle Starr on an episode of *Death Valley Days.*

Barton MacLane, who played Chalk Reynolds, was a big tough guy who made memorable impressions in many a film. Among them are his fight with Tim Holt and

Stanley Andrews, Zachary Scott and Steve Darrell are allies in *Treasure of Ruby Hills.* Andrews was the Old Ranger on television's *Death Valley Days.*

Humphrey Bogart in 1948's *The Treasure of the Sierra Madre* and his gunning down Randolph Scott in 1941's *Western Union.*

As the main bad guy in this Western, Dick Foran, like Zachary Scott, lacked the strength of presence the part demanded. Foran was perhaps just too likable of a performer over a long career on TV and in the movies. During the 1930s, he was billed as Dick Foran the Singing Cowboy in a series of films. By the early 1960s, he had the recurring role of fire chief Ed Washburne on the *Lassie* TV series.

A really strong bad man in Westerns, and seen in that capacity in this one, was Lee Van Cleef. After making his film debut menacing Gary Cooper in the 1952 classic *High Noon,* he also menaced Kirk Douglas in 1957's *Gunfight at the O.K. Corral* and Gregory Peck in 1958's *The Bravados.*

Although director Frank McDonald did what he could to salvage *Treasure of Ruby Hills,* it did not play well then and has not worn well over the years. Like *Four Guns to the Border,* it was deemed a B Western despite the solid cast. McDonald directed plenty of B Westerns, including a whole series he did with Roy Rogers and Republic Pictures in the 1940s. Among their best was 1946's *My Pal Trigger.* His directional work with Allied Artists also included 1953's *Son of Belle Starr.*

Tom Hubbard and Fred Eggers were the screenwriters who adapted L'Amour's earlier story. *Daniel Boone, Trail Blazer* (1956) was another of Hubbard's film scripts. Between 1951 and 1955, he also wrote four episodes of the TV series *Adventures of Wild Bill Hickok.* Eggers wrote for television as well, although his credits were fewer. They included episodes of both *Have Gun, Will Travel* and *Maverick.*

In 1986, Bantam published a book called *The Rider of the Ruby Hills* which contained Louis's original magazine story as well as three other stories he wrote. In that book's foreword, L'Amour wrote, "Once accepted as a novelist I was able to realize my long-held wish to redo my magazine novels for publication as books."

Called a novella, "The Rider of the Ruby Hills" fit that particular word's description of either a short novel or a long short story. Turned into at the most a routine Western film, L'Amour's two stories, which preceded and followed it, displayed the writer's penchant for suspenseful if sometimes wordy tales brimming with characters and flavored with action.

Climax

1955. A Chrysler Corporation Presentation.
CBS Television.
60 Minutes/Black and White.

Episode: "The Mojave Kid."

Credits: Bretaigne Windust (Producer), William H. Brown, Jr. (Director), Gil Doud (Teleplay). Based on a story by Louis L'Amour.

Cast: Ricardo Montalban (Pete McLean), Ward Bond (Sheriff Ab Kale), Barbara Ruick (Judith Kale), John Lupton (The Mojave Kid).

Synopsis: The Mojave Kid, an infamous gunman, seeks revenge against Sheriff Ab Kale for the death of his brother. The sheriff is unable to stand up to the Kid when threatened by his fast draw. Befriending vagrant Pete McLean, the sheriff teaches him to use a gun. Meanwhile, the Mojave Kid is terrorizing the town.

The sheriff does muster up his courage against the gunman, but it is Pete's own gun hand which makes the Kid show fear. The Mojave Kid then leaves town.

Original Source: The short story "The One for the Mohave Kid."

Plotline: Marshal Ab Kale doesn't want the killer known as the Mohave Kid in his town of Hinkley. Welcomed, however, is gunsmith Riley McLean, who falls in love with Ab's daughter, Ruth. Riley also helps the marshal against the Kid.

Commentary: The dramatic anthology series *Climax* was presented by Chrysler Corporation for CBS-TV between October 1954 and June 1958. William Lundigan hosted the series for the entire run, and was joined by Mary Costa in the last two seasons. It alternated with another series hosted by Lundigan, *Shower of Stars*, which revolved around musicals and comedies.

The works of various authors were adapted for *Climax*, including Ian Fleming, whose James Bond novel *Casino Royale* was the basis for one episode. The British spy was Americanized, however, with Barry Nelson playing Bond. Over time, this series moved away from live black-and-white telecasts; filmed and taped entries were seen, some of which were in color.

Episode 13 during the first season, "The Mojave Kid," was based on a short story by L'Amour. In the September 1954 issue of *Western Short Stories* magazine, Louis's tale was printed as "The One for the Mohave Kid." (Bantam Books included it in the 1986 L'Amour collection *Dutchman's Flat.*) The story was altered quite a bit when it was adapted by writer Gil Doud for its telecast on January 27, 1955. William H. Brown, Jr., directed the episode.

The differences right away are the title and name spellings — Mojave Kid for the show and Mohave Kid for the short story. Ab Kale is given a stronger constitution by Louis when first facing the Kid than the TV lawman. Riley McClean in the story becomes Pete McLean in the show. And Ab's daughter is Judith for the show and Ruth for the story.

But the biggest difference is the Kid's fate. Instead of facing a tragic end as in the L'Amour story, the show's Kid is made to feel the same sense of fear he used to humiliate the marshal.

Variety's reviewer felt that "Gil Doud's adaptation of Louis L'Amour's original was confused and protracted." The review erred in calling the tale original since it was taken from the magazine story.

Doud also wrote for motion pictures, *Saskatchewan* (1954) starring Alan Ladd among them. As a director, William H. Brown, Jr., helmed other episodes of *Climax*, including "Casino Royale" on October 14, 1954.

While three fine actors — Ricardo Montalban, John Lupton and Ward Bond — starred in "The Mojave Kid," they perhaps were not seen to their best advantage. Montalban was later seen on other shows co-starring Lupton or Bond. In '56, Lupton and Montalban appeared in the "Broken Arrow" episode of the TV series *20th Century–Fox Hour*. And in '57, Ricardo was a guest star on Bond's series *Wagon Train*.

Stranger on Horseback

1955. A Leonard Goldstein Production.
Released by United Artists.
66 Minutes/Ansco Color.

Credits: Robert Goldstein (Producer), Jacques Tourneur (Director), Herb Meadow, Don Martin (Screenplay), Ray Rennahan (Photography), William B. Murphy (Editor), Albert Hogsett (Art Director), Victor Gangelin (Set Decorator), Jack Byron, Wilton Fields (Makeup), Paul Dunlap (Music). Based on a story by Louis L'Amour.

Cast: Joel McCrea (Rick Thorne), Miroslava (Amy Lee Bannerman), Kevin McCarthy (Tom Bannerman), John McIntire (Josiah Bannerman), John Carradine (Buck Streeter), Nancy Gates (Caroline Webb), Emile Meyer (Marshal Nat Bell), Robert Cornthwaite (Arnold Hammer), Jaclynne Greene (Paula Morison), James Bell (Vince Webb), Roy Roberts (Sam Kettering).

Synopsis: Circuit judge Rick Thorne arrives in the Western town of Bannerman to go over its records. Thorne sees that the businesses in town are all owned by cattle baron Josiah Bannerman and his family. Through Marshal Nat Bell, Thorne learns of a recent shooting which has left a citizen, Sidney Morison, dead. While this shooting (done by Tom Bannerman, Josiah's son), was supposedly in self-defense, Thorne still wants Tom to stand trial.

The marshal believes no one in town will be part of a posse to go after Tom. When Tom and some of his ranch hands come into town, Thorne asks Bell for help in arresting young Bannerman. Thinking Thorne should do it alone, Bell declines. Standing up to Tom, Thorne beats him to the draw and hauls him off to jail. Now respecting Thorne, Bell fires a shot as a warning to the ranch hands.

The following day, Thorne is told by district attorney Buck Streeter that he (Streeter) will prosecute the case against Tom. Thorne realizes this is a conflict of interest since Streeter is Josiah's personal counsel. At the jail, Josiah's niece, Amy Lee Bannerman, confronts Thorne over locking up Tom, angry about Thorne daring to challenge the Bannermans' control on the town. Thorne visits Paula Morison, the slain man's widow, and learns that he never even carried a gun and that Tom was harassing her. Paula was even paid to leave town after the killing.

Back in town, district attorney Streeter hints that Josiah Bannerman will give Thorne political support if Tom is let go. Thorne refuses the offer. Gunsmith Vince Webb reveals to Thorne that both he and his daughter Caroline saw an unarmed Sidney Morison gunned down by Tom. Caroline admits that she refrained from stepping forward because she was hoping Tom would marry her.

Out riding, Amy Lee lies that her horse has run off so that Thorne will take her back to the Bannerman ranch. Josiah orders Thorne to release his son to him (Josiah) for punishment.

Thorne warns Marshal Bell that Tom will have to be moved that night to the neighboring town of Cottonwood so that Tom can be brought to trial. Confronted once more by Amy Lee before leaving, Thorne is kissed by her after being warned that he is in danger. Thorne feels this is another ploy to see Tom freed.

The marshal and Thorne leave with Tom and the Webbs, who will testify against him. When Josiah realizes this, he rides with his men to stop Thorne along a mountain pass. Meanwhile, Amy Lee rides to warn Rick of the approaching riders. Not realizing that her feelings for Thorne are sincere, Tom admits to Amy Lee that he murdered Morison. Moving along the mountain pass, Tom manages to shove Webb over the edge and to his death. Amy Lee is shocked by this action and, when Josiah appears with his men, says that her loyalty is now with Thorne.

Overwhelmed by so many men against him, Thorne begins to ride away, leaving Tom behind. Reaching cover, however, he starts a gun battle with his adversaries. Thorne is joined by the marshal. Amy Lee then forces Tom's horse, to which he is tied, to gallop to Cottonwood.

Surrendering to Thorne and Bell, Josiah leaves with his riders and Amy Lee. Later, in the courtroom, Amy Lee is there as Thorne starts the trial.

Commentary: Like 1953's *East of Sumatra*, the film *Stranger on Horseback* was based on an original story written for the big screen by L'Amour. It was produced by Robert Goldstein over a three-week period starting on July 12, 1954. With this schedule, a running time of just over one hour, and a budget of $380,000, the film had all the earmarks of just another B Western.

Like *Treasure of Ruby Hills*, it was partly shot in Placerita Canyon in Newhall, California — on Gene Autry's Melody Ranch, to be exact. Location filming also took place in Sedona, Arizona.

"A routine Western with a better-than-average theme," was how *National Parent-Teacher* labeled the film after its release by United Artists in February 1955.

The Herb Meadow–Don Martin screenplay, derived from the L'Amour story, was seemingly a familiar one. What raised this motion picture above the ordinary to almost the extraordinary were the people behind it.

Jacques Tourneur's astute direction and Joel McCrea's equally adept acting, in a role to which he was perfectly suited, were the strongest assets. While *Variety* noted that the direction was "good," it began its review with the following statement. "Joel McCrea brings law and order to the range in *Stranger on Horseback* and the stalwart, unflinching manner with which he tackles the chore makes for good viewing for the outdoors action fan."

Joel McCrea's Rick Thorne in *Stranger on Horseback* was the first of two roles he would play in movies based on Louis L'Amour stories. (The other was *The Tall Stranger*.)

McCrea so believed in the film that he waived his usual high salary in the face of the small budget and tight schedule. Instead he opted to take a percentage deal, and the Western proved successful.

Like L'Amour, McCrea had grandparents who were part of the Western experience: His maternal grandmother traveled west in a covered wagon, and his paternal grandfather battled Apache Indians. On the advice of humorist-actor Will Rogers, Joel invested in land during his many years in the film business. He became not only a successful rancher but also a superb horseman. In his later years making Westerns, he used one of his own horses, Dollar.

Stranger on Horseback was Joel's second of three films with director Tourneur. In 1950, they did a movie that became a personal favorite of McCrea's, *Stars in My Crown*. Although Western-flavored, it was actually set in the Old South. Their last film was another Western, *Wichita* (1955), in which McCrea portrayed Wyatt Earp.

Joel's leading lady, Miroslava (her last name was Stern), was originally from Czechoslovakia. After moving to Mexico, she became a film star in that country. She committed suicide in Mexico City on March 10, 1955, when she was only 30 years old. In 1993, her life story became a film called *Miroslava*.

In *Stranger on Horseback,* Joel McCrea and John Carradine size each other up.

As the patriarch, John McIntire once again proved his credibility as a fine character actor. His range lent special depth to roles like this one, rough yet sympathetic. In the early 1960s, McIntire made his mark on television when he took over as wagonmaster on *Wagon Train.*

A few years before making this Western, Kevin McCarthy received an Oscar nomination for Best Supporting Actor as one of the sons in 1951's *Death of a Salesman.* McCarthy more than held his own against the seasoned McCrea.

The actor playing the lawman who finds self-respect, Emile Meyer, was a forceful presence in films. He made an especially memorable villain as the corrupt cop who busts Tony Curtis in 1957's *Sweet Smell of Success* and as the nemesis of Alan Ladd and Van Heflin in 1953's *Shane.*

Still another notable character actor in this film was John Carradine. His speaking voice and style lent distinction to such roles as Hatfield in 1939's *Stagecoach* and Dracula in 1944's *House of Frankenstein* and 1945's *House of Dracula.*

Suspense was another key factor in *Stranger on Horseback*'s success. Jacques Tourneur

Joel McCrea and Emile Meyer's lawman become allies in *Stranger on Horseback.* Meyer also co-starred in L'Amour's *Taggart* when it was turned into a film.

started his directorial career with three cult horror films, and creating suspense became his forte. The films were 1942's *Cat People* and 1943's *I Walked with a Zombie* and *The Leopard Man.* Tourneur also directed the marvelously entertaining *The Flame and the Arrow* in 1950.

Writers Don Martin and Herb Meadow undoubtedly should receive praise for their contribution to this Western. Other writing credits for Martin included two 1957 television episodes for the series *Sheriff of Cochise.* He also wrote the story for a 1968 Lee Van Cleef film, *Commandos.*

In 1950 and '51, Meadow wrote ten episodes of the TV series *The Lone Ranger.* When Clayton Moore reprised his famous role in the 1956 feature film *The Lone Ranger,* Meadow wrote the screenplay.

While *Stranger on Horseback* is a little gem of a Western, Jacques Tourneur felt the Ansco Color process gave it a flat look. Warm praise was given to Joel McCrea by L'Amour: Louis told McCrea that he played Rick Thorne just as the character was intended.

City Detective

1955. A Revue Production.
On Syndicated Television.
30 Minutes/Black and White.

Episode: "Man Down, Woman Screaming."

Credits: Herschel Daugherty (Director), Lawrence Kimble (Teleplay). Based on a story by Louis L'Amour.

Cast: Rod Cameron (Lt. Bart Grant). Guest cast: Jack Kelly (Arthur), Beverly Garland (Jeanne), Lee Van Cleef (Hardtman).

Synopsis: A construction engineer named Arthur is kidnapped so that a criminal can steal his identity and get out of the country. The hired kidnappers are named Jeanne and Hardtman. But Arthur manages to plant a clue for the police. Detective Bart Grant rescues Arthur, and the guilty parties are brought to justice.

Commentary: Revue Productions' syndicated TV series *City Detective* ran for two seasons between 1953 and 1955. Each of its 64 episodes was 30 minutes long. Big and brawny, Rod Cameron starred in this series as two-fisted detective lieutenant Bart Grant, who was New York City–based but fought crime wherever he was needed. A staunch trouper in B Westerns of the 1940s and early 1950s, Cameron was especially popular on a later syndicated television show, *State Trooper* (1956–59). Whether as a law enforcer on TV or riding the range in films, Cameron had all the markings of a typical L'Amour hero. Yet his acting persona was at times so rock-like that it might have kept him from becoming an even bigger star.

Episode 28 of the second season of *City Detective* was entitled "Man Down, Woman Screaming." Its airdate was on April 26, 1955. The Lawrence Kimble teleplay was derived from a story by Louis L'Amour. Kimble worked on five episodes over the course of the series. In 1960, he was a writer on another Rod Cameron series, *Coronado 9*, about a private eye.

In later years, Herschel Daugherty's work as a director included the TV Westerns *Wagon Train, Rawhide,* and *Bonanza.* He also directed the 1958 Walt Disney film *The Light in the Forest.*

According to the *Official Louis L'Amour* Website, L'Amour wrote a couple of stories which were used on the *Cowboy G-Men* television series. But like the *City Detective* episode, it could not be discerned if they were original or from earlier magazine stories by the author. *Cowboy G-Men* aired in syndication between September 1952 and June 1953. Telemount Mutual made the 39-episode series with Henry B. Donovan and Russell Hayden co-producing. Hayden also co-starred with actor Jackie Coogan. The two performers played, respectively, undercover Federal agents Pat Gallagher and Stoney Crockett, who in the 1880s traveled incognito as cowboys to catch the bad guys. *Cowboy G-Men* was fun to watch and enjoyed some popularity.

Televised only on the West Coast and from Four Star Productions, *Chevron Hall of*

Stars also featured an episode during 1956 based on a L'Amour short story. Called "The Defense of Sentinel," it was initially written in 1952 for *5 Western Novels* magazine.

Blackjack Ketchum, Desperado

1956. A Clover Production.
Released by Columbia Pictures.
76 Minutes/Black and White.

Credits: Sam Katzman (Producer), Earl Bellamy (Director), Luci Ward & Jack Natteford (Screenplay), Fred Jackman, Jr. (Photography), Saul A. Goodkind (Editor), Paul Palmentola (Art Director), Sidney Clifford (Set Decorator), Mischa Bakaleinikoff (Music). Based on a novel by Louis L'Amour.

Cast: Howard Duff (Tom "Blackjack" Ketchum), Victor Jory (Jared Tetlow), Maggie Mahoney (Nita Riordan), Angela Stevens (Laurie Webster), David Orrick (Bob Early), William Tannen (Dee Havalik), Ken Christy (Sheriff Macy), Martin Garralaga (Jaime Brigo), Robert Roark (Ben Tetlow), Don C. Harvey (Mac Gill), Pat O'Malley (Doc Blaine), Jack Littlefield (Burl Tetlow), Sydney Mason (Matt Riordan), Ralph Sanford (Happy Harrow), George Edward Mather (Andy Tetlow), Charles Wagenheim (Jarry Carson), Wes Hudman (Grat Barbey).

Synopsis: At the Oxhorn stage station in New Mexico, gunfighter Tom "Blackjack" Ketchum is forced to kill the brother of Jared Tetlow, a cattle baron, to protect his friend Jaime Brigo. Tom and Jaime then ride to the Double R ranch in Horseshoe Valley. The ranch is run by another friend, Matt Riordan, and Matt's daughter Nita. After buying his own land for a ranch, Tom would like to marry Nita although he feels his gunfighting past might be a problem.

Wanting control of the whole range for his cattle, Jared Tetlow becomes angered when the other ranchers don't feel the same way. Ben, his younger brother, wants him to work things out with the ranchers. When Jared finds out about Burl's death at the stage station, he wants revenge. Yet he follows Ben's advice, offering to buy the grazing land he needs. But when a rancher named Carson refuses, Jared allows Dee Havalik, a hired gunman, to kill him.

Sheriff Macy has a coroner's jury convene on the killing, despite Jared's claim that it was in self-defense. Tetlow has men beat Matt Riordan to make the jury free Havalik. Trying to stop Tetlow's destructive course, the sheriff seeks help from Ketchum. Attorney Bob Early and Doc Blaine help by driving Jared's men off the Double R.

Havalik and other men are sent by Jared to kill Tom. But Ketchum is too crafty, luring his adversaries into the desert where he can get the drop on some of them. Worried about Tom, Nita sneaks into Tetlow's campsite and uncovers a plot to stampede cattle on her ranch. But she is too late to prevent it and her father is killed.

Havalik guns down the sheriff when he attempts to arrest him for Matt's death.

Jaime Brigo tries to get the town to go against Tetlow and his gang, but Tom urges caution since Jared is hoarding all the munitions.

When the munitions are located, Tom leads a group of citizens to recover them by stampeding Tetlow's cattle against him. Andy, another brother of Jared's, dies in the process. Back in town, Tetlow shoots a man for trying to send word to the territorial marshal. Taking a stand against his own brother, Ben Tetlow informs Tom that Havalik is out to get Nita. With Ben helping to stop Jared's men, Tom goes after Dee Havalik. In their showdown, Tom Ketchum is faster and kills his adversary.

Jared's arrest finally ends the violence, and Ben gives his brother's cattle to the town as compensation. Tom and Nita's marriage plans can now move forward.

Original Source: The novel *Kilkenny.*

Plotline: A son of cattleman Jared Tetlow is killed in a gunfight. Lawyer Bob Early's niece, Laurie Webster, witnessed it; only later do the townsfolk of Horsehead recognize the other gunman as Lance Kilkenny. The first is Dolan, a shady businessman whose life was once saved by the gunfighter.

Victor Jory, Howard Duff, Angela Stevens, and David Orrick in a tense moment from *Blackjack Ketchum, Desperado.*

Kilkenny becomes the catalyst in the fight to keep Tetlow, his other sons and a hired killer, Dee Havalik, from taking over the whole range. Jared's son Ben Tetlow backs Kilkenny, as does Lance's old flame Nita Riordan, whose own ranch is being threatened. Providing especially strong support for Nita and Lance are her foreman, Jaime Brigo, and ranch hand Cain Brockman.

Commentary: Louis L'Amour's novel *Kilkenny* was published in 1954 by Ace Books. Various reprints followed, including one from Bantam Books in 1983.

The story was the third one about gunslinger Lance Kilkenny. He initially appeared in the April and December 1947 issues of *West* magazine. They were novellas Louis wrote (as Jim Mayo) entitled "The Rider of Lost Creek" and "A Man Called Trent."

In 1976, Bantam published *The Rider of Lost Creek* as a novel after it was expanded a bit by L'Amour. The novella "A Man Called Trent" became part of Bantam's 1986 collection *The Rider of the Ruby Hills*; the story was also expanded by Louis into a 1978 novel for Bantam, *The Mountain Valley War.*

Three more Kilkenny tales were also written — a pair of short stories and another novella — and became part of Bantam collections. They were "A Gun for Kilkenny" in 1986's *Dutchman's Flat* and "West of Dodge" and "Monument Rock" in 1996 and 1999 books of the same titles.

Nita Riordan, Jaime Brigo and Cain Brockman are all featured in the novellas as well. The initial two novellas (and later expanded novels), like *Kilkenny*, have a range war theme, which was commonly used by L'Amour to good advantage throughout his writing career.

"The Rider of Lost Creek," and the novel of the same title, do bear a similarity to both "The Rider of the Ruby Hills" and *Where the Long Grass Blows.* Whereas Star Levitt is the main villain instigating trouble between ranchers Pogue and Reynolds in these latter two tales, it is Royal Barnes stirring things up between cattlemen Chet Lord and Webb Steele in the former ones. While Nita owns a saloon in the first Kilkenny story and a gambling house in the second, with Brigo as her bodyguard, the biggest development is with Brockman. Cain and brother Abel are renegades working for Barnes in the first story. Kilkenny and Cain are therefore initially enemies. But in "A Man Called Trent" and the follow-up novel, Cain Brockman is talked out of making further trouble for Kilkenny, who uses the name Trent instead of his own. (He uses the name early on in *Kilkenny* as well.)

Without then having to worry about Cain, Kilkenny finds he has his hands full with King Bill Hale. Like Jared Tetlow, King Bill wants the range for his cattle. The difference between the two cattlemen is that Hale already lives in the area and Tetlow is searching elsewhere for land.

In each of the initial stories, there are murderous sons. Chet Lord's son, Steve, in the first one and King Bill's son, Cub, in the second are both killers.

Nita and Lance fall in love in the first story. Yet it's not until the third story that Kilkenny is able to come to terms with his gunfighter status. After that, their future together is finally on the right path.

When L'Amour's *Kilkenny* was turned into a motion picture, it was called *Blackjack Ketchum, Desperado.* Tom Ketchum was a real man whose life had nothing to do with the events in Louis's story although, like Kilkenny, he packed two guns and had a notorious reputation.

Jilted by his lady fair, Tom Ketchum took it so badly that he beat himself senseless and turned to a life of crime. With other outlaws, including his brother Sam, he robbed stages and trains. Both brothers were called Blackjack at various times.

In 1899, Sam and two others had a shootout with the law and he was shot in the shoulder. When gangrene set in, the arm was crudely amputated and he soon died.

Tom was alone that same year when he attempted to rob another train. Hit with buckshot, he was captured and sentenced to hang as train robbery was then a capital offense in some parts of the West. In Clayton, New Mexico, on April 25, 1901, Tom "Blackjack" Ketchum was hanged in a horrid execution which in fact decapitated him. His last words as he stood on the gallows were, "Let her rip."

Blackjack Ketchum, Desperado was made between September 19 and October 1, 1955. It was released in March 1956 by Columbia Pictures. According to the *New York Times,* it was "without fanfare" and "filling the lower half of the bill." Howard Duff starred in the title role and did a good job. In the tradition of Kilkenny, he wore black and carried two guns. His appearance "obviously was confusing to some young students of Western film lore at one theatre yesterday," further noted the *Times.* "Since when, they wanted to know, does the good guy wear black?"

For L'Amour, the color of a man's clothes did not determine whether he was bad or good. But Hollywood did not always feel the same way. Both Robert Taylor and Burt Lancaster were among the actors playing bad guys and wearing black in (respectively) 1941's *Billy the Kid* and 1954's *Vera Cruz.*

As radio's private eye Sam Spade, Duff first made his mark during the 1940s. His film debut was as one of Lancaster's cellmates in 1947's *Brute Force.* Duff fit well in both dramas and Westerns. The actor portrayed Samuel Clemens, a.k.a. Mark Twain, in a 1959 episode of *Bonanza.* A solid stature and strong voice made Duff's presence always notable whether in films or television.

Maggie Mahoney, who played Nita Riordan in *Blackjack Ketchum,* was formerly known as Margaret Field. Actress Sally Field is her daughter. Many television appearances are credited to Maggie Mahoney–Margaret Field. As Margaret, she played in two 1954 episodes of *The Gene Autry Show,* and as Maggie she played Bridget Malone in three 1958 episodes of her husband Jock Mahoney's series *Yancy Derringer.*

Victor Jory and William Tannen were the bad guys in this Western. Their extensive film credits go back to 1930 and 1934, respectively. Jory was particularly effective etching out remarkable villains with his sinister persona. Two of his best were Injun Joe in 1938's *The Adventures of Tom Sawyer* and Ike Clanton in 1942's *Tombstone, the Town Too Tough to Die.* He also had the title role in the 1940 serial *The Shadow.*

Tannen's work included comedy, adventure and Western films. Between 1950 and

1955, the actor made a few Jungle Jim movies with Johnny Weissmuller, and during the 1957–58 TV season, he played Deputy Hal Norton on *The Life and Legend of Wyatt Earp.*

Earl Bellamy began his motion picture career as an assistant director. One of the films he worked on in this capacity was 1953's *From Here to Eternity.* He directed his first Western film, *Seminole Uprising,* in 1955. *Blackjack Ketchum, Desperado* was his second. Also directing for TV, Bellamy's credits included *The Adventures of Rin Tin Tin* in 1954 and *Young Dan'l Boone* in 1977. In between these shows, he also showed a flair for comedies like *The Andy Griffith Show* and *M*A*S*H.*

The fact that cattle baron Jared Tetlow remains alive at the end of *Blackjack Ketchum* was considered a bit of a letdown. Yet L'Amour interpreted his story that way so the climax could be the riveting showdown between Dee Havalik and the hero. The film also interprets it that way.

Skillful writers able to bring out the very best in B Westerns were Luci Ward and Jack Natteford. Their screen credits were most impressive. Several early John Wayne Westerns attest to Luci Ward's capabilities. Included were the 1938 oaters featuring

In a romantic respite from the gunplay in *Blackjack Ketchum, Desperado* are its heroine and hero, Maggie Mahoney and Howard Duff.

The Three Mesquiteers (*Overland Stage Raiders, Santa Fe Stampede* and *Red River Range*). *Calling Wild Bill Elliott* (1943) was another of her writing credits.

Both *The Lonely Trail* and *The Oregon Trail* were Wayne films that Jack Natteford scripted in 1936. He wrote the screenplay for 1938's *Rawhide,* the Western made by baseball immortal Lou Gehrig. Natteford, who collaborated with L'Amour on *East of Sumatra,* also worked with Ward on *Black Bart* and *Return of the Badmen* (both 1948).

Out of the entries that make up the Louis L'Amour filmography, *Blackjack Ketchum, Desperado* is perhaps the oddest. Perhaps it was felt to be a more commercial title. During this same period, there were a number of B Westerns undoubtedly attempting to capitalize on the appeal of outlaws of the Old West. Such films included two in '54, *Jesse James vs. the Daltons* and *The Law vs. Billy the Kid.*

Aside from not using Kilkenny's name for this '56 Western, the overall theme of a gunfighter versus a cattleman was adhered to from its source. Each version opens at a stage station with the hero's shooting of a Tetlow (Bud in the book, Burl in the film). In the novel, Jamie Brigo is not seen until later when Lance Kilkenny rides by Nita's ranch.

As in the book, the film has the hero wanting to settle down and marry Nita Riordan but at odds with his past as a gunman. Of course, in both the issue is happily resolved. Her father, however, is killed by a Jared Tetlow–ordered cattle stampede in the movie; while he has already died before the novel even begins.

There are two lawmen in the book, only one in the film. Marshal Lott in the novel is the victim of Dee Havalik rather than the film's Sheriff Macy. Macy is still a pivotal character in both. Other townsfolk featured in both versions included Laurie Webster, Bob Early and Doc Blaine. Left out of the film is Dolan, who backs Kilkenny's stand against Tetlow in the book.

Andy and Ben Tetlow are Jared's sons in the L'Amour novel, his brothers in the movie. While Andy is the victim of a stampede in the latter, he meets his end in the book's gunfight against Cain Brockman. Another son, Phin Tetlow, is also not included in the film.

Schlitz Playhouse of Stars

1956. A Meridian Production.
CBS Television.
30 Minutes/Black and White.

Episode: "Flowers for Jenny."

Credits: William Self (Producer), Don Weis (Director), Jameson Brewer (Teleplay), George T. Clemens (Photography), Sam Gold (Editor), Serge Krizman (Art Director). Based on a story by Louis L'Amour.

Cast: Dale Robertson (The Arizona Kid), Claudia Barrett (Jenny), Elisha Cook, Jr., James Griffith, Richard Reeves (Outlaw Brothers).

Synopsis: In the Wild West, schoolmarm Jenny and the Arizona Kid are sweet on each other. Despite the threat of three outlaw brothers, she makes the Kid refrain from using his fists or guns against them. Instead, Jenny sends the Kid to find flowers although the area is troubled by drought. In accomplishing this task, he also manages to capture the outlaws.

Original Source: The short story "Love and the Cactus Kid."

Plotline: To prove his love to pretty Jenny Simms, the Cactus Kid agrees to find her flowers. Due to a drought, the Kid must travel afar in his quest. Proving an even bigger obstacle, however, are outlaw brothers Red, Joe and Benny Herring.

Commentary: CBS-TV's *Schlitz Playhouse of Stars* debuted as a live dramatic anthology series in 1951. It was made by Meridian Productions and sponsored by the Schlitz Brewing Company. Established stars guested on the series; actress Irene Dunne was its hostess in 1952. It had an eight-year run. The running time was changed in '52 from 60 minutes to 30 and the live broadcasts were dropped in '56. Its title was even shortened to just *Schlitz Playhouse.* And while the quality of the programs was felt to have diminished over the years, interesting episodes and surprising stars occasionally showed up.

"Flowers for Jenny" aired on August 3, 1956. It was episode 44 of season five. The source story, "Love and the Cactus Kid," first appeared in the fall 1950 issue of the magazine *Thrilling Ranch Stories.* It was the second of several Cactus Kid yarns that Louis wrote. In 1990, Bantam published it as part of the L'Amour collection *The Outlaws of Mesquite.*

The Cactus Kid becomes the Arizona Kid in the TV episode and Jenny becomes a schoolmarm. In both versions, she does not want her fellow to shoot anybody while gathering the flowers. But he is forced to use his firepower against the outlaws, albeit without killing them, in the short story.

"This *Schlitz* entry is weak," noted *Variety,* "with the [story] suffering from a serious case of gaposis." Although *Variety* also felt that Dale Robertson "doesn't expand too much effort on his role," he conveyed both a charm and strength as the Arizona Kid. These qualities were put to much better use in another story for *Schlitz Playhouse*: On December 14, 1956, the actor appeared in the *Playhouse*'s pilot for a proposed Western series which became *Tales of Wells Fargo.* As special agent Jim Hardie, Robertson starred in this popular series from 1957 to 1962.

Robertson appeared as Jesse James in the first Western film he made. It was 1949's *Fighting Man of the Plains* starring Randolph Scott. Another Scott Western followed in 1950, *The Cariboo Trail.*

Like L'Amour, Robertson came from a Western background, as he was raised on a ranch in Oklahoma, and was even a prizefighter in his youth. With his fine physical stature and grace, and Oklahoma accent, he embodied the perfect Westerner.

Robertson never did a feature film based on one of L'Amour's stories, but his co-star in this TV episode did: Claudia Barrett, who played Jenny, had a role in 1964's *Taggart.* The actress had roles in other Westerns as well as *Robot Monster* (1953), a science fiction movie. In 1960, she was in the Audie Murphy horse opera *Seven Ways from Sundown.*

Jameson Brewer's other TV writing credits included two 1962 episodes of *Alcoa Premiere.* One of them, "Flashing Spikes," had James Stewart in a guest spot and John Wayne doing a cameo.

Director Don Weis had a flair for combining comedy and drama which he showed on other television shows. They included four episodes of *Batman* during 1966–67, and four episodes of *Kolchak: The Night Stalker* in 1974.

The Burning Hills

1956. A Warner Brothers–First National Picture.
Distributed by Warner Brothers.
93 Minutes/WarnerColor/CinemaScope.

Credits: Richard Whorf (Producer), Stuart Heisler (Director), Irving Wallace (Screenplay), Ted McCord (Photography), Clarence Kolster (Editor), Charles H. Clarke (Art Director), Frank Miller (Set Decorator), Marjorie Best (Costumes), Gordan Bau (Makeup), David Buttolph (Music). Based on a novel by Louis L'Amour.

Cast: Tab Hunter (Trace Jordan), Natalie Wood (Maria Cristina Colton), Skip Homeier (Jack Sutton), Eduard Franz (Jacob Lantz), Earl Holliman (Mort Bayliss), Claude Akins (Ben Hindeman), Ray Teal (Joe Sutton), Frank Puglia (Tio Perico), Hal Baylor (Braun), Tyler McDuff (Wes Parker), Rayford Barnes (Veach), Tony Terry (Vicente Colton), Jack Williams (Farrell), Robert Herron (Faber), Dale Van Sickel (Johnny Jordan), Julian Rivero (Miguel).

Synopsis: Trace Jordan seeks the men who murdered his brother, Johnny, and stole their horses. The guilty men work for Joe Sutton, a prominent rancher who wants to control the range. Confronting Sutton at his ranch, Jordan threatens to report the theft and murder to the U.S. cavalry at Fort Stockton. Gunplay breaks out and both men are wounded. Sutton then sends his son Jack to kill Jordan. The other men with young Sutton include ranch foreman Ben Hindeman and tracker Jacob Lantz.

Unconscious due to his injury, Jordan is cared for in a hidden cave by Maria Cristina Colton. She herds sheep with her Uncle Perico and a brother, Vicente. Her father was killed opposing the Suttons. As Jordan recovers from his wound, Maria temporarily diverts the men hunting him and helps him to escape to a secluded ranch. Blaming Hindeman for the setback, an angry Jack Sutton shoots him down.

Mort Bayliss, one of Johnny's killers, gets into a fight with Jordan at the ranch and is killed. Maria and Jordan ride off together but soon realize that Lantz is tracking them down. With hostile Indians approaching, Jordan lures them into a fight with his pursuers. A few of the men escape from the Indians and continue after the fleeing couple. At a hazardous river crossing, Jordan and Maria find their path is blocked and are forced

As the hero in ***The Burning Hills,*** Tab Hunter proved he could take care of himself with guns and on horseback.

to make a stand. After another pursuer, Wes Parker, is killed, Jordan fights and drowns Sutton in the river. Parker and Sutton were also responsible for his brother's death.

Before Jordan and Maria is Lantz holding a gun. Revealing that his job was only to find Jordan, he lets them go on to the fort.

Original Source: The novel *The Burning Hills.*

Plotline: Attempting to recover horses after his partner Johnny Hendrix is killed for them, Trace Jordan is forced to flee for his life. His assailants include rancher Bob Sutton's sons Joe and Jack, Ben Hindeman, Mort Bayliss, Wes Parker and their tracker Jacob Lantz.

After saving Jordan's life, Mexican senorita Maria Cristina Chavero ends up also fleeing with him. As the killers of Johnny are revealed to Trace and Maria during the chase, Apaches prove a danger as well.

Commentary: The Louis L'Amour novel *The Burning Hills* was originally serialized in *The Saturday Evening Post* magazine in 1955 (November 26, December 3, 10, 17, and

Natalie Wood's heroine in *The Burning Hills* tends to the injured Tab Hunter when he does need help.

24). In May 1956, Jason Press published the novel in hardcover; in August, Bantam Books published it in paperback. At the time of Louis's death, over 30 years later, it was recognized as one of his top ten best sellers. *Hondo* was number one.

Warner Brothers, which released the film *Hondo*, also made *The Burning Hills*, this time using the widescreen CinemaScope format. The release date was September 1, 1956.

Although the theme of a hunted white man being helped by a Mexican woman is present in both novel and film, many contrasting elements do exist between the two. Perhaps the biggest is the elimination of villain Jack Sutton by hero Trace Jordan.

In the novel, Sutton shoots it out with Jordan earlier on, while the film's barehanded struggle between the two is the climactic highlight. The raging river used for their fight in the movie was the Kern River near Bakersfield, California. The Western was filmed in February and March of '56.

The fates of Ben Hindeman and Jacob Lantz are the next biggest differences. In the L'Amour tale, Ben survives and calls off the hunt against the wronged man. The film's

Another scene with Natalie Wood and Tab Hunter from *The Burning Hills*. The film and *Hondo*, both Warner Brothers releases were the best produced of the L'Amour entries during the 1950s.

scenario, written by Irving Wallace, has young Sutton killing Hindeman. Although Lantz survives in the film, he falls victim to the Apaches in the novel. Wes Parker is shot down by Vicente Chavero in the book and by Jordan in the film.

Maria Cristina's last name is Colton in the film and Chavero in the novel. While she only has one brother and an uncle in the movie, there are two brothers, a mother, and a sister-in-law in the book. In the movie, Johnny Jordan is Trace's brother. He was Jordan's friend Johnny Hendrix in the novel.

In the novel but not the film is a daring rescue led by "a small square-shouldered man with cold gray eyes," who is none other than John Slaughter. Only 5'6", the real John Horton Slaughter was a fearless man not to be taken lightly. Before becoming one of the great cattle ranchers, he was a private in 1872 with the Minute Men of Texas Rangers. Two years later, he served with the Rangers in their Brown and San Saba Company. In 1884, Slaughter bought the San Bernardino ranch (the site of the rescue in the novel), which consisted of 65,000 acres in Arizona and Mexico. He was also elected sheriff of Cochise County, Arizona, in 1886 and 1888. At the time of this death in bed, at age 80 in 1922, he was a honorary deputy.

The two young stars of *The Burning Hills* were Tab Hunter and Natalie Wood. At the time of its release, he was 25 and she was 18. Their popularity with the teen market prompted another Warner Brothers film that same year, the comedy *The Girl He Left Behind.* Both films, according to Hunter in his autobiography, had "booming grosses."

The reviews, at least in regards to the Western, were mixed. *Time* was especially sarcastic: "Tab Hunter and Natalie Wood speak pidgin English to each other and sleep out on the prairie without a chaperone." But the *New York Times* felt they met the challenges of the film: "As a matter of fact, the testing that has been arranged for them [in this movie] is a good, lively one by comparison with what we usually get in Westerns these days."

Wood was considered miscast as the Mexican girl. She was hampered with heavy makeup to darken her skin and an unrealistic accent. Both leading actor and actress found Stuart Heisler not especially helpful as a director. Heisler, who helmed Hunter's first film *Island of Desire* (1952), directed another Warner Brothers Western in 1956, *The Lone Ranger.*

While *The Burning Hills* was still in production, Tab escorted Natalie to the 28th Academy Awards show. She was nominated as Best Supporting Actress for 1955's *Rebel Without a Cause.*

The supporting cast for the Western was top-notch. Two other young actors of the 1950s, Skip Homeier and Earl Holliman, played the punk killers. Holliman had previously been seen with Jeff Chandler in 1953's *East of Sumatra*, while Homeier menaced Gregory Peck in 1950's *The Gunfighter*. *Gunfight at the O.K. Corral* (1957) and *Last Train from Gun Hill* (1959) were among Holliman's two finest Westerns. Kirk Douglas was Earl's friend in the first and his foe in the second one. Homeier ran up against Randolph Scott in two good ones: 1957's *The Tall T* and 1960's *Comanche Station.*

Also seen in the latter Scott Western, and as the foreman in *The Burning Hills,* was Claude Akins. One of the most recognizable of all Western players, this big and burly actor appeared in many of the TV oaters during the 1950s and 1960s. Akins was unforgettable in the Western films *Rio Bravo* (1959) and *Return of the Seven* (1966).

Eduard Franz claimed to have "14 different wise looks" for the characters he portrayed. Two of the actor's favorite film roles were in Westerns—1954's *Broken Lance* and 1955's *White Feather.*

Writer Irving Wallace began his career working on films and then moved on to television. Like L'Amour, he is probably best known as a novelist. His novels included *The Chapman Report* and *The Prize,* which became films in 1962 and 1963 respectively.

Maria Cristina is regarded as one of the strongest heroines in all of L'Amour's stories. Trace Jordan is another in a long line of sturdy L'Amour heroes, forced to face insurmountable obstacles.

One great satisfaction Tab Hunter got out of *The Burning Hills* was riding his own mare, Swizzlestick, in it; he felt the horse was the "best thing" about the film.

Utah Blaine

1957. A Clover Production.
Released by Columbia Pictures.
75 Minutes/Black and White

Credits: Sam Katzman (Producer), Fred F. Sears (Director), Robert E. Kent, James B. Gordon (Screenplay), Benjamin H. Kline (Photography), Charles Nelson (Editor), Paul Palmentola (Art Director), Sidney Clifford (Set Decorator), Ross DiMaggio (Music Conductor). Based on a novel by Louis L'Amour.

Cast: Rory Calhoun (Mike "Utah" Blaine), Susan Cummings (Angie Kinyon), Angela Stevens (Mary Blake), Max Baer (Gus Ortmann), Paul Langton (Rip Coker), George Keymas (Rink Witter), Ray Teal (Russ Nevers), Ken Christy (Joe Neal), Gene Roth (Tom Corey), Norman Frederic (Jug Davis), Steve Darrell (Lud Fuller), Terry Frost (Gavin), Jack Ingram (Clel Miller), Pierce Lyden (Ray Forbes), Dennis Moore (Ferguson).

Synopsis: A group of vigilantes work for Russ Nevers, who is killing anyone who interferes with his plan to take control of the range. Finding that Rink Witter, a former friend, is a hired gunman for Nevers, Utah Blaine becomes Joe Neal's ranch manager to put an end to the trouble. Blaine had saved Neal from them.

With Neal hiding out, Blaine goes to the town of Red Creek. Trying to see Neal's friend, Ben Kinyon, Blaine discovers that he was killed by the vigilantes. Blaine is invited to Kinyon's ranch by his daughter, Angie. He reveals to her the plans made with Joe Neal. Nevers and his men ride up and Angie is threatened. When Blaine surprises Nevers as the manager of Neal's 46 Plus ranch, he takes his riders and leaves.

In Red Creek, Nevers tricks big Gus Ortmann into engaging in a fistfight with Blaine; Blaine beats the man. When Rink Witter tries to shoot Blaine, friend Rip Coker disarms him with a shotgun blast.

Leading lady Susan Cummings can count on her leading man, Rory Calhoun, and their friend Paul Langton in *Utah Blaine*.

Having filed his papers at the bank as ranch manager, Blaine rides out accompanied by both Rip and Gus. Witter is sent by Nevers to find Neal and kill him. Bar B ranch owner Mary Blake is alerted by Blaine that her own foreman is in cahoots with Nevers. When Nevers has her horses stampeded, Blaine rides with Mary to Angie's place. After capturing a few of the vigilantes, Blaine and his allies find Witter in town boasting of shooting down Neal. More shooting breaks out and Gus is injured.

Mary brings news that Neal had legally left his ranch to Blaine and Angie. Mary advises Blaine to form a coalition against Russ Nevers with the good citizens of Red Creek. Returning to Angie's ranch, Nevers and his gang start trouble. Attempting to protect her, Gus is shot down by Witter. The killer gets away as Blaine and Rip fire their guns at him.

Backing Blaine, the townsfolk hold an election to try and bring some law to the area. But with Nevers rustling B stock, Blaine has the town newspaper run the story about his inheriting the 46 Plus with Angie and his ad looking for ranch hands.

Desperate to stop the opposition, Nevers and Witter lead their gang into town.

However, the citizens are armed on the rooftops and disarm the enemy. Witter is killed by Blaine in a shootout.

Original Source: The novel *Utah Blaine.*

Plotline: Gunman Utah Blaine saves rancher Joe Neal from vigilantes and then helps him to protect his land. Neighbor Mary Blake's father, Gid, isn't as fortunate. Joe's own foreman, Lud Fuller, and Mary's foreman, Clell Miller, are among those responsible. The worst are rancher Russ Nevers and his hired gun, Rink Witter. Also posing a threat are Lee Fox, a rancher, and Red Creek banker Ben Otten.

Blaine finds ample support: Rip Cocker is a ranchhand of Joe's, while Tom Kelsey and Dan Timm are Mary's staunch hands. Angie Kinyon, who lives on Joe's land, shares a mutual attraction with Blaine. Meantime, Mary forms a bond with Ralston Forbes, who runs the town's paper. Pitted against Blaine initially is yet another rancher, Ortmann, but he becomes a strong ally. Although good lives are sacrificed in the power play, justice does prevail.

For *Utah Blaine,* Rory Calhoun, Susan Cummings, Max Baer and Paul Langton seem ready for any gunplay. The film was based on one of L'Amour's longer novels.

Commentary: *Utah Blaine* was the second Columbia–Sam Katzman feature film made from a L'Amour story (the first was *Blackjack Ketchum, Desperado*).

Using the pseudonym Jim Mayo for the last time, Louis wrote the novel *Utah Blaine* for publication by Ace Books in 1954. It was reprinted under his own name in 1983 by Bantam Books. (As his fame grew during the 1950s, the pseudonym fell by the wayside.) A longer book, it had an epic sense with the range war theme that Louis so enjoyed using. This quality was shared by the shorter novels *Kilkenny* and *Where the Long Grass Blows*, as well as the novella "The Rider of the Ruby Hills."

Utah Blaine, more the novel than the film, spun its range war yarn around a gunfighter trying to protect two big ranches from a swarm of bad men. Range warfare had also been part of the films *Treasure of Ruby Hills* and *Blackjack Ketchum, Desperado.*

Produced between late July to August 10, 1956, *Utah Blaine* saw a February '57 release. As a producer, Katzman was known for making his films as cheaply as possible. This particular Western was of better than average quality but *National Parent-Teacher* still referred to it as "run-of-the-mill."

"Sam Katzman has garmented the tense Robert E. Kent–James B. Gordon screenplay with values which blend tough characters with fast movement," praised *Variety*, "capturing the spirit of the Louis L'Amour novel to keep the bell ringing."

Often in Western stories, it is actually the small rancher being victimized by the big cattleman. But in this L'Amour tale, and carried over for the film, it is the big rancher, Joe Neal, who is mistreated. Yet another twist in the novel is that Neal actually helped to organize the vigilantes who then turned on him (as was their plan all along). This was after he found himself going along with the lie that fellow rancher Gid Blake was a rustler and had to be eliminated. Thus the film's characterization of Neal is whitewashed a bit compared to the book. While Russ Nevers and Rink Witter are the pivotal villains in each, others lurked in L'Amour's version. They included Lee Fox, Ben Otten and the giant Ortmann.

Of these last three characters, only Ortmann makes it into the movie (with the first name of Gus). In each version there is an exciting fistfight between him and the title character, whose actual first name is Michael. After becoming Utah's ally, Ortmann is killed off in the film but survives in the book.

Rip Coker, Utah's other staunch ally, is left standing at the film's conclusion to hug Mary Blake; Utah Blaine pairs with Angie Kinyon. In the novel, both men are so shot up, particularly Rip, that it's a miracle they survive. In the novel, it is newpaperman Ralston Forbes whom Mary is attracted to rather than Coker. Ray is used as the first name for Forbes in the film.

More characters included in both versions are bad guys Lud Fuller and Clell Miller (whose first name is listed in the *AFI Catalog* as Clel). Dan Timm and Tom Kelsey, both allies of Utah and Rip in the book, are not part of the movie.

Heroine Angie Kinyon's father, Ben, substitutes for Mary's father, Gid, in the movie as the first victim of the vigilantes. Gid Blake's death actually happened before the start of the novel, while Ben Kinyon's is referred to during the film. Part of the book is a shared animosity between Angie and Mary, some of it jealousy over Utah, which is resolved over time.

In the L'Amour novel, Angie's homestead is the setting for the climactic gunplay, while the town serves that purpose in the film. Russ Nevers, another target for Blaine's gun hand in the book, survives in the film to be brought to justice.

While L'Amour has readers believe initially that Lud Fuller is leading the vigilantes, Nevers is revealed to have been with them all along, inciting everyone to violence. For the movie, the latter's leadership was clearly established early on.

In the film as well, Witter is referred to as having been a partner of Blaine's until he (Witter) pulled a double-cross. This then is the catalyst which brings Blaine to help Neal. Blaine's motivation for aiding Joe in the novel is not this noble; he simply wants a piece of the rancher's property to start his own, yet in an honest way, unlike those who would kill and steal for it.

Blaine is trusted by the rancher for a number of reasons. L'Amour compares his "gun skill with Wes Hardin, Clay Allison and Earp." Blaine also drove cattle for John Slaughter.

"Westerns are the great love of my life," Rory Calhoun once said, and admitted that most of them were B films. Having already starred in one derived from a L'Amour story, *Four Guns to the Border,* he made two more: *Utah Blaine* and *Apache Territory* (1958).

In 1955, Calhoun collaborated on a screenplay with Clark E. Reynolds for another B Western, *Shotgun,* starring Sterling Hayden. Calhoun co-starred with Jeff Chandler, the first actor to play a L'Amour hero on the big screen, in the 1955 version of *The Spoilers.* According to *Variety,* Calhoun "effectively" handled the role of hero Utah Blaine.

His heroine in the Western was played by Susan Cummings. Her acting credits included another Western film that same year, *Tomahawk Trail,* and she appeared in many 1950s television shows including *The Adventures of Kit Carson* and *Perry Mason.*

Angela Stevens, the other actress of note in *Utah Blaine,* previously played Laurie Webster in *Blackjack Ketchum, Desperado.* The character Mary Blake, however, was a larger role. Her other film credits included *Jack McCall, Desperado* (1953). Using the name Ann Zika, she appeared in two 1951 TV episodes of *The Cisco Kid.*

Main villain Russ Nevers was enacted by longtime character actor Ray Teal. In *The Burning Hills,* he was patriarch Joe Sutton; and in 1958, the actor was in another Tab Hunter Western, *Gunman's Walk.* Although a great heavy in films, Ray is best remembered as Sheriff Roy Coffee on the *Bonanza* TV series in the 1960s.

Gus Ortmann was portrayed by former heavyweight boxing champion Max Baer, who won the title from Primo Carnera in 1934. With his first title defense the following year, he lost it to James J. Braddock. His son is Max Baer, Jr., who played Jethro on the 1960s television comedy hit *The Beverly Hillbillies.*

Ken Christy, who was the sheriff in *Blackjack Ketchum, Desperado,* played Joe Neal in *Utah Blaine.* His TV Western credits included *Broken Arrow* and *Tales of Wells Fargo.*

Writers Robert E. Kent and James B. Gordon did indeed do a fine job on the script for *Utah Blaine.* In 1960, Kent produced a Western, *Noose for a Gunman,* from a screenplay by Gordon. The 1955 Jim Bridger adventure *The Gun That Won the West* was another screenplay Gordon wrote for producer Sam Katzman. Other scripts written by Kent for Katzman were turned into a pair of George Montgomery vehicles in 1953, *The Pathfinder* and *Fort Ti.* Writer Gordon worked with Fred F. Sears, *Utah Blaine*'s director, on other films, including 1956's *The Werewolf.*

A director of many B movies, Fred F. Sears died the year *Utah Blaine* came out. At least eight more films he had made were released throughout 1958.

Sugarfoot

1957. A Warner Brothers Television Production.
ABC Television.
60 Minutes/Black and White.

Episode: "The Strange Land."

Credits: Leslie H. Martinson (Director), Russell S. Hughes (Teleplay). Based on a story by Louis L'Amour.

Cast: Will Hutchins (Tom "Sugarfoot" Brewster). Guest Cast: Morris Ankrum (Cash Billing), Rhodes Reason (Burr Fulton), Jan Chaney (Anne), Walter Barnes (Hefferman), Stuart Randall (Higgins), Daniel White (Kennedy).

Synopsis: Cash Billing, an embittered old rancher, gets entangled with a gunman who makes things worse. Arriving to help Billing and stop the gunman is Tom "Sugarfoot" Brewster.

Original Source: The short story "Regan of the Slash B."

Plotline: Hunting mountain lions for the Slash B outfit is Dan Regan. Cash Billings owns the spread and is being cheated by his nephew and foreman. Also rustling cattle are Burr Fulton and Bill Hefferman. But Dan helps to set everything right.

Commentary: *Cheyenne* became the first hit television series for Warner Brothers. Two years after its 1955 debut, *Sugarfoot* became the studio's newest horse opera. It ran on ABC for four seasons, from September '57 to July '61.

For the first couple of seasons, it alternated with *Cheyenne.* When Clint Walker, who played Cheyenne Bodie, became involved in a contract dispute with Warner Brothers, Ty Hardin substituted for him on that show as Bronco Layne during the 1958-59 season. Walker returned to *Cheyenne* for the 1959-60 season while Hardin received his own series, *Bronco,* which then alternated with *Sugarfoot.* All three shows rotated weeks in the 1960-61 season, *Sugarfoot's* last, under the banner title *The Cheyenne Show.*

Will Hutchins starred as Tom "Sugarfoot" Brewster, a corresponding law student who went West looking for adventure. He received his nickname because of being "one grade lower than a tenderfoot" as a cowpoke. *Sugarfoot,* unlike *Cheyenne* and *Bronco,* took

Publicity pose of Will Hutchins in the title role on *Sugarfoot*, one of the solid Western TV shows produced by Warner Brothers.

a more lighthearted approach. While Sugarfoot could be heroic, he had more of a knack for rhetoric.

The third episode of its opening season aired on October 15, 1957. It was called "The Strange Land" and was based on a short story written by L'Amour.

Under his Jim Mayo pseudonym, Louis wrote the tale, "Regan of the Slash B," for the October 1949 issue of *Thrilling Western* magazine. It was published by Bantam in the 1988 L'Amour collection *Lonigan.*

The show's Tom Brewster substitutes for the short story's Dan Regan. Both versions have unsavory types named Hefferman and Burr Fulton, and Cash Billings is also incorporated into the show minus the "s" in his last name. The heroine is called Anne here, while she is Jenny in L'Amour's story.

Leslie H. Martinson directed the TV episode. He also directed the forthcoming *Maverick* episode in this filmography.

Writing this *Sugarfoot* script was Russell Hughes, who wrote another called "Hideout" in '58. He also wrote episodes for *Maverick, Bronco,* and *Cheyenne.*

Maverick

1957. A Warner Brothers Production.
ABC Television.
60 Minutes/Black and White.

Episode: "Stage West."

Credits: Roy Huggins (Producer), Leslie H. Martinson (Director), George Slavin (Teleplay), David Buttolph, Paul Francis Webster (Theme Music). Based on a story by Louis L'Amour.

Cast: James Garner (Bret Maverick). Guest Cast: Ray Teal (Mart Fallon), Edd Byrnes (Wes Fallon), Peter Brown (Rip Fallon), Erin O'Brien (Linda Harris).

Synopsis: Mart Fallon and his sons, Wes and Rip, are looking for a map to a gold mine. After killing two miners in a failed attempt to get the map, they go after Linda Harris, the widow of one of the slain men.

She is taken prisoner by the Fallons along with gambler Bret Maverick. The Fallons are soon confronted by Indians.

Commentary: Along with *Cheyenne, Sugarfoot* and *Bronco,* Warner Brothers produced other Western shows for the ABC television network. Certainly among the most popular was *Maverick*, which ran for 124 episodes between September 1957 and July 1962.

"Stage West," which aired October 27, 1957, was episode six of season one and it supposedly was based on a L'Amour magazine story. But *which* story remains a mystery. This episode, directed by Leslie H. Martinson, had a teleplay written by George Slavin.

James Garner and Jack Kelly, who came in with episode eight, were the original stars

James Garner in a publicity pose as Bret Maverick. Warners' *Maverick* TV series enjoyed greater popularity than *Sugarfoot.*

of the series. Weekly appearances were usually alternated by the pair, but sometimes they were seen together. They played gambler-brothers Bret and Bart Maverick, traveling the West and getting into all kinds of adventures. In this particular episode, Garner was featured. Included in the guest cast was Ray Teal, the bad guy in both *Utah Blaine* and *The Burning Hills*, and once more filling that role. Teal's sons here were played by rising young performers Edd Byrnes and Peter Brown. Byrnes went on to co-star on the *77 Sunset Strip* series, and Brown on *Lawman*.

In 1960, Garner had a falling-out with Warner Brothers over his contract. Winning a release, the actor was replaced by Roger Moore as cousin Beau. Robert Colbert also joined the cast as Bret and Bart's brother, Brent.

After leaving *Maverick*, Garner concentrated mainly on his movie career in the 1960s. A standout year for the actor was 1963, with a pair of comedies with Doris Day (*The Thrill of It All* and *Move Over, Darling*) and the rousing wartime drama, *The Great Escape*.

Director Leslie H. Martinson helmed a good many episodes of *Maverick* through 1961. A number of episodes of *The Roy Rogers Show* also benefited from his direction. In 1979, he directed an episode of the short-lived *Young Maverick* series.

George Slavin's writing credentials included film and television Westerns. A 1951 Alan Ladd vehicle, *Red Mountain*, was one of the films. Between 1959 and 1961 he wrote five episodes of *Bat Masterson*. Slavin also wrote for the 1967 series version of *Hondo*.

The Tall Stranger

1957. An Allied Artists Production.
Released by Allied Artists.
82 Minutes/Deluxe Color/CinemaScope

Credits: Walter Mirisch (Producer), Thomas Carr (Director), Christopher Knopf (Screenplay), Wilfred M. Cline (Photography), William Austin (Editor), David Milton (Art Director), Joseph Kish (Set Decorator), Bert Henrikson (Wardrobe), Emile LaVigne (Makeup Artist), Hans Salter (Music). Based on a story by Louis L'Amour.

Cast: Joel McCrea (Ned Bannon), Virginia Mayo (Ellen), Barry Kelley (Hardy Bishop), Michael Ansara (Zarata), Whit Bissell (Adam Judson), James Dobson (Dud), George Neise (Mort Harper), Adam Kennedy (Red), Michael Pate (Charley), Leo Gordon (Stark), Ray Teal (Cap), Philip Phillips (Will), Robert Foulk (Pagones), Jennifer Lea (Mary Judson), George J. Lewis (Chavez), Guy Prescott (Barrett), Ralph Reed (Murray), Mauritz Hugo (Purcell).

Synopsis: In 1865, Ned Bannon, an ex–Union soldier, is shot and left to die by cattle rustlers. Ned is cared for until he recovers by a widow, Ellen, and her boy Will, who are part of a wagon train bound for California.

Trail guides Mort Harper and Purcell take the wagons to Bishop's Valley instead.

Before they become allies in *The Tall Stranger*, Barry Kelley and Joel McCrea must settle some issues.

Ownership is claimed by Hardy Bishop, Ned's half brother. A falling-out between the two men occurred when Ned was accused of the death of Bishop's son Billy during the Civil War.

Harper wants the wagoners to homestead in the valley, saying it is government land. While suspicious of Harper's motives, Ned is concerned that fighting will break out between Bishop and any homesteaders. Trying to warn the wagon train of the risks, Ned is driven away at gunpoint by Purcell.

When Ned confronts Hardy about the dilemma, he gets into a fistfight over the man's dead son. Defeated, Bishop listens to both Ned and Stark, his own ranch foreman, and accepts that Billy was executed for riding with renegades. Bishop still wants to make the wagon train leave the valley. Ned, however, is able to buy some time and hopes to convince the people to move on peacefully.

Zarata, the rustler who actually shot Ned earlier on, plots with Mort Harper to steal

This advertisement for *The Tall Stranger* also mentions the author's involvement with the novel *Hondo.*

Bishop's land. To prevent the wagon train families from accepting Ned's offer of help and supplies, Harper and Zarata incite the wagoners into a frenzy.

One of Bishop's riders, Red, is goaded into gunplay by Harper and is mortally wounded. To make it appear like Red fired his gun at the wagoners, Zarata kills a woman and later fights with Ned, causing Ellen to shoot Purcell. Zarata escapes after injuring young Will and again incites the wagoners against Ned.

Fleeing to the ranch with Ellen and Will, Ned learns she was a former dance hall girl and had her son out of wedlock. It doesn't matter to Ned as he and Ellen share a mutual attraction. Charley, a ranch hand, helps tend to Will's injury. Hardy threatens to attack the wagoners.

There is an attack on the ranch by Harper and the rustlers. Zarata mortally wounds Hardy during the struggle, but in turn is strangled. When Will and Ellen are threatened by Harper, Ned throws down his gun. Outmaneuvering Harper, Ned grabs a rifle and kills him. As the wagon train later prepares to move on under the leadership of Adam Judson and Cap, Ned extends an invitation for all the folks to settle in the valley since he is the new owner. He personally goes after Ellen and Will's wagon to bring it back.

Original Source: The novella "Showdown Trail."

Plotline: Injured by Indians, Rock Bannon is cared for by Sharon Crockett, who is traveling with her father Tom in a wagon train. While Cap Mullholland is the wagon-master, entrepreneur Morton Harper leads the wagons to settle on range belonging to Hardy Bishop. Rock turns out to be Hardy's son. Others aiding Mort Harper in this reckless pursuit include a killer, Zapata, and wagoners Pike Purcell and Lamport. Torn between both sides, Rock must decide where his true loyalties belong.

Commentary: The novella "Showdown Trail" first appeared in the winter 1948 issue of *Giant Western* magazine. It became one of L'Amour's stories featured in Bantam Books' 1986 collection *The Rider of the Ruby Hills.*

Calling it *The Tall Stranger*, Louis restructured some of the story's words and paragraphs for novel publication by Fawcett–Gold Medal in September 1957. In 1986, the novel was reprinted by Bantam.

In November 1957, Allied Artists released their version of *The Tall Stranger*, based on the initial title. "Good Western in an old-fashioned shoot-em-up vein," said *Variety.* The review also pointed out that it was "modernized" to fit with the current (1950s) trend toward adult Westerns.

This adult approach was keenly felt in the film with the heroine's being an unwed mother. At the time, it was a bit risqué. Ellen, the mother, and son Will are not part of Louis's actual story. While Sharon, the heroine in his tale, is part of a wagon train, she is traveling with her father, Tom Crockett. Rock Bannon, in the story, is called Ned Bannon in the film.

Although *Variety* felt Joel McCrea played the male lead with his "customary authority and conviction," it should be noted that he was much older than L'Amour's 27-year-

In *The Tall Stranger,* Virginia Mayo has the appropriate reaction to Michael Ansara's assault upon her.

old hero. The film's script undoubtedly included the child and mother to help make it more plausible with its mature hero.

Differences between the L'Amour source and motion picture were many, despite the main plotline of his tale being realized. Wagons rolling west is shared with the oft-used one of range conflict. In the novella, Rock's wounds were the result of a "lone" encounter with Indians (a sequence which had already transpired). As the film begins, Ned's being cared for by Ellen is the result of injuries caused by Zarata. And again to reflect Bannon's maturity in the film, he is a half brother rather than a son of rancher Hardy Bishop.

The half-breed Zarata (Zapata in the novella) meets his fate at Bishop's hands in the film, and Hardy is shot down by him. While Hardy is shot by an enemy during the ranch attack in the story, he does survive. Zapata's fate in L'Amour's story is decided earlier on by Ned. (Sometimes L'Amour surprised readers by eliminating a major bad guy earlier than anticipated. He also did it with Jack Sutton in *The Burning Hills.*)

There is no town built in the movie like in the story, and no crooked storekeeper, Joe Kies, working with equally crooked Mort Harper to take advantage of the settlers.

Unlike Harper and the half-breed in each account, Kies survives the story but is driven away by Bannon.

Another villainous character in the novella, Lamport, is not part of the movie; his slugfest in the story with Rock is replaced in the film with one between Ned and Hardy. There is no son of Bishop's named Billy in the story as there is in the film.

Cap and Purcell, misguided in their loyalty to Harper, are in each version. Other settlers in each include Pagones, Dud and Mary (her last name is Pagones in the story and Judson in the film). The film's Adam Judson, not in the story, helps to guide the settlers on the right path after being led astray by Harper. Ranch hands in each version include Red, Stark and Chavez.

L'Amour's customary descriptions of scenic backgrounds prevailed in the story. While CinemaScope showcased some excellent exteriors for the film, not everything could be visualized. Particularly captivating in the novella was the hero's treacherous ride over a mountain.

While the film's climax is the big fight on the ranch between a number of men, the climax in the story is an intimate one as Bannon faces another dangerous ride to rescue Sharon from Harper. Ellen and Will are both held hostage in the movie, but it is during the depiction of the ranch fight.

Harper triggers warfare in each version. In L'Amour's, he actually fires a fatal shot and provokes an instance in the film where a woman's death by Zarata is blamed on a ranch hand.

The film *The Tall Stranger* was set after the Civil War. Its protagonist is a former Yankee and the prospective settlers are Southerners uprooted from their homes to begin new lives in the West. L'Amour did not include this aspect in his story; it is a nice one by screenwriter Knopf, adding tension to what already exists.

Working titles for this Western were *The Rifle* and *Walk Tall.* It began production in May 1957 and utilized locations near Agoura, at the Morrison Ranch and at Ventura County's Triunfo Ranch.

In 1949, Joel McCrea and Virginia Mayo co-starred in the Western *Colorado Territory*. A versatile actress, Mayo was especially captivating in costume adventures. They included 1950's *The Flame and the Arrow,* 1951's *Captain Horatio Hornblower* and 1952's *The Iron Mistress*. Her leading men in these films were, respectively, Burt Lancaster, Gregory Peck and Alan Ladd.

The two main villains in *The Tall Stranger* were played by George Neise and Michael Ansara. Neise's television credits included a regular role on McCrea's *Wichita Town* TV series (1959–60). He also had a recurring role during 1959 on the *Zorro* series.

In the 1950s, Ansara was especially prominent as Cochise on the *Broken Arrow* television series. The actor also carved a niche as a villain with Western films like 1956's *The Lone Ranger* and 1961's *The Comancheros.*

Barry Kelley, who played the tough rancher in this Western, excelled in authoritative roles. His varied films include Westerns, dramas and comedies. Among them were

Buchanan Rides Alone (1958), *The Manchurian Candidate* (1962) and *The Love Bug* (1969).

Both seen in *Hondo,* Michael Pate and Leo Gordon had roles in *The Tall Stranger.* Pate's character, Charley, was not included in the initial story. Seen in three of the previous four entries of the L'Amour filmography, Ray Teal played Cap in this one.

Director Thomas Carr may be best remembered for his extensive work on the *Adventures of Superman* television series in the '50s. He also directed the 1948 serial *Superman.* Many episodes of the *Rawhide* series were directed by Carr between 1962 and 1965.

While writer Christopher Knopf worked on other movies besides this Western, including 1957's *20 Million Miles to Earth,* his TV credits were more extensive. They included two episodes of *Wanted: Dead or Alive* and six episodes of *Dick Powell's Zane Grey Theatre.* Speaking of Grey, despite his popularity as a Western writer, the sales of his stories were surpassed by those of both Max Brand and Louis L'Amour. It was L'Amour who achieved the status as the best-selling Western writer in the world.

Apache Territory

1958. A Rorvic Production.
Released by Columbia Pictures.
72 Minutes/Eastmancolor.

Credits: Rory Calhoun, Victor M. Orsatti (Producers), Ray Nazarro (Director), Charles R. Marion, George W. George (Screenplay), Frank Moss (Adaptation), Irving Lippman (Photography), Al Clark (Editor), Cary Odell (Art Director), Mischa Bakaleinikoff (Music Conductor). Based on a novel by Louis L'Amour.

Cast: Rory Calhoun (Logan Cates), Barbara Bates (Jennifer Fair), John Dehner (Grant Kimbrough), Carolyn Craig (Junie Hatchett), Thomas Pittman (Lonnie Foreman), Leo Gordon (Zimmerman), Myron Healey (Webb), Francis De Sales (Sgt. Sheehan), Frank DeKova (Lugo), Reg Parton (Conley), Bob Woodward (Graves), Fred Krone (Styles).

Synopsis: Drifter Logan Cates rides across a desert toward Yuma, Arizona. Finding the lone survivor of an Indian massacre, Junie Hatchett, he then takes her to the water and shelter at Papago Wells. The two discover another survivor of an attack by Indians, Lonnie Foreman. Heading to Yuma to be married, and stopping to rest, are Jennifer Fair and Grant Kimbrough. Cates and Jennifer were once close until he decided she deserved better than life with a drifter.

They are joined by soldiers who survived an Indian attack: Sgt. Sheehan and privates Conley, Graves, Styles, Webb and Zimmerman. But Sheehan has his men follow Cates' orders. Cates reasons that Churupati is killing all in his path with other renegade Apaches. In short order, the renegades have surrounded Papago Wells.

Able to sneak into Papago Wells is a part–Pima Indian, Lugo, on the run from the law. Zimmerman and Sheehan object to his presence, the former because he dislikes all Indians, the latter because Lugo is wanted for murdering a soldier. (Lugo killed in self-defense to safeguard gold nuggets he dug from a mine and which he carries in a bag.) Cates know Lugo will be a good man to have in the fight with the renegades.

An Apache sniper kills Sheehan. Zimmerman then tries to usurp Cates' leadership and is beaten in a fight. Stealing Lugo's bag of gold, Zimmerman is prevented from killing him by Lonnie. The Apaches kill Zimmerman when he attempts to ride out. Lugo admits that he hid the gold and filled the bag with rocks.

Before his death, Zimmerman had planned to leave with Kimbrough and Jennifer. She reveals this to Cates, who risks his life to find food for everyone. Water is rationed when the well begins to dry up.

Having fallen in love with Junie, Lonnie plans a life with her in California. Cates admits he still loves Jennifer.

Graves is killed by an Apache arrow. An upset Webb confronts the Indians and is captured. As Webb is slowly being tortured to death, Cates shoots him to free him from the torment. As a windstorm approaches, Cates creates bombs by having the canteens

Rory Calhoun's Logan Cates is aware of the damage caused by Indians in *Apache Territory*. This was his third and final Western motion picture derived from a L'Amour tale.

As the leader in ***Apache Territory,*** Rory Calhoun keeps a lookout for danger as Tom Pittman fills the canteens.

filled with blasting powder. With Lugo then protecting the two women, Cates leads Lonnie and Kimbrough against the renegades.

But Kimbrough backs out, wanting Jennifer to leave with him. Refusing, she calls him a coward. Trying to flee on a horse, Kimbrough is killed by Lugo, again in self-defense. While Conley is killed fighting the Indians, Cates and Lonnie's bombs defeat them. Lonnie is given gold by Lugo to buy a house for Junie. Jennifer and Cates realize they belong together.

Original Source: The novel *Last Stand at Papago Wells.*

Plotline: Drifter Logan Cates becomes the leader of a group of civilians and soldiers when they are trapped by Apaches at Papago Wells. Initially with Cates are Jennifer Fair, Grant Kimbrough, Junie Hatchett and Lonnie Foreman. The soldiers include Sgt. Sheehan, Styles and Zimmerman. Outlaws Tony Lugo and Jim Beaupre and posse member Taylor also seek protection from the hostile Indians.

Finding her way to Papago Wells is Big Maria, who has made off with stolen gold. The Apaches use cunning diversion to try and eliminate everyone. Yet danger also comes from Zimmerman and Kimbrough, further testing Cates' leadership.

Commentary: L'Amour's *Last Stand at Papago Wells* was first published by Fawcett–Gold Medal in 1957. Bantam reprinted the novel in 1983. It was one of Louis's strongest stories at the time it was written. The narrative expertly blended action and characterization. The tale of a group of diverse souls facing their destinies at a desert stronghold drew its strength from both the external and internal forces at play. The external were the savagery of the Indians and the unrelenting elements of nature; the internal, the conflicts imposed upon those trapped between the two.

In October 1958, Columbia Pictures distributed a film version, *Apache Territory.* The working title during production in December '57 was *Papago Wells.* While the gist of the novel was faithfully adhered to, there *were* differences. Many of the characters appear in both versions, but a few from the novel are not included in the film. And the film has at least one new character, the soldier named Graves. Like all the other soldiers in both — Zimmerman, Webb, Styles, Sheehan and Conley — he is killed off in the course of the action.

Not seen in the film are the book's Beaupre, Taylor and Big Maria. The scene of the latter bringing gold into Papago Wells is replaced in the movie by one with Lugo, who acquires it fairly and not from robbery and possibly murder like Maria.

Junie Hatchett is not found by Cates in the novel as she is in the film; L'Amour has her rescue dependent upon the soldiers. While there is a posse in the book made up of civilians, including Taylor and a sheriff who cannot face being stranded in the desert, there is no posse in the film. Lonnie Foreman is already at Papago Wells in the movie when Grant Kimbrough and Jennifer Fair come riding in. The three are together in the book.

Since there is no Beaupre in the film, Lugo acted alone as a wanted man. While Lugo had killed a soldier in the film, the demise of a troublemaking civilian is attributed to the pair of outlaws in the book.

Kimbrough is killed in the movie by Lugo rather than Cates in the novel. Any final confrontation between the two rivals for Jennifer thus is a letdown for the film version. In the motion picture, Cates and Jennifer were once involved romantically unlike the novel where they are strangers when they first meet. Her father, Jim Fair, is also not part of the film.

One of the biggest differences is the climax. *Variety* referred to the movie as having an "exciting climax," with the concocted explosives ending the Indian danger. But L'Amour in his novel leaves the fate of the remaining Apaches a mystery. Following the climactic sandstorm, only an arrowhead lies in the sand, and it "might have been a thousand years old." The arrowhead could be interpreted as a sign that the Indians were buried by the sand. However, it could just as easily be that the arrival of Jim Fair and his men scared them away.

Another big difference is the relationship between Jennifer and Cates. In the novel, he is initially very blunt with her because he feels she lacks grit. But in the motion picture, Cates feels that he wasn't good enough for her.

Fulfilling the same duties as on *Apache Territory*, Rory Calhoun, Victor M. Orsatti and Ray Nazarro also collaborated on a pair of 1957 Westerns, *The Domino Kid* and *The Hired Gun*. In the fall of '58, Calhoun and Orsatti began making television history (in partnership with Desilu Productions) with a Western series called *The Texan*. Initially aired for two seasons until September 1960, *The Texan* made Calhoun more popular than his prior film work. He portrayed Bill Longley, who in actuality was an outlaw in the Old West, but for the show was a staunch hero defending those in distress.

As Logan Cates, another staunch hero, in *Apache Territory*, Rory was credited by *Variety* with a "good performance." (The same review called the film a "routine oater.") Fine performances were given by the other cast members as well. The pair of ladies seen in this Western, Barbara Bates and Carolyn Craig, appeared both in films and on television. Uncredited when she first appeared in movies, Barbara's early roles included 1948's *Adventures of Don Juan* starring Errol Flynn. In the 1952 Western *The Outcasts of Poker Flat*, the actress co-starred with Dale Robertson and Anne Baxter. Carolyn's 1950s TV credits included episodes of *Annie Oakley* and *The Life and Legend of Wyatt Earp*.

Both John Dehner and Leo Gordon had easily recognizable faces from numerous 1950s films, a good many of them Westerns. Dehner tormented Burt Lancaster in 1954's *Apache*. In the same year he appeared in *Apache Territory*, the actor co-starred with Gary Cooper in *Man of the West* and with Paul Newman in *The Left Handed Gun*. In the latter, Dehner played Pat Garrett to Newman's Billy the Kid.

Hondo and *The Tall Stranger* were other Westerns for Gordon. He also had a recurring role in the TV series *Circus Boy* between 1956 and '58. A second career as a writer began in '57 when Gordon had a screenplay produced: the Western *Black Patch*, in which he co-starred with George Montgomery.

Frank Moss, George W. George and Charles R. Marion wrote for television and films. Marion's writing credits included dramas, Westerns and comedies. For TV he worked on *The Untouchables* and *The Adventures of Jim Bowie.* He also wrote Bowery Boys films. George's film writing jobs included the 1953 drama *Thunder Bay* starring James Stewart. His TV Western credits included episodes of *The Rifleman* and *Bonanza.* The television writing credits for Moss included Westerns (*The Lone Ranger*, *Wagon Train*) and dramas (*Combat!*).

As a prolific director of B Westerns, Ray Nazarro was among the best. His films included *Al Jennings of Oklahoma* (1951) and *Cripple Creek* (1952). Among his television credits of the 1950s are *Annie Oakley, The Gene Autry Show* and *Fury.* Action was always a key factor in Nazarro's direction. Undoubtedly it was one of the reasons that Calhoun and Orsatti utilized his services for their Rorvic production company.

Calhoun has the distinction of being the first leading man to star in three motion pictures based on the writings of Louis L'Amour. Joel McCrea had two to his credit as the decade of the 1950s ended. Many years later, Tom Selleck starred in three television productions from L'Amour's work. Four TV productions starred Sam Elliott. (Two of the four were with Elliott and Selleck *together.*)

Lending further credence to L'Amour's imprint on Rory Calhoun's work, the author contributed to at least two episodes of *The Texan* in its first season. Their titles were "The Marshal of Yellow Jacket" and "No Place to Stop."

THE 1960S

Guns of the Timberland

1960. A Jaguar Production.
Distributed by Warner Brothers.
91 Minutes/Technicolor.

Credits: Aaron Spelling (Producer), Robert D. Webb (Director), Joseph Petraca, Aaron Spelling (Screenplay), John Seitz (Photography), Tom McAdoo (Editor), John Beckman (Art Director), Frank M. Miller (Set Decorator), Marjorie Best (Costume Design), Gordon Bau (Makeup Supervisor), David Buttolph (Music). Based on a novel by Louis L'Amour.

Cast: Alan Ladd (Jim Hadley), Jeanne Crain (Laura Riley). Gilbert Roland (Monty Welker), Frankie Avalon (Bert Harvey), Lyle Bettger (Clay Bell), Noah Beery, Jr. (Blackie), Verna Felton (Aunt Sarah), Alana Ladd (Jane Peterson), Regis Toomey (Sheriff Taylor), Johnny Seven (Vince), George Selk (Amos Stearnes), Paul E. Burns (Bill Burroughs), Henry Kulky (Logger).

Synopsis: Jim Hadley and Monty Welker, partners in the logging business, arrive in the town of Deep Well and find that the stableman will not rent his horses to them. Teenager Bert Harvey, however, takes Jim to the ranch where he lives so that Jim can inquire about horses. Jim gets into an altercation with Laura Riley, the owner, over the logging destroying her cattle range.

To fulfill their government contract, the loggers begin cutting down the trees. Bert shows an interest in becoming a lumberjack. Laura and the townsfolk plan secretly against the logging outfit. At a dance, a fight is started with the lumberjacks; it is a diversion as explosives are used to cause an avalanche and block the logging road. With the only other road to the timber lying through Laura's ranch, Jim plans to build another road. This doesn't go over well with his partner and Jim even offers to buy Laura's ranch.

Ranch foreman Clay Bell is accused of causing the avalanche. Laura takes Jim to a town, now deserted, where Clay was raised. Logging destroyed the watershed there when the trees were cut down and the soil washed away. Jim finds himself attracted to Laura and kisses her. With Welker's goading, a temporary application is made for passage across her land.

Their entry is blocked by Clay and the loggers are forced to wait. Sheriff Taylor tries to make Hadley understand just how damaging logging is to the entire town. Welker uses dynamite to open the road. As a result, young Bert is hurt badly. Seeing that Welker will only continue the violence, Jim beats him in a fight.

Deciding to leave town, Jim visits Bert and Laura. Set upon by gunfire by Welker and other loggers, Jim shoots back in self-defense. A logger named Vince is killed and Welker is wounded. Welker then sets fire to the forest. With Laura rushing for help in town, Jim and Clay join forces. They set dynamite in the trees around the fire's edge in a desperate move to stop it. As the dynamite is detonated by Clay, Jim rescues a trapped Welker.

Welker dies after asking to be forgiven for his actions. Jim and his lumberjacks leave on the train. Turning the ranch over to her Aunt Sarah, Laura joins Jim.

Original Source: The novel *Guns of the Timberlands.*

Plotline: Rancher Clay Bell must fight to protect his grazing land against Jud Devitt and his lumberjacks. Those willing to kill to let Devitt have his way are Tinkersville's banker Noble Wheeler and lumberjack Pete Simmons. In his desperation, Devitt even turns to gunmen Jack Kilburn and Stag Harvey.

Devitt's fiancée, Colleen Riley, falls for Bell. Others supporting Bell in the struggle are the town's founder, Sam Tinker, and cowboys Bert Garry, Shorty Jones and Montana Brown.

Commentary: *Guns of the Timberlands* was originally written by L'Amour for the September 1950 issue of *West* magazine. The pseudonym Jim Mayo was used. Jason Press published an expanded novel version in June 1955. Bantam Books also published the novel that November. The novel was the source for the 1960 motion picture *Guns of the Timberland.*

Aaron Spelling and Joseph Petracca's screenplay used the bare bones concept of L'Amour's land rivalry story. Here it is a rancher versus a logging outfit. But there are monumental changes in the film from its source. The town is called Deep Well in the film and Tinkersville in the novel. Only one full character name is used in the movie from the book — and it is Clay Bell. While Bell is the central figure in L'Amour's story, in the movie he is a secondary character.

The film's main figure, Jim Hadley, and partner Mort Welker are composites of the book's Jud Devitt. Unlike Devitt, both Hadley and Welker come to regret the harm done by their logging. Jim discovers it earlier on and becomes the big hero, while Welker pays for the discovery with his life.

Bert Harvey (Bert Garry in the novel) is injured due to Welker's actions in the film. Harvey survives, unlike Garry whose condition worsens due to the savagery of lumberjack Pete Simmons. A character named Vince in the film seems to fill the boots for more than one shady character from the book. This includes Simmons and even the hired guns left out of the film, Stag Harvey and Jack Kilburn.

The book's lawman, Morton Schwabe, is a vindictive character not really on hand but only referred to in the course of events. Sheriff Taylor, the film's law official, is seen as a decent man.

In the film, the law is forced to comply with the logging faction. This is unlike the novel where the rancher ultimately wins the rights to the land being fought over. The

Alan Ladd and Gilbert Roland are the partners in *Guns of the Timberland* who become bitter enemies.

rancher only succeeds in the film because the loggers simply look elsewhere to fulfill their contractual obligation. The fisticuffs in L'Amour's climax between Bell and Devitt are transferred to the earlier fight in the motion picture between Hadley and Welker. Therefore no raging fire exists in the novel. The fire is the film's climactic set piece; the movie thus has a stronger climax.

Schwabe, Devitt and banker Noble Wheeler are among the logging alliance forced to leave town in the novel at different times. In the movie, Hadley pulls out with the lumberjacks willingly. At film's end, Laura gives up her ranch life over her love for Jim. The novel's ending is more realistic with Colleen and Bell sharing together the ranch life.

Guns of the Timberland was released by Warner Brothers in March 1960. Locations included Quincy, California, and Reno, Nevada. Overall the film was considered a minor effort despite being an A production. It was the first Alan Ladd movie since his breakthrough role in 1942's *This Gun for Hire* not to be reviewed by the *New York Times*.

Ladd was supposedly drinking heavily at the time the Western was made in 1959. *Variety* remarked that he "has looked better, and he's had better roles than this one." The

Western was his last film on a contract with Warner Brothers which began with 1952's *The Iron Mistress* (with Ladd as Jim Bowie). Ladd is best remembered for 1953's *Shane,* which was his last film under a Paramount contract. In '54, he starred in the Western *Drum Beat,* which was his initial film for his own Jaguar Productions. The company also helped make *Guns of the Timberland.*

Ladd originally planned to have his *Shane* co-star and friend, Van Heflin, as his partner in *Guns.* But Gilbert Roland was given the part instead and gave a strong account. Roland's big screen career included a series of Cisco Kid adventures.

Credited with the best performance in this Western was Jeanne Crain. She played another ranch owner in the Kirk Douglas Western *Man Without a Star* (1955). Lyle Bettger made his mark portraying bad guys during the 1950s. He gave impressive performances in 1952's *The Greatest Show on Earth,* 1956's *The Lone Ranger,* and 1957's *Gunfight at the O.K. Corral* (as Ike Clanton).

Teen idol Frankie Avalon was put in the movie as box office insurance. In 1959,

Jeanne Crain and Lyle Bettger are forced to fight for their land in *Guns of the Timberland.*

In *Guns of the Timberland,* opponents Alan Ladd and Lyle Bettger find themselves fighting together to stop a raging fire.

Avalon scored one of his greatest hits as a singer: The song "Venus" undoubtedly helped to pave his way into films. "Gee Whiz Willikers Golly Gee" by Mack David and Jerry Livingston was one of the songs Avalon sang in *Guns.*

Alana Ladd, Alan's daughter, made her film debut in the movie playing Frankie Avalon's girlfriend. The Ladds also appeared in a 1964 release, *Duel of Champions. Guns of the Timberland* and *Duel of Champions* were regarded as Alan Ladd's worst films.

The action was certainly helped along by the film's director, Robert D. Webb. He had the distinction of directing young Elvis Presley's first feature in 1956, *Love Me Tender.* Webb also directed a couple of films with another rising young star of the '50s, Robert Wagner, 1953's *Beneath the 12-Mile Reef* (co-starring Gilbert Roland) and 1955's *White Feather.*

Screenwriter Joseph Petracca's other Western films included one with Alan Ladd, 1958's *The Proud Rebel.* (He also worked on '59's *The Jayhawkers!* which starred Jeff Chandler and Fess Parker.) His co-writer Aaron Spelling worked on another Ladd Western in '60, *One Foot in Hell*, Spelling went on to become one of the greatest names in television production. His extensive list of successful shows included *Daniel Boone* (1964–70), *Charlie's Angels* (1976–81) and *Dynasty* (1981–89). Spelling's very first television series as a producer was 1959's *Johnny Ringo. Guns of the Timberland* was his initial motion picture as a producer.

Heller in Pink Tights

1960. A Ponti-Girosi Production.
Released by Paramount Pictures.
100 Minutes/Technicolor.

Credits: Carlo Ponti, Marcello Girosi (Producers), George Cukor (Director), Dudley Nichols, Walter Bernstein (Screenplay), Harold Lipstein (Photography), Howard Smith (Editor), Hal Pereira, Eugene Allen (Art Directors), Sam Comer, Grace Gregory (Set Decorators), Edith Head (Costumes), Wally Westmore (Makeup Supervisor), Daniele Amfitheatrof (Music). Based on a novel by Louis L'Amour.

Cast: Sophia Loren (Angela Rossini), Anthony Quinn (Tom Healy), Margaret O'Brien (Della Southby), Steve Forrest (Clint Mabry), Eileen Heckart (Lorna Hathaway), Ramon Novarro (DeLeon), Edmund Lowe (Manfred "Doc" Montague), George Mathews (Sam Pierce), Edward Binns (Ed McClain), Warren Wade (Hodges), Frank Silvera (Santis), Robert Palmer (McAllister), Cal Bolder (Goober), Frank Cordell (Theodore), Cactus McPeters (William), Geraldine Wall (Madam), David Armstrong (Achilles), Alfred Tonkel (Calchas), Bryn Davis (Venus), Cathy Cox (Juno), Howard McNear (Photographer).

Synopsis: Having stolen costumes from Hodges, a theater owner in Nebraska, the Great Dramatic and Concert Company is chased to the Wyoming border. In Cheyenne, the site of its next job, company owner-player Tom Healy introduces the other members of his troupe. They are Doc Montague, Lorna Hathaway, her daughter Della Southby, and Angela Rossini. All the members are a bit startled at the sight of two men laid out after being killed by gunman Clint Mabry. The deceased were killed for a mining claim sought by shady businessman DeLeon; their partner, Santis, knows Mabry was hired to do the job and fears for his own life.

Sam Pierce, owner of Cheyenne's theater, protests the troupe's rehearsal of a play with adultery as part of the scenario. Although Tom wants Angie to marry him, she is too free-spirited to accept the idea.

A new play, *Mazeppa*, is a success, particularly when Angie in pink tights is strapped to the back of a moving horse. Mabry is among those entertained by the show. Hodges arrives backstage and tries to have Tom arrested. Tom is given until morning to pay off the debt for the costumes. Angie's arrangement with Pierce to pay the debt and then be repaid in just a short period only means that the troupe must flee again.

Townspeople watch as show folk Anthony Quinn and Sophia Loren arrive with their traveling troupe in *Heller in Pink Tights.*

That evening Angie tries to win the money for the debt in a poker game. Losing to Mabry, she even puts herself up as part of the betting. When Santis comes after Mabry with a gun, and is then killed, Angie gets away.

Mabry goes to their rooms, soon followed by Pierce, but the performers have skipped town. Hearing they are headed for the town of Bonanza, Mabry catches up to them along the trail. Despite Angie's plea, Tom invites him to join them because of the possible Indian danger.

Indians threaten the group and Mabry kills two. As the Indians have slain their wagon drivers, the performers leave the wagons behind and follow Mabry. More Indians find the deserted wagons and ransack them. Mabry takes the troupe over a snow-covered mountain to a safer area. At their campsite, Angie tells Tom about the earlier bet lost to the gunman. Tom's annoyance is fueled when he sees the two were alone together.

Meanwhile, DeLeon sends out several men to kill Mabry because he doesn't want to pay all the money owed to him. One of the henchmen mistakes Tom for Mabry and shoots him in the leg. At a mission, Tom collapses from his wound. He later informs Angie that he is breaking up the troupe. Young Della tries in vain to seduce Tom into letting her take Angie's place in the company.

Utilizing Angie's seductive powers, Mabry pays her to entice DeLeon to hand over the money due or be exposed for having men killed. While the ploy works, Angie instead uses the entire amount to buy Tom a theater in Bonanza.

At first refusing the gift after learning of Angie's scheme, Tom does agree to stage *Mazeppa* to pay his debts. Mabry comes backstage during the show and is angry at Angie for stealing his money. Interfering with her performance, Mabry is beaten by Tom in a fistfight. Although drawing a gun on Tom, Mabry accepts his help to escape DeLeon's henchmen. Replacing Angie on the horse in the show, Mabry gets away.

Believing Angie has gone with Mabry, Tom realizes that she has returned to the theater as he puts out the stage lights. Upon learning she paid Mabry off with a loan signed Mrs. Thomas Healy, Tom carries Angie off in his arms.

Original Source: The novel *Heller with a Gun.*

Plotline: Gunfighter King Mabry comes across a traveling show at a wayside stop called Hat Street Station. Run by Tom Healy, the troupe of players includes Janice Ryan and Dodie Saxon. Both gals show an interest in Mabry when he follows their wagons, concerned about the intentions of guide Andy Barker.

Barker's interest is in the gold Tom is carrying and has hired gunmen to rob the troupe. Plaguing *everyone* are renegade Indians. In the journey over harsh winter terrain, Tom, Dodie and King show their strengths.

Commentary: *Heller with a Gun* was initially published by Fawcett–Gold Medal in 1955. Bantam first published the novel in 1984. The 1960 film version *Heller in Pink Tights* is actually more interesting than the novel and profoundly different. Only Healy's name is left untouched, with Mabry's first name changed to Clint and the other characters having different names from the book. Janice is Angela Rossini, Dodie is Della

Southby and Maggie is Lorna Hathaway. Guilford is Doc Montague, who survives with his other companions, unlike the book's character. Maggie and Dodie are not mother and daughter like their screen counterparts.

L'Amour offered a better look at the world of the thespian in two later novels, 1970's *Reilly's Luck* and 1981's *Comstock Lode.* There is only a brief sequence in *Heller with a Gun*— in a room at a station stop — in which the thespians perform. The motion picture, however, highlights several colorful sequences depicting on-stage and backstage escapades.

Snow is the main backdrop in the novel; the theater is in the film. In fact, the film only shares a brief interlude where the performers and Mabry are hampered by wintry elements.

Hardly a substitute for the book's main villain, Andy Barker, is the film's DeLeon. DeLeon appears suave and gentlemanly on the surface; Barker is brusque and far more threatening. Yet Mabry, looked on as a villain of sorts since he is depicted as a professional killer in the film, feels threatened during the climax when he is trapped by DeLeon and his cronies in the theater.

The book's climax occurs in a barn where Mabry, who much earlier turned down a job as a hired killer, fights Barker and his henchmen. Although Dodie shows interest in King, that she is revealed as the gal for him comes as a nice surprise. In the movie, Mabry doesn't end up with any of the ladies.

Janice's rejection of the West's code of kill-or-be-killed becomes grating. She ends up with Tom, just as Angie does in the film. As in the L'Amour novel, Tom loves his lady all along. Janice and Angie share an attraction to Mabry in each version.

Healy plays a significant part in both, even saving Mabry's life. He is a stronger presence in the film, even physically. Angie seems rather surprised when he proves to be tougher than Mabry with his fists.

The novel's central figure is King Mabry, but the movie showcases Angie Rossini. Like Healy, she is a stronger figure than the book's counterpart despite her frivolous nature. Angie's shenanigans, although somewhat tiresome, are the film's true strength. She is not really a bad woman; her beauty and spirit are so exhilarating, so intoxicating, that every man seems enslaved by her and her reckless abandon.

While a fictional character, Angie was inspired by a very real person: Adah Isaacs Menken died from peritonitis in 1868. In 1861, in Albany, New York, the legendary entertainer made her first appearance in the play *Mazeppa.* It made her famous and the touring engagements included frontier towns in the West. Angie dons pink tights for the film; Adah donned flesh-colored ones and utilized her equestrian skills for the exciting bareback ride wherever she played. The *New York Times* noted that Sophia Loren "may be a bit more chic than was Miss Menken." The reviewer also felt that she was "warm and natural" in her role.

Miss Loren and her equally adept leading man, Anthony Quinn, played in two previous films together, 1954's *Attila* and 1959's *The Black Orchid.* Following *Heller in Pink Tights,* the actress won the 1961 Best Actress Oscar for *Two Women.* In '57, Quinn received a Best Actor nomination for *Wild Is the Wind,* which was helmed by *Heller*'s director, George Cukor.

Cukor was one of the greatest of all Hollywood film directors. The stars who won Academy Awards for performances in his films include James Stewart in 1940's *The Philadelphia Story,* Judy Holliday in 1950's *Born Yesterday,* and Rex Harrison in 1964's *My Fair Lady.* "Director Cukor filled many of his [*Heller in Pink Tights*] scenes with full-blown diversion, others with high action, and his skills blend the two without weakening either of them," opined a *Variety* critic.

As the movie's gunslinger, Steve Forrest held his own with the two stars. The role was supposedly intended for Alan Ladd. Forrest, the younger brother of actor Dana Andrews, had a knack for Westerns; that same year he was in Elvis Presley's *Flaming Star.* In 1977 and '78, Forrest played James Fenimore Cooper's Hawkeye in a pair of TV movies, *The Last of Mohicans* and *The Deerslayer.*

One of the great silent screen stars, Ramon Novarro, portrayed the film's elegant villain. His silent film roles included the villainous Rupert of Hentzau in the 1922 version of *The Prisoner of Zenda* and the heroic title role in the 1926 version of *Ben-Hur.*

Edmund Lowe, Eileen Heckart and Margaret O'Brien contributed ample support as the rest of the theater troupe. Like Novarro, Lowe was a silent star and moved on to sound films; *Heller in Pink Tights* was the last film for both men.

Heckart was initially a theater actress; she was in the '54 play and '56 film version of

Seen in the title role for *Heller in Pink Tights* is the beautiful Sophia Loren.

In *Heller in Pink Tights,* Steve Forrest, Anthony Quinn, Sophia Loren and companions find themselves caught along a snowy mountain pass.

The Bad Seed and the '69 play and '72 film version of *Butterflies Are Free.* For the latter film, she won the Oscar as Best Supporting Actress.

Among the most famous of all juvenile stars, Margaret O'Brien is warmly remembered as Judy Garland's little sister in 1944's *Meet Me in St. Louis.* Her other notable films of that era included *The Canterville Ghost* (1944) and *Our Vines Have Tender Grapes* (1945). In 1944, Miss O'Brien received her very own special Oscar as Outstanding Child Actress.

Paramount Pictures bought the film options in 1958 to L'Amour's novel for $25,000. Zoe Adkins was initially hired to write an outline, then passed away. Dudley Nichols worked on the script, and Walter Bernstein took over when he became ill. Nichols died before the film's March '60 release. Both Nichols and Bernstein received joint credit for the screenplay, which supposedly was still being written during production. An uncredited writer on 1960's *The Magnificent Seven,* Bernstein also worked on the Loren films *That Kind of Woman* (1959) and *A Breath of Scandal* (1960). Known for his collaborations with directors John Ford and Howard Hawks, Dudley Nichols had an exceptional writing career. Among his films with Ford were 1939's *Stagecoach* and 1940's *The Long Voyage Home.* His work with Hawks included '38's *Bringing Up Baby* and '52's *The Big Sky.*

For *Heller in Pink Tights,* Paramount utilized its famed Western Street and also built a frontier theater complete with balcony, box seats, gaslights and stage. Location filming sites included Bronson Canyon in Griffith Park and Tucson, Arizona.

Despite the talent and skill that went into the motion picture, it was not a box office success. Yet *America* magazine reflected, "[T]he picture captures with surprising authenticity the flavor of the theatrical entertainment our grandfathers used to like in the days before the movies."

How the West Was Won

1962. A Metro-Goldwyn-Mayer and Cinerama Presentation.
Released by Metro-Goldwyn-Mayer.
165 Minutes/Metrocolor.

Credits: Bernard Smith (Producer), John Ford, George Marshall, Henry Hathaway (Directors), James R. Webb (Screenplay), William H. Daniels, Milton Krasner, Charles Lang, Jr., Joseph LaShelle (Photographers), Harold F. Kress (Editor), George W. Davis, William Ferrari, Addison Hehr (Art Directors), Henry Grace, Don Greenwood, Jr., Jack Mills (Set Directors), Walter Plunkett (Costumes), William Tuttle (Makeup), A. Arnold Gillespie, Robert R. Hoag (Special Visual Effects), Alfred Newman (Music), Ken Darby (Music Associate). Suggested by the series in *Life* magazine.

Cast: Spencer Tracy (Narrator), Carroll Baker (Eve Prescott), Lee J. Cobb (Lou Ramsey), Henry Fonda (Jethro Stuart), Carolyn Jones (Julie Rawlings), Karl Malden (Zebulon Prescott), Gregory Peck (Cleve Van Valen), George Peppard (Zeb Rawlings), Robert Preston (Roger Morgan), Debbie Reynolds (Lilith Prescott), James Stewart (Linus Rawlings), Eli Wallach (Charlie Gant), John Wayne (William T. Sherman), Richard Widmark (Mike King), Brigid Bazlen (Dora Hawkins), Walter Brennan (Colonel Hawkins), David Brian (Attorney), Andy Devine (Corporal Peterson), Raymond Massey (Abraham Lincoln), Agnes Moorehead (Rebecca Prescott), Henry (Harry) Morgan (Ulysses S. Grant), Thelma Ritter (Agatha Clegg), Mickey Shaughnessy (Deputy Marshal), Russ Tamblyn (Rebel Soldier).

Synopsis:

The Rivers

Out West, mountain man Linus Rawlings rides into a friendly Indian village. With a canoe filled with beaver pelts, he is soon paddling upriver.

At the Erie Canal, the Prescott family is waiting to board a barge to take them west-

MARYLAND PREMIERE TODAY 8:30 P.M.

"Brilliant, exciting, spectacular and totally absorbing"

METRO-GOLDWYN-MAYER and

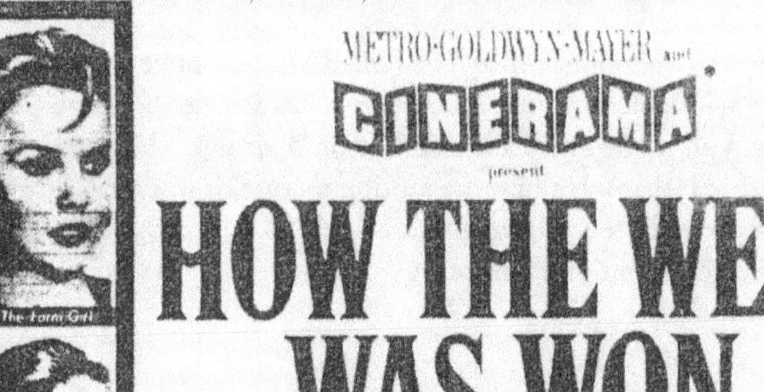

The Farm Girl · The Tinhorn

STARRING

CARROLL BAKER · LEE J. COBB · HENRY FONDA · CAROLYN JONES
KARL MALDEN · GREGORY PECK · GEORGE PEPPARD
ROBERT PRESTON · DEBBIE REYNOLDS · JAMES STEWART
ELI WALLACH · JOHN WAYNE · RICHARD WIDMARK · NARRATED BY SPENCER TRACY

TECHNICOLOR®

Frontier Marshal · The Sod Buster

Buffalo Hunter · Marshal's Wife

Horse Soldier · Wagon Master · Gambler's Bride · Mountain Man · The Desperado · The General · Empire Builder

CO-STARRING
BRIGID BAZLEN · WALTER BRENNAN · DAVID BRIAN · ANDY DEVINE
RAYMOND MASSEY · AGNES MOOREHEAD · HENRY (HARRY) MORGAN
THELMA RITTER · MICKEY SHAUGHNESSY · RUSS TAMBLYN

WRITTEN BY JAMES R. WEBB · DIRECTED BY HENRY HATHAWAY, JOHN FORD, GEORGE MARSHALL

PRODUCED BY BERNARD SMITH · MUSIC ALFRED NEWMAN

★

RESERVED SEATS BY MAIL OR BOX OFFICE

SCHEDULE OF RESERVED SEAT PERFORMANCES & PRICES

MATINEES: 2:00 P. M. (Wednesday)—Orc. & Mezz. $1.75—Bal. $1.50
MATINEES: 2:00 P. M. (Sat., Sun. & Hols.)—Orc. & Mezz. $2.25—Bal. $1.75
EVENINGS: 8:30 P. M. (Mon. thru Thurs.)—Orc. & Mezz. $2.00—Bal. $1.65
EVENINGS: 8:30 P. M. (Fri., Sat. & Hols.)—Orc. & Mezz. $2.50—Bal. $2.00
EVENINGS: 7:30 P. M. (Sundays)—Orc. & Mezz. $2.50—Bal. $2.00.

FOR GROUPS & THEATRE PARTIES CALL LE. 9-7139

MAKE CHECKS OR MONEY ORDER PAYABLE TO:

trans-lux town

LE. 9-2294
318 WEST FAYETTE ST.

Please send me ______ tickets for ALTERNATE CHOICE
Date ______ or ______
Time of Performance ______ or ______
At $ ______ each, or ______
Enclosed is my check or money order for $ ______
NAME ______
ADDRESS ______
CITY ______ ZONE ______ STATE ______

PLEASE ENCLOSE REMITTANCE AND A STAMPED, SELF-ADDRESSED ENVELOPE
No cash or stamps please

ward. Zebulon is the father, Rebecca the mother, and their offspring are Eve, Sam, Lilith and Zeke.

Another family, the Harveys, travel with the Prescotts through the canal; they build rafts to take them down the Ohio River. Linus comes in with his canoe as the families are camped out. Although there is a strong attraction between Linus and Eve, he leaves the next morning on his journey east.

Stopping to buy whiskey along the river, Linus is waylaid by river pirates and left for dead. He survives and follows them. Linus then joins the Prescotts and the Harveys to defeat the pirates. Although Eve wants him to go with her, Linus moves on.

On their raft, the Prescotts are caught in rapids and Lilith is swept overboard. She reaches the shore safely, but Rebecca and Zebulon are drowned. Hearing of the tragedy, Linus returns to help bury them. He decides to stay with Eve and build a farm together.

The Plains

Lilith Prescott is a performer in a St. Louis music hall. Among her admirers is gambler Cleve Van Valen, who overhears she has inherited a gold claim in California. On a wagon train bound for California, Lilith joins another woman, Agatha Clegg; Cleve follows. To keep him out of a fight with wagonmaster Roger Morgan, Agatha allows him to work for her.

Although she realizes he is interested in her claim, Lilith is still attracted to Cleve. During an Indian attack on the wagons, Cleve proves his worth in the fighting. But with the gold claim just a pocket played out, Cleve leaves Lilith. Morgan, who had earlier proposed to her, does so again. Once more she refuses. When Lilith is heard by Cleve singing on a riverboat, he turns down a winning hand in a card game to see her. She accepts his proposal.

The Civil War

On the Rawlings farm, Eve receives a letter from her sister, Lilith. Cleve, who has become successful in San Francisco with the railroad, has an opening for Eve and Linus' oldest son, Zeb. With his father already in the Union army, Zeb's mother reluctantly lets him go to war instead.

At Shiloh, Zeb discovers there is no glory with all of the killing. Although not aware of it, his father is among the dead. When a newfound friend turns out to be a rebel soldier trying to shoot General Grant, Zeb is forced to kill him.

Returning home after the Civil War, Zeb learns that both his folks are dead. Saying farewell to his brother Jeremiah, Zeb plans to go west with the army.

Opposite: **This advertisement for *How the West Was Won,* the most popular entry in the L'Amour filmography, showcases its all-star cast. The names are alphabetized.**

THE RAILROAD

In a race to put down the most track are the Central Pacific and Union Pacific railroad lines. Union Pacific man Mike King is upset when the track layers stop their work; it seems their attention is drawn to Jethro Stuart, a buffalo hunter who has found two men slain by Indians.

Cavalry officer Zeb Rawlings tries to keep the peace with the Indians. They are preparing for war since their hunting grounds have been violated. Urged by King to secure a treaty, Zeb does with Jethro's help as an interpreter. It is with the promise that no settler or hunter will violate the hunting grounds. But the treaty is broken once the railroad brings people west. Failing to prevent an Indian attack, Zeb warns the railroad camp. Buffalo are stampeded by the Indians against the camp. The broken treaty causes Zeb to resign from the army. But he pays a visit to Jethro, who was an old friend of his father.

THE OUTLAWS

After Cleve Van Valen's death, Lilith travels to Arizona where she has ranch land. Her nephew Zeb is retiring as a lawman to run the ranch. Lilith is met at the railroad station by Zeb, his wife Julie and their children, Eve, Linus and Prescott. Also at the station is an old enemy of Zeb's named Charlie Gant.

Zeb warns lawman Lou Ramsey about Gant. At first Lou doesn't want to be involved in any fight between the two men. But with the train carrying a gold shipment, Lou and Zeb work together to stop any possible robbery.

When the train comes under attack by Gant and his outlaw gang, Zeb, Lou and a deputy fight them off. Stuck holding onto a flatcar, Zeb still manages to shoot down Gant as part of the train is derailed. Zeb and his family, including Lilith, set out toward the ranch to begin their new life together.

Commentary: *How the West Was Won* was written directly for the screen by James R. Webb. His story was inspired by a seven-part series of historical articles which ran between April 6 and May 18, 1959, in *Life* magazine. While the film's characters and their adventures were fictional, actual historical incidents and people were sources of inspiration.

The film had a London opening in November 1962, a Los Angeles opening in December, and a widespread release in March 1963. At the time of the widespread release, the novelization of the screenplay was published by Bantam Books. L'Amour was the author. Louis's novel of the same title was a faithful treatment of Webb's script, but he then added details and characterizations not found in the film. In Part 1, *The Rivers,* the novel includes a fight that Linus Rawlings and other mountain men have with the Ute Indians. More insight into the nature of the river pirates is given by L'Amour; for example, one named Marty would like to travel to the West for new land like the pioneers.

Colonel Jeb Hawkins, the pirate leader, is revealed as Marty's father in the book; both are killed in the fight between the pioneer families and the pirates. Their deaths and the wounding of Sam Prescott during this conflict are also seen in the film.

The destruction of the raft in the rapids and the aftermath are more vivid in the book. The Prescott family is separated by the raging waters; Eve and Sam are reunited first, then much later Zeke and Lilith find them. As in the movie, their parents are drowning victims.

In both versions, Linus returns to Eve. Not mentioned in the movie, however, are the plans to care for her brothers as well. Also unmentioned is Linus' desire to fulfill Lilith's wish to return east with the money generated from the beaver pelts he has brought out of the mountains.

In L'Amour's *The Plains,* it is revealed that down-on-his-luck gambler Cleve Van Valen killed two men in past duels; the first man was a crooked business partner of his

Gregory Peck and Debbie Reynolds manage a quiet moment on their wagon train journey in *How the West Was Won.*

late father. A member of the wagon train that Cleve joins is a friend of his, Gabe French, who does not figure at all in the film. They initially meet in St. Louis when French carries Van Valen piggyback across a muddy street.

In the book, when the wagons come under attack by the Cheyenne, Cleve has just knocked out wagonmaster Roger Morgan with one punch when caught gambling. Van Valen then helps to circle the wagons in the place of the still unconscious wagonmaster.

After Morgan stops Cleve from gambling in the film, there is no fistfight as the wagons make a dash to get away from the Indians. The lead horses and cattle are abandoned to prevent the massacre of the entire train.

Part 3 of the L'Amour novel is called *The War*. In both versions, Linus Rawlings and his son Zeb fight against the Confederacy in the War Between the States. The book reveals how Linus was killed at Shiloh (he is shot and bayoneted by the enemy). The book further mentions that Zeb was with Sherman on his March to the Sea to help end the war.

Civil War generals Ulysses Simpson Grant and William Tecumseh Sherman are briefly part of each version. Ten months into the actual conflict, they were both at Shiloh, Tennessee, in April 1862, when 1,754 Union forces and 1,723 Confederate forces were killed. Over 16,000 more men were wounded in the two days of fighting.

For anyone who might wonder what the Civil War is doing in a story called *How the West Was Won*, L'Amour summed it up nicely: Reflecting on the increase of people who went westward after the war, he wrote in the novel, "It was the Union that finally opened the West, a free, united nation where all men were equal, where each had his right to his own."

The Iron Horse is the title of Part 4 of the book. As in the film, buffalo hunter Jethro Stuart brings in the two railroad men killed by Indians, but the novel points out that one of the victims is Sam Prescott.

Lieutenant Zeb Rawlings protects the railroad in both; and Mike King is his adversary in yet another way in the book: They are both interested in the same woman, Julie, who is Jethro's daughter.

When the railroad moves onto the hunting grounds of the Arapahoes in both film and novel, King claims that their buffalo herds will not be killed off in a lifetime. The railroad, of course, soon brings people westward to hunt and settle there. In the book, Julie chooses Zeb over King as a husband.

The last segment of the film opens with the death of Cleve Van Valen, and wife Lilith's giving up their San Francisco mansion and auctioning off their belongings to pay debts. In the novel, this episode is still part of *The Iron Horse*. Here Gabe French also reminisces with Lilith over old times. He married Agatha Clegg, now also deceased; Agatha was Lilith's traveling companion on that California wagon train in *The Plains*.

To begin Part 5 of the novel, *The Outlaws*, L'Amour describes an episode not seen in the motion picture: Making his way into the wilderness, Jethro Stuart comes across the home of Brutus Harvey, whose family had traveled with the Prescotts many years before in *The Rivers*. Brutus was one of the three sons traveling with their father in both versions.

Journeying on in the novel, Jethro gets into a fight; outlaws and a grizzly bear are involved. Jethro and outlaw leader Zeke Ralls are related as he is actually the youngest of the Prescott siblings. Both Zeke and Jethro are mortally wounded.

There are three sequences in the book concerning fights with bears. Along with the grizzly in *The Outlaws,* Cleve Van Valen kills one rummaging around the wagons in *The Plains,* and *The War* includes a reminiscence of Linus Rawlings tracking down a club-foot bear.

Bad man Charlie Gant's past troubles with Rawlings are thoroughly revealed in the book. They include Zeb forcing Gant and his nefarious gambling establishment out of a Texas town. Floyd Gant, Charlie's brother (mentioned in the movie), seemed to be forced by him into a gunfight with Rawlings; in the gunfight Floyd is killed.

A grizzled John Wayne as General Sherman in *How the West Was Won.* Wayne also played the man in an episode of TV's *Wagon Train* series.

There is no train derailment nor subsequent wreck in the novel like in the film. But Zeb is trapped in each version on a flatcar with logs falling off. In the film, Gant is shot by Rawlings and flung from the moving train; the final gunfight in the book, where Zeb is wounded and Charlie killed, occurs off the train after it has stopped. Concluding both versions is the passage where Aunt Lilith, Zeb, Julie and children Prescott, Linus and Eve ride in the wagon to their new ranch.

"Home in the Meadow" is the song everyone shares at the end of movie and novel. Other songs were part of the film, but none were better than this one with lyrics by Johnny Mercer. The song seems a fitting tribute to the westward-bound families depicted here.

Both Debbie Reynolds and George Peppard embodied youthful daring and then, in scenes set years later, wise maturity. Known for her song-and-dance skills, which were nicely blended with her acting abilities, Debbie's talents always brightened the films she was in. Her other movies included 1952's *Singin' in the Rain* and 1964's *The Unsinkable Molly Brown*; for the latter, she received a Best Actress Oscar nomination.

How the West Was Won was George Peppard's first Western. He made others, including 1967's *Rough Night in Jericho*, and had a flair for action roles. But he was also a fine romantic lead as was proven by *Breakfast at Tiffany's* (1961).

Carroll Baker conveyed tenderness in her portrayal of Eve, as did Carolyn Jones as Julie. Both actresses were past Academy Award nominees — Baker as Best Actress for 1956's *Baby Doll*, and Jones as Best Supporting Actress for 1957's *The Bachelor Party*. In the epic Western *The Big Country* (1958), Baker co-starred with Gregory Peck. He won the Best

George Peppard and Henry Fonda enjoy each other's company in this scene from *How the West Was Won*. In the book, their characters are related.

Actor Oscar in 1962 for *To Kill a Mockingbird.* Peck and James Stewart gave roguishly charming performances in *How the West Was Won*, as did Henry Fonda, whose Jethro was an old friend of the Stewart character. (The two actors were friends in real life. They were both up for the 1940 Best Actor award, Fonda for *The Grapes of Wrath* and Stewart for *The Philadelphia Story.* Although Jimmy won the Oscar, he admitted that he voted for his pal Hank.)

The one cast disappointment in *How the West Was Won* was that John Wayne only made a brief appearance. Still, as General Sherman, he gave a gritty performance.

Metro-Goldwyn-Mayer joined forces with Cinerama, utilizing the latter's widescreen process. This production was considered the first with a dramatic narrative to do so. (In Cinerama, three separate cameras filmed images which were later projected side-by-side-by-side on theater screens.)

In reference to the film, *Variety* said, "It's a story which naturally puts the spotlight on action and adventure, and the three directors between them have turned in some memorable sequences." All three of the directors — John Ford, George Marshall and Henry Hathaway — first worked on movies during the silent era. Over the years, Westerns were among their most accomplished. Ford, who directed the "Civil War" episode, made *Fort Apache* (1948) starring Fonda and Wayne. Another one by Ford, 1962's *The Man Who Shot Liberty Valance,* starred Wayne and Stewart.

Destry Rides Again (1939), starring Stewart, was Marshall's favorite of all those he directed. He also did a pair of comedies with Debbie Reynolds, including 1960's *The Gazebo.* Marshall helmed the episode "The Railroad" in *How the West Was Won.*

Hathaway directed three episodes, "The Rivers," "The Plains" and "The Outlaws." He made a number of films with the Duke, including 1965's *The Sons of Katie Elder.* In 1971, Hathaway directed Gregory Peck in another Western, *Shoot Out.*

A number of outstanding locations were utilized, among them Battery Rock along the Ohio River in Illinois, Custer State Park in South Dakota, and Monument Valley on the Arizona-Utah border. The motion picture was produced by Bernard Smith for around $15,000,000. Its domestic earnings were nearly $21,000,000; worldwide, it eventually made some $50,000,000. These were colossal figures in that era.

Eight Academy Award nominations were received by this wonderfully entertaining film, including Best Picture of 1963. It won three Oscars: Franklin E. Milton's sound, Harold F. Kress's film editing and James R. Webb's screenplay. Webb's other writing credits included *The Big Country* and a third epic Western, *Cheyenne Autumn* (1964), which was director John Ford's last in that genre. *The Iron Mistress* (1952) and *Trapeze* (1956) were also written by Webb. Webb's scenario, and L'Amour's novelization, touchingly conveyed the aspirations of the many characters over a 50-year period. There were some people who supposedly thought that the film was derived from one of Louis's stories instead of the other way around.

More on *How the West Was Won* can be found in this author's book *The Golden Corral: A Roundup of Magnificent Western Films* (McFarland, 1997).

Taggart

1964. A Gordon Kay & Associates Production.
Released by Universal Pictures.
85 Minutes/Technicolor.

Credits: Gordon Kay (Producer), R.G. Springsteen (Director), Robert Creighton Williams (Screenplay), William Margulies (Photography), Tony Martinelli (Editor), Alexander Golitzen, Raymond Beal (Art Directors), Bud Westmore (Makeup), Herman Stein (Music). Based on a novel by Louis L'Amour.

Cast: Tony Young (Kent Taggart), Dan Duryea (Jason), Dick Foran (Stark), Elsa Cardenas (Consuela), Jean Hale (Miriam), Emile Meyer (Ben Blazer), David Carradine (Cal Dodge), Peter Duryea (Rusty Bob Blazer), Tom Reese (Vince August), Ray Teal (Ralph Taggart), Claudia Barrett (Lola), Stuart Randall (Sheriff), Harry Carey, Jr. (Lt. Hudson) Bill Henry (Army Sergeant), Sarah Selby (Maude Taggart), George Murdock (Army Scout), Arthur Space (Colonel), Bob Steele (Cook).

Synopsis: Western land is bought by the Taggart family — Ralph, Maude and their son, Kent. Greedy rancher Ben Blazer wants their land, and with his own son, Rusty Bob, attacks the Taggarts. Kent's folks are killed by Rusty Bob, and Kent is hurt. Following after the Blazers, Kent injures Ben and kills Rusty Bob.

A gunman named Jason and his partners Cal Dodge and Vince August are hired by the dying Ben Blazer to get Taggart. Kent kills one of Jason's men and wounds the other one. Killing his own injured partner because he is a burden, Jason tracks Kent into Indian country. Kent has found a mission where an old gold miner, Stark, lives with his daughter Miriam and young wife Consuela.

Kent helps Stark and the women against dangerous Apaches. In appreciation, Stark makes Jason a prisoner. Failing in her seduction of Kent, an embittered Consuela releases Jason and helps him steal Stark's gold. Joining a wagon train with Jason, Consuela then tries to make off with the gold. But she is killed by attacking Indians.

The Indians also pose a threat to an army fort, as does Jason to Kent and Stark when they face off. After killing Stark, Jason is shot at by Kent and crushed beneath the weight of his falling horse and the stolen gold. Kent now plans for a future life with Miriam at his side.

Original Source: The novel *Taggart.*

Plotline: Digging for gold in Apache country is prospector Adam Stark. Accompanying him are his wife Consuelo and his sister, Miriam. Soon joining them is wrongly accused fugitive Swante Taggart and Pete Shoyer, the lawman on his trail.

Fighting together against the Indian danger, the small group rides out with packhorses loaded with gold. Deception then occurs over the gold with Shoyer and Taggart's own confrontation temporarily on hold.

Commentary: Bantam first published L'Amour's novel *Taggart* in 1959. Part of it was derived from an earlier short story by Louis. It was called "Trap of Gold," and initially

Jean Hale and Dick Foran seem to be sizing up a somewhat distracted Tony Young in *Taggart.* In the earlier *Treasure of Ruby Hills,* Foran played the main villain.

was printed in the August 1951 issue of *Argosy* magazine. This story can also be found in Bantam's L'Amour collections *War Party* (1975) and *Law of the Desert Born* (1983). The story tells of a man digging for gold beneath an unstable towering rock formation. In the short story, his name is Wetherton; he is Adam Stark in the novel. Also in the 1964 Universal film *Taggart*, a man named Stark is a gold miner.

In L'Amour's initial story, Wetherton's plan is to extract some $10,000 in gold. Stark's plan in the book is for the much greater sum of $100,000. Neither man reaches his goal.

The digging in the short story causes the rock to shift, burying the miner; he barely escapes with his life. In the novel, the miner is forced to abandon his digging on account of Indians. While hostile Indians are also part of the film, they are not in the short story. Besides Wetherton here, the only other characters mentioned are his wife Laura and son Tommy.

Stark in both film and novel has a stunning Mexican wife whose sexuality is noticed by one and all. Her name slightly differs in each account — it is Consuela for the movie

This ad placed *Taggart* at the bottom half of a double feature which highlighted Doris Day and Rock Hudson's third big-screen pairing.

and Consuelo for the book. Miriam is Stark's sister in the novel and daughter in the film. In both versions, the title character's first name is different — it is Swante in the book and Kent in the film. His parents — Ralph and Maude for the movie — die earlier on in the novel, and their deaths are not related to the film's scenario.

In the film, like the book, Taggart becomes a wanted man for fighting back for land to live on. His main antagonist in the novel is Pete Shoyer and Jason in the film. While there is some substance that Shoyer is a lawman, at least according to Swante Taggart, Stark recognizes him as a bounty hunter. Jason is also a bounty hunter.

Vince August and Cal Dodge, Jason's cronies, are not in the novel, but the film's Rusty Bob Blazer is mentioned. Rather than father Ben joining him like in the film, Jim Bennett, one of three brothers, does so only to be stopped by Taggart. Unlike the novel where they do survive, Stark and his wife are killed off in the movie.

Stark's wife in the novel is told by Miriam that he was forced to kill another man who supposedly loved her. L'Amour allows Consuelo to realize before it's too late that her husband is the better man.

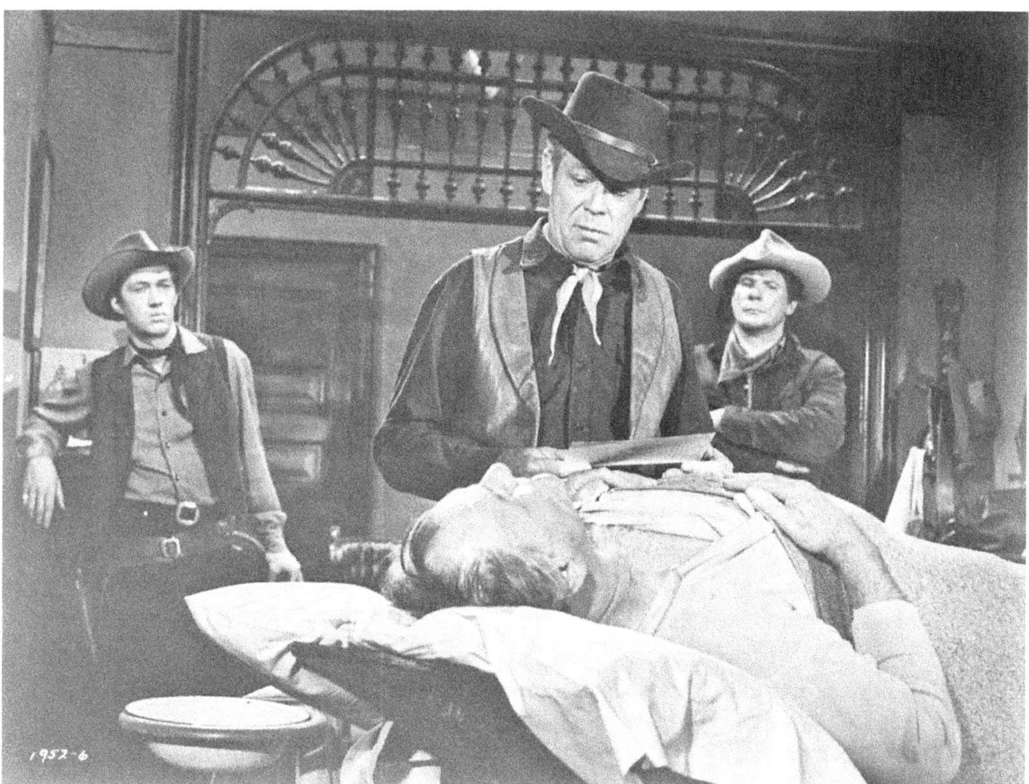

David Carradine, Dan Duryea and Tom Reese look down on Emile Meyer for this scene from *Taggart*. Duryea was certainly one of the classic villains in Westerns.

In both accounts, Miriam and Taggart's love is realized after the bad guy meets his fate. For the novel, the couple will go on to share a ranch with her brother and sister-in-law.

As the L'Amour novel reached its climax, he utilized the services of Wells Fargo in the story. The actual company, founded in 1852 by Henry Wells and William G. Fargo, became the greatest express service in the 19th century West.

Producer Gordon Kay, director R.G. Springsteen, screenwriter Robert Creighton Williams and actors Tony Young and Dan Duryea all collaborated on another 1964 Western for Universal, *He Rides Tall.* Young, who had the title role in *Taggart,* starred in the short-lived Western series *Gunslinger* (1961). Other TV Westerns on which he appeared included *Bronco* and *Cheyenne* during 1962.

Dan Duryea and his son, Peter, played bad guys in this Western. The younger Duryea appeared in a number of TV shows including a two-part *Star Trek* and two episodes of *Family Affair.*

An actor famous for conveying charming yet deadly menace, Dan Duryea's presence always highlighted a film or television show. He co-starred with Jimmy Stewart in several films, including *Winchester '73* (1950) and *Night Passage* (1957). While *The New York Times* categorized *Taggart* as "mediocre" and Tony Young's hero as "deadpan," it added, "[O]nly Mr. Duryea contributes a steady pitch amidst all the neighing, mayhem and dust."

Seen as one of Duryea's henchmen in the movie was a young David Carradine. Son of the great actor John Carradine, David scored in later films. Among his strongest roles were as Caine on the *Kung Fu* TV series of the 1970s and Cole Younger in the 1980 movie Western *The Long Riders.*

Jean Hale and Elsa Cardenas were the attractive actresses in *Taggart.* Especially striking was Cardenas, whose character's sexiness was relayed in film and novel. After appearing in such American films as 1963's *Fun in Acapulco* (with Elvis Presley) and 1969's *The Wild Bunch* (with William Holden), Cardenas became a Mexican film star.

Hale's film credits included the female lead in 1967's *The St. Valentine's Day Massacre.* An impressive list of TV credits included three episodes of the 1965–66 series *Bob Hope Presents the Chrysler Theater.*

Dick Foran, Emile Meyer and Ray Teal were all seen in *Taggart.* They had all appeared in earlier films based on L'Amour's frontier adventures.

"Sex is only unusual facet of Robert Creighton Williams' script," opined *Variety.* Director R.G. Springsteen was credited as having "molded this grab-bag of clichés into smooth flowing narrative that does hold viewer interest."

Both Williams and Springsteen were old hands working on B Westerns the caliber of *Taggart.* Williams was also an uncredited writer on the 1962 classic *Ride the High Country.* As Bob Williams, his work included a 1955 episode of the *Jungle Jim* TV series and the 1957 sci-fi flick *20 Million Miles to Earth.*

Springsteen's films included the A.C. Lyles Westerns of the 1960s, among them

Apache Uprising (1966) and *Hostile Guns* (1967). His television work as a director included five episodes of *Bonanza* during the 1960s.

Kid Rodelo

1966. A Trident Films–Fenix Production.
Released by Paramount Pictures.
91 Minutes/Black and White.

Credits: Jack O. Lamont, James J. Storrow, Jr. (Producers), Richard Carlson (Director), Jack Natteford (Screenplay), Manuel Merino (Photography), Allan Morrison (Editor), Jaime Perez Cubero, Jose Luis Galicia (Art Directors), Peris (Wardrobe), Fernando Martinez (Makeup), Johnny Douglas (Music). Based on a novel by Louis L'Amour.

Cast: Don Murray (Kid Rodelo), Janet Leigh (Nora), Broderick Crawford (Joe Harbin), Richard Carlson (Link), Jose Nieto (Thomas Reese), Julio Pena (Balsas), Miguel Del Castillo (Chavas), Jose Villa Sante (Cavalry Hat), Alfonso San Felix (Gopher), Emilio Rodriguez (Warden), Fernando Hilbeck (Perryman), Roberto Rubenstein (Doctor), Bill Christmas (Guard).

Synopsis: Kid Rodelo is released from Yuma Prison after serving a one-year sentence. He was imprisoned because of his involvement with thief and murderer Joe Harbin, who is serving a life sentence. Before his capture, Harbin hid $50,000 in stolen gold which Rodelo now wants to find. Harbin escapes and also goes after the gold. Joining him are convicts Thomas Reese and Gopher.

Along the trail, Rodelo joins up with three others — Link, Nora and Balsas — who have an interest in the gold. It is hidden somewhere in an abandoned town which Rodelo leads them to. They find a chest and believe it holds the gold; an argument ensues and Balsas shoots Link dead. The contents are rocks. Coming into town are Harbin, Reese and Gopher. Tracking them is a band of Indian bounty hunters led by Cavalry Hat.

Harbin reveals the gold; Reese is killed by the greedy Balsas. In order to get a share of the gold, Rodelo offers to lead the group through the desert to the Gulf of Mexico.

When hostile Indians poison a waterhole, Gopher tries to take Harbin's water and is killed. After Rodelo helps his group to escape from the Indians, Harbin and Balsas tell Nora the lie that Rodelo is dead. She then accompanies the two men to the Gulf.

After finding there are no boats on which to get away, Balsas is shot down by Harbin. Having caught up with them, Rodelo is fired at. Harbin is then shot by Cavalry Hat. Rodelo kills the Indian leader as the rest of the Indians ride off with Harbin's body. Nora and Rodelo are left together with the gold.

Original Source: The novel *Kid Rodelo.*

Plotline: Released from prison, Dan Rodelo accompanies strangers Nora Paxton, Jake Andrews and Clint Wilson to a ghost town searching for gold. Having hidden the stolen gold, convict Joe Harbin breaks out of prison and finds it with fellow cons Tom

Sharing a tender respite in ***Kid Rodelo*** are Janet Leigh and Don Murray. The scene is reminiscent of the interplay between a younger Leigh and James Stewart in ***The Naked Spur.***

Badger and Gopher. The two parties collide, and death and deceit await them. During an arduous trek across the desert, Yaqui Indians also pose a threat.

Commentary: The novel *Kid Rodelo* was first published by Bantam Books in March 1966. Beating out the L'Amour story on which it was based by a month, however, was the film version of the same title.

A short story Louis wrote, "Desperate Men," bore similarities to the novel and the film. It went unpublished until 1997; that year it was one of the eight L'Amour stories in the Bantam collection *End of the Drive.*

Louis's novel and short story both deal with four men crossing the desert with stolen gold. In the novel, the amount is $50,000, and the men are Dan Rodelo, Joe Harbin, Tom Badger and Gopher. For the short story, it is $15,000, and the men are Otteson, Isager, Rydberg and Rodelo. There is no woman accompanying the men in the short story. In the story, Rodelo is an escaped convict; he has been released from prison in the novel and the film.

In the short story, Rydberg succumbs to the brutal desert heat. Isager kills Otteson and is then mortally wounded by Indians. As in the novel, Rodelo escapes with the gold in a boat. He is with Nora in the novel; the Yaqui leader Hat watches them sail off. A pursuing sheriff sees the boat sail away in the short story.

And unlike the novel, where the bodies of Badger and Harbin are taken aboard the boat (thus robbing Hat of the bounty on them), Harbin's body is taken by the Indians in the film. In the novel, Hat is the only Indian actually still around, while his screen counterpart, Cavalry Hat, is killed.

In the movie, the character Balsas fills the boots of two of the novel's characters, Badger and Clint Wilson. Like Wilson, who kills Jake Andrews over the gold, Balsas kills his partner Link. Balsas then continues the journey like Tom Badger does in the book. Jake's screen counterpart therefore is Link. This includes being involved with Nora.

The film's escaped convict, Thomas Reese, is also a counterpart for the book's Andrews; he is gunned down by Balsas. Reese fills Badger's boots as well in that both initially break out of prison with Harbin in each account. Gopher is featured in each and is killed off. Sam Burrows, who runs a store in the book's ghost town, does not figure in the film.

L'Amour begins his novel with Yaquis collecting a bounty on escaped prisoner Isager, who is not a part of the film. In the short story, Isager is the last man left with Rodelo. While Harbin's fate is sealed by the movie's Indian leader, it is determined by Rodelo in the book.

The novel lays out Dan and Nora's reasons for making the journey with the escaped cons. In both film and novel, they are together at the fade-out, but added is some speculation as to where the gold will wind up.

"Amateurish Western filmed in Spain" was the headline of *Variety*'s review of the motion picture, which they called "adequate for kiddie matinees." While supposedly geared for juvenile audiences, *Kid Rodelo* had all the makings of the soon-to-be-trendy

Spaghetti Westerns. This was particularly evident with the mixture of American and foreign performers, the hammy acting and violent content. *Kid Rodelo* was filmed in black and white; the whole idea was to economize. Thus the Western had the look and feel of a low-budget B film.

Richard Carlson filled the director's seat. This was Carlson's second film to use L'Amour as a source, for he also helmed *Four Guns to the Border* in 1954. Carlson also played a small role as Link, who is killed off early. The *New York Times*, which called the film "feeble fiction," gibed that as an actor in it "he must be credited with some wisdom for making a hasty exit." Over the years as an actor, Carlson appeared in movies and on television. One series of note was *Mackenzie's Raiders* (1958–59).

Don Murray had the title role and received some criticism for going in and out of a Texas drawl during the course of the story. Murray always seemed a fine choice for any of the Westerns he made and conveyed a strong persona. In 1958, he starred in one of his best Western films, *From Hell to Texas. The Outcasts* was a TV series he did in the 1968–69 season.

Murray's co-stars in *Kid Rodelo*, Janet Leigh and Broderick Crawford, also received

Broderick Crawford, Don Murray, Julio Pena and Janet Leigh take time out from the calamity in *Kid Rodelo*.

criticism. *Variety* commented that Crawford "grimaces and groans every chance he gets," and Leigh "looks continuously startled." Yet these very things served the performers well in other, better films. Leigh was especially memorable in 1958's *Touch of Evil* and 1960's *Psycho.* For the latter, she received an Oscar nomination as Best Supporting Actress. Crawford won a Best Actor Oscar for *All the King's Men* (1949). TV fans will remember him as Chief Dan Matthews on the *Highway Patrol* series during the 1950s.

Kid Rodelo was writer Jack Natteford's third L'Amour film. The others were *East of Sumatra* and *Blackjack Ketchum, Desperado.* Natteford made his mark on a great many B Westerns, like 1945's *Trail of Kit Carson.* His last Western was 1967's *Ride to Hangman's Tree.* Like Louis L'Amour, Natteford had a high degree of success writing exciting and entertaining frontier stories, albeit for the movies.

Hondo

1967. Batjac Productions/Fenady Associates.
ABC Television.
17 Episodes/Color.

Credits: Andrew J. Fenady (Producer). Lee H. Katzin, William Witney, Michael D. Moore, Arthur H. Nadel, Harry Harris, Alan Crosland, Jr., Eddie Saeta, Michael Caffey (Directors). Andrew J. Fenady, George Schenck, Frank Chase, Frank L. Moss, Don Mullally, Nathaniel Tanchuck, Frank Paris, Palmer Thompson, George F. Slavin, Peter Germano, Tunley Walker, William Froug, Max Hodge (Writers). Richard Markowitz (Music). Based on the screenplay by James Edward Grant. From the short story by Louis L'Amour.

Cast: Ralph Taeger (Hondo Lane), Kathie Browne (Angie Dow), Noah Beery, Jr. (Buffalo Baker), Buddy Foster (Johnny Dow), Michael Pate (Vittoro), Gary Clarke (Captain Richards).

Episodes and Airdates: "Hondo and the Eagle Claw," 9/8/67; "Hondo and the War Cry," 9/15/67; "Hondo and the Singing Wire," 9/22/67; "Hondo and the Superstition Massacre," 9/29/67; "Hondo and the Savage," 10/6/67; "Hondo and the Apache Kid," 10/13/67; "Hondo and the War Hawks," 10/20/67; "Hondo and the Mad Dog," 10/27/67; "Hondo and the Judas," 11/3/67; "Hondo and the Comancheros," 11/10/67; "Hondo and the Sudden Town," 11/17/67; "Hondo and the Ghost of Ed Dow," 11/24/67; "Hondo and the Death Drive," 12/1/67; "Hondo and the Hanging Town," 12/8/67; "Hondo and the Gladiators," 12/15/67; "Hondo and the Apache Trail," 12/22/67; "Hondo and the Rebel Hat," 12/29/67.

Commentary: Like its motion picture counterpart, *Hondo* the television series was based on the James Edward Grant screenplay derived from Louis L'Amour's short story "The Gift of Cochise." John Wayne's Batjac Productions was behind the series along with producer Andrew J. Fenady's company.

Ralph Taeger was chosen to portray Hondo Lane. He had already starred in two other series, *Klondike* (1960–61) and *Acapulco* (1961), both co-starring James Coburn. Like television's *Hondo*, they also were short-lived due to poor ratings.

Hondo ran as a series from September to December 1967; a total of seventeen 60-minute episodes were made. The first two episodes were compiled into the feature film *Hondo and the Apaches* and released by MGM in Europe in '67. Its scenario had Hondo rescuing Angie Dow and her son Johnny from renegade Apaches. Mother and child were returning to Fort Lowell after delivering a wagonload of supplies. This is different from the 1953 film where Hondo first meets them on their ranch. Hondo is trying to find Apache chief Vittoro and arrange peace talks with the U.S. Army. At the fort, Hondo meets Gallagher, a mine owner, and has trouble with Angie's husband Ed Dow, who is the storekeeper there.

When Ed later tries to ambush Hondo, he is shot. (A similar situation occurred in the earlier movie.) Dow also takes an arrow in the back when the renegades attack. Vittoro appears to stop renegade Silva from torturing Hondo. For having killed his brother, Silva demands a fight with Hondo, who wins and spares his life. These incidents were also reflected in the first film. The chief agrees that Hondo can set up the peace talks.

Back at the fort, Hondo tells Angie about her husband's death and she understands. In the '53 film, when he brings the news to her ranch, she does not accept it so readily. When supplies need to be delivered to Gallagher, Johnny accompanies Hondo.

Silva leads the renegades against Gallagher and his crew but Hondo and soldiers from the fort stop them. Vittoro helps, and kills Silva. In the earlier version, Silva is slain by Hondo. The peace talks can now move ahead.

The Lowes became the Dows for the '67 version, and own a general store instead of a ranch. Chief Vittoro is now Hondo's former father-in-law; his daughter was killed during an army massacre.

Fellow scout Buffalo Baker and Hondo's dog, Sam, were part of the series as well. This time, Sam is not killed by Silva. One of the major new characters, Gallagher, was played by former MGM star Robert Taylor in the initial two shows.

Secondary plotlines here involved Gallagher being united with his grown son, Sean (played by Randy Boone), and a shady businessman named Randall Tribolet (played by Michael Rennie) trying to buy the general store from Angie.

Kathie Browne's charm and beauty graced other television Westerns. Perhaps no frontier woman looked this good. She had the recurring role of Laura Dayton on *Bonanza* in 1964. Another series she appeared on a couple of times was *Laramie* in 1962 and '63.

John Smith, who played Ed Dow, was one of the regular characters, Slim Sherman, on *Laramie.* He also co-starred in *Circus World*, a 1964 film with John Wayne. Along with the initial pair of TV episodes (and feature film), Smith was part of episode 12 which relates how his father, Ben Dow (played by David Brian) accepts the truth about his son's death after causing problems for Angie, Johnny and Hondo.

Unlike the 1953 film, romance between Hondo and Angie is left unresolved. But they do share a mutual attraction in the series.

The roles played by Geraldine Page and Duke Wayne in the earlier film were assumed by Kathie Browne and Ralph Taeger in the television version of *Hondo.*

A young Buddy Foster watches Ralph Taeger, who is clearly primed for action in TV's ***Hondo.***

Guns of the Timberland (1960) was one of the many films in which Noah Beery, Jr., appeared. Beery added a comic touch as Buffalo Baker; other TV series on which he played a regular included *Circus Boy* (1956–58) and *Riverboat* (1959–61).

Jodie Foster's older brother Buddy was seen as little Johnny. TV fans may remember him as Ken Berry's son Mike on *Mayberry R.F.D.* (1968–71).

Reprising the role of the great Apache chief from the '53 movie was Michael Pate. His character's name went from Vittorio to Vittoro; it was based on a real chief actually named Victorio. During the troubles between the Apache Indians and U.S. Army in the American Southwest, Victorio did raid with his followers. General Crook (depicted by William Bryant as a colonel on the TV *Hondo*) was involved in securing the peace. But when the Apaches were ultimately forced from their reservation in Warm Springs, New Mexico, the raiding began again. Both American and Mexican troops were deployed to stop it.

Two versions of Victorio's 1880 demise exist. One account said that he was killed by an Indian scout working with the Mexicans. The other, believed by the Apaches, was that Victorio took his own life.

Andrew Fenady not only produced *Hondo* but wrote scripts for three episodes: the first two ("Hondo and the Eagle Claw" and "Hondo and the War Cry") and episode 4 ("Hondo and the Superstition Massacre"). The latter guest-starred Robert Reed as Frank Davis, the man responsible for leading the army in the massacre that caused the death of Hondo's Indian wife. While Hondo beats him badly, Davis reveals his side of the tragedy which has tormented him.

Hondo Lane was an ex–Confederate soldier, and episode 9 ("Hondo and the Judas") deals with William Quantrill reuniting his old Civil War outfit, including Hondo, not only to steal an army payroll but to find out who tried to kill him. Needless to say, Hondo wants no part of the robbery. The guest stars included Forrest Tucker as Quantrill and John Agar and Ricky Nelson as Frank and Jesse James.

In the same television season as *Hondo*, ABC aired another Western series, *Custer*, which also bit the dust after only a few months. Despite strong heroes and solid stories, both series failed to excite viewers.

Comparing the two actors who portrayed Hondo, *Variety*'s review of the opening episode included the remark, "Taeger doesn't have Wayne's dominance, but he could catch on."

It was unfortunate that he wasn't given more time to prove it.

Shalako

1968. A Kingston Films–Palomar Pictures International Presentation.
A Dimitri de Grunwald Production.
Released by Cinerama Releasing Corp.
113 Minutes/Technicolor/Franscope.

Credits: Euan Lloyd (Producer), Edward Dmytryk (Director), J.J. Griffith, Hal Hopper, Scot Finch (Screenplay), Clarke Reynolds (Screen Story), Ted Moore (photography), Bill Blunden (Editor), Herbert Smith (Art Director), Cynthia Tingey (Costumes), Robert Farnon (Music). Based on a novel by Louis L'Amour.

Cast: Sean Connery (Shalako Carlin), Brigitte Bardot (Countess Irina Lazaar), Stephen Boyd (Bosky Fulton), Jack Hawkins (Sir Charles Daggett), Peter Van Eyck (Frederick von Hallstatt), Honor Blackman (Lady Julia Daggett), Woody Strode (Chato), Eric Sykes (Mako), Alexander Knox (Henry Clarke), Valerie French (Elena Clarke), Julian Mateos (Rojas), Donald Barry (Buffalo), Rodd Redwing (Chato's Father), "Chief" Tug Smith (Loco), Hans De Vries (Hans), Walter Brown (Pete Wells), John Clark (Hockett).

Synopsis: In the Old West, a European hunting party violates a treaty with the Apaches by being on their reservation. Riding alone, ex–Army man Shalako Carlin rescues one of the Europeans, Countess Irina Lazaar, from a few Indians. Unfortunately, the wagonmaster with her dies a horrible death.

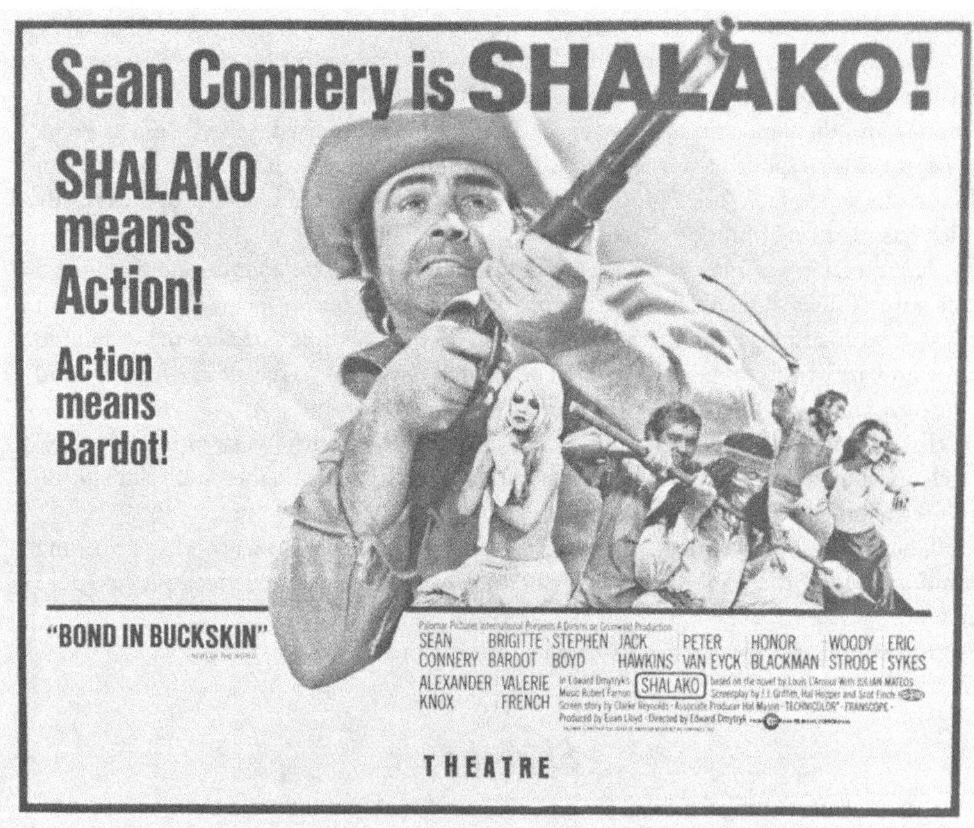

Advertisement for ***Shalako***, Sean Connery's first Western.

As they are riding to her camp, Shalako and Irina are stopped by a large band of Apaches. Only Shalako's promise to the old chief, to get the hunting party to leave the reservation, saves their lives. Chato, the chief's son, vows to fight Shalako one day.

The hunting party's leader, Frederick von Hallstatt, resists Shalako's urging to move on. As the party's guide, Bosky Fulton knew of the treaty violation. There is a vote and the group decides to stay.

Precautions are made to defend the camp and Shalako rides on with a plan to tell the Army of the situation. When the Indians attack the camp, smoke signals are sent up by Shalako to trick the Apaches into investigating.

At gunpoint, Fulton and his men rob and abandon the others. Going with him is Lady Julia, the adulterous wife of Sir Charles Daggett. Shalako returns to help those remaining escape from the Indian danger.

Crossing rugged terrain, Shalako utilizes the climbing skills of Frederick to get over

Undoubtedly because their characters were so despicable in *Shalako*, Honor Blackman and Stephen Boyd generated more sexual excitement than co-stars Connery and Bardot.

a mountain to save time. During the journey, Irina and Shalako begin to fall in love. Although not in love with each other, Frederick planned on marrying Irina.

Scouting ahead, Bosky Fulton witnesses the killing of his entire group by the Apaches. Julia dies from being forced to swallow her own diamond necklace. After his horse runs off, Fulton joins Shalako and the others with him to fight the Indians. Daggett, upset over his wife's fate, kills Fulton but is mortally wounded in the process.

A friend of Shalako's, Buffalo, is killed by the Indians, as is Frederick's servant Mako. The others are held captive. Forced to fight Chato with spears, Shalako defeats him. The chief gets his son's life spared and the Apaches ride off. As Shalako separates from the others now leaving the reservation, Irina joins him.

Original Source: The novel *Shalako.*

Plotline: In 1882 New Mexico, Lady Irina Carnarvon is the first member of an elite hunting party warned by a lone rider, Shalako Carlin, of the Indian menace. Commanded by Baron Frederick von Hallstatt, other members are Charles and Edna Dagget, Laura Davis, Count Henri, Roy Harding and Julia Paige. Hans Krueger is the baron's aide, while Mako is their cook and Buffalo Harris a hunter.

The group's treacherous guide, Bosky Fulton, has a gang of men. Despite this threat and the Apaches, an even deadlier danger is a rogue Indian called Tats-ah-das-ay-go.

Commentary: Bantam Books first published L'Amour's novel *Shalako* in 1962. The World Premiere of the motion picture of the same name was in Germany in September 1968. Louis attended the film's Royal Premiere in London.

A December review in *The London Times* called the film "just about the biggest British Western to date." (The international production included a British ensemble of players and financing.) But the reviewer also felt *Shalako* was "formula bound, curiously dispirited and slow."

Shalako was made in Almeria, Spain. The intention was to possibly create another classic like *Shane*, but such was not the result. One of the choice items which pre-sold this $5,000,000 Western to over 30 countries was the anticipated pairing of Scots-Irish Sean Connery and French Brigitte Bardot as hero and heroine. Their screen chemistry was found lacking, however.

Following the film's United States opening in November '68, the *New York Times* felt it was "a good, long, old-fashioned, wide-screen Western." Nonetheless, its reported domestic box office earnings were under $1,000,000.

L'Amour's tale of a lone rider helping aristocrats against Apaches was reflected in the film version but there are a number of dissimilarities beginning with the names of some characters: Irina's last name is Lazaar in the film and Carnarvon in the novel.

In the film, Charles Daggett gets an extra "t" in his name. His wife is Edna in the book and Julia in the film. L'Amour does not have Edna nor his Julia Paige running off with Bosky Fulton like Julia Daggett does in the movie.

Other characters not seen in the film are Sir Henri and Laura Davis. Their composites for the movie are Senator Henry Clarke and his wife, Elena. Laura is depicted in the book as the daughter of a senator. Von Hallstatt's adjutant, Hans, has a larger role to play in the book. So too does Fulton's confederate, Rio Hockett.

The book's Roy Harding seems to be the film counterpart for Rojas, another friend of Shalako's. Unlike Harding, Rojas survives at the end.

The biggest difference is the Apache antagonist. For the film, Chato fills this central role which culminates in the fight with Shalako. While Chato's Indians are a driving force in both, the feared Apache Tats-ah-das-ay-go battles to the death with the hero in the novel.

With this dreaded warrior, L'Amour makes his climactic encounter against Shalako more riveting than the one in the film. Yet more riveting in the movie is the death of the wagonmaster. In the book, Shalako finds him already shot dead, while in the film he is tied down, and still alive, with a spear slowly penetrating through his back. Also riveting is the film scene where Julia perishes swallowing her jewelry. Such brutal scenes were reminiscent of the Spaghetti Westerns of that time.

Variety said that Connery "reveals himself as a natural for dramatic, outdoor adventures." Such future productions as 1975's *The Man Who Would Be King* attest to this last reflection. *Shalako* was his first film after claiming he was through playing James Bond, a character he brought to the screen in *Dr. No* in 1962. But he later returned as Bond in 1971's *Diamonds Are Forever* and 1983's *Never Say Never Again.*

For her participation in *Shalako,* Brigitte Bardot received perhaps more than her share of criticism. Included was the heavy eye makeup she wore. A foreign performer with impeccable allure, Bardot became a film star after she appeared in 1957's *And God Created Woman.* She was quite good in a 1965 Western called *Viva Maria.*

Anglo-Irish actor Stephen Boyd had the range to play both heroes and villains. He was a bad guy in the 1958 Western *The Bravados*; especially unforgettable was his performance as the evil Messala in 1959's *Ben-Hur.*

Jack Hawkins and Honor Blackman headed the list of British supporting players in the Western. She was Pussy Galore in the 1964 Bond film *Goldfinger.* Before the British TV series *The Avengers* came to America in the 1960s, Blackman was Patrick Macnee's original partner, Cathy Gale.

Unfortunately for the esteemed actor Hawkins, he had to have his lines dubbed due to an operation for throat cancer. He was also in *Ben-Hur* and *The Bridge on the River Kwai* (1957).

Shalako was German actor Peter Van Eyck's last film (he died the following year). His fine work included roles in *The Longest Day* (1962) and *The Spy Who Came In from the Cold* (1965).

Portraying Chato in the film was Woody Strode, a great presence in many fine films over the years. He played the title role in 1960's *Sergeant Rutledge* for director John Ford.

While director Edward Dmytryk's best work was behind him, his work on *Shalako* was nothing of which to be ashamed. Writers J.J. Griffith and Scot Finch also worked on 1971's *Catlow,* derived from Louis's novel. Finch wrote the script for a third L'Amour tale, *The Man Called Noon,* two years later.

These two scenes from ***Shalako*** showcase Sean Connery and Brigitte Bardot. Their big-screen pairing seemed a bit too tame, although Sean made a great L'Amour hero.

Finch and *Shalako*'s third screenwriter, Hal Hopper, were actors as well. Hopper appeared on such television Westerns as *Maverick*; in 1957 he composed the theme music for the Warner Brothers series *Colt .45*. Working on the screen story, Clarke Reynolds wrote teleplays for many 1950s TV Westerns including *Cheyenne* and *Broken Arrow*.

The film *Shalako* begins with an on-screen prologue written by L'Amour. It tells of the actual European hunting expeditions in the American West during the 19th century. One expedition occurred in the mid–1850s, and among the huge number of animals killed for sport were buffaloes. This particular party under Sir George Gore was guided by frontiersman Jim Bridger. (Either Louis or the filmmakers made a mistake here, however, for instead of Sir George the name mentioned is Sir *Richard* Gore.) L'Amour closes this insightful passage with these words: "They and their descendents helped the peoples of North America to build the adventurous West...."

During the course of both novel and film, it is revealed that Shalako got his name from the Zuni Indians. It was the name of their rain god in the book and meant "rain bringer" in the movie. Whenever Shalako rode into their territory in either account, it would rain. This was only one of the revelations which differentiated the title hero from other mysterious riders like Shane. Although Connery preferred to play the part with more mystery, other revelations surfaced in each version about the character's past.

For the film, Bosky Fulton refers to Shalako's army background, as does Rojas (who calls him "colonel"). In L'Amour's version, he was involved in the earlier Franco-Prussian War, as were Frederick von Hallstatt and Sir Henri; the latter even thinking he first saw Shalako then.

The motion picture *Shalako*, whether for its good points or bad, certainly deserves a better fate than it received after it was released. However, additional recognition was given many years later on cable TV's Encore Western channels.

THE 1970S

Catlow

1971. A Frontier Films Production.
Released by Metro-Goldwyn-Mayer.
101 Minutes/Metrocolor.

Credits: Euan Lloyd (Producer), Sam Wanamaker (Director), Scot Finch, J.J. Griffith (Screenplay), Ted Scaife (Photography), John Glen, Alan Killick (Editors), Herbert Smith (Art Director), Ron Patton, German Quejido (Set Decorators), Agustin Jiminez (Costumes), Ramon de Diego, Jose Antonio Sanchez (Makeup), Roy Budd (Music). Based on a novel by Louis L'Amour.

Cast: Yul Brynner (Jedidiah Catlow), Richard Crenna (Marshal Ben Cowan), Leonard Nimoy (Orville Miller), Daliah Lavi (Rosita), Jo Ann Pflug (Christina Calderon), Jeff Corey (Merridew), Michael Delano (Rio), Julian Mateos (Diego Recalde), David Ladd (Caxton), Bessie Love (Mrs. Frost), Bob Logan (Oley), John Clark (Keleher), Dan Van Husen (Dutch), Cass Martin (Sanchez), Jose Nieto (General Calderon), Angel Del Pozo (Rafael Vargas), Victor Israel (Pesquiera), Erika Lopez (Sara), Tito Garcia (Pedro), Antonio Padilla (Jose), Rafael Albaicin (Alberto), Alejandro Enciso (Fernandez), Ralph Brown (Roots), Walter Coy (Parkman), Allen Russell (Otis), Florencio Amarilla (Tarahumara), Raul Castro (Tonkawa Indian).

Synopsis: Tracking down Jedidiah Catlow for cattle rustling is his old friend Marshal Ben Cowan. When Ben is wounded by attacking Indians, he is rescued by Catlow and his men. Looking after the injured marshal, Catlow relates that the cattle are a maverick herd and not rustled. Nonetheless, a big rancher, Parkman, has sent gunman Orville Miller to kill Catlow. With a derringer hidden in a boot, Catlow gets the drop on Miller. The gunman and his cronies are then driven off.

Followed to Abilene by Ben, Catlow insists on being arrested. But he soon escapes with the help of a Mrs. Frost. Catlow's party turns up in the border town of Nogales, where a girlfriend, Rosita, is waiting. Ben chases after him and tries to convince Catlow to surrender before Miller catches up and shoots him. But Catlow wants Ben to join him in a scheme to steal a shipment of gold.

A Mexican, Sanchez, brings word to Catlow that the gold's destination is Hermosillo, south of the border. Prior to leaving Nogales, Catlow tangles with Miller and injures him with a clay jug.

Although a trap is set by Ben, the marshal is instead captured by Catlow and tied over his horse. Miller appears and attempts to force the horse over a precipice. Ben frees himself in the nick of time. Ben then helps save injured Mexican officer, Diego Recalde, from Apaches. Fighting the Indians, the pair are rescued by the Mexican Army. Grateful to Ben, Diego takes him to Hermosillo. There he meets Diego's uncle, General Calderon, and the general's daughter, Christina. Hiding out in town, in the house of Rosita's father, are Catlow and his men.

As the gold-carrying mule train nears town under army guard, commanding officer Rafael Vargas receives a message from Christina inviting him to a ball that night. But the bogus message was sent by Catlow. The deception works and the enamored Vargas rushes to town. The mule train sentries are soon subdued by Catlow's waiting men. Ben realizes the ploy yet is stopped by Catlow.

As Ben is held captive by Rosita, Catlow abandons her and flees into the desert with his gang and the mule train. Ben escapes and quickly gives chase. During the desert trek, gang member Rio tries to usurp Catlow's leadership. Danger from Tonkawa Indians unites the gang and Ben arrives to help. Ben even warns Catlow when an upset Rosita threatens with her own gang.

As Michael Delano argues his case to boss Yul Brynner, the other members of their outlaw gang look on in this scene from *Catlow*.

Yul Brynner, in the title role in *Catlow,* has a derringer hidden in his boot.

Ben informs Catlow that he plans to return the gold to the United States (it was originally stolen from the Confederate Army during the Civil War). In cahoots, Rio and Rosita steal all the guns in camp. Attempting to take the gold, Rio is killed by Catlow's Indian guide.

With Miller hiding nearby, the Tonkawas prepare to attack the unarmed men. The Mexican Army saves the day. Back in Hermosillo, the arrested Catlow is put by Ben aboard a stagecoach bound for trial. Christina is there to accompany Ben. When Miller appears and wounds Ben, Catlow kills the gunman.

Pinning on the marshal's badge, Catlow promises with a smile to follow his course of action.

Original Source: The novel *Catlow.*

Plotline: Once boyhood friends, Bijah Catlow is now an outlaw and Ben Cowan a deputy marshal. Yet Ben initially helps him against rancher Parkman, whose hired gun, Matt Giles, is after the outlaw.

Catlow wants Cowan to help steal gold and silver in Mexico. Duty-bound to capture his old friend, Ben gives chase and is ably assisted by a rancher's daughter, Rosita Calderon, and the Mexican Army. With a girl in seemingly every town, Catlow also faces constant double-crosses from Cordelia Burton and her uncle Miller and from Pesquiera and his daughter Christina.

Commentary: *Catlow* was initially published by Bantam in 1963. The L'Amour novel was the first after his novelization of the film *How the West Was Won.* In October 1971, MGM brought out a film version of *Catlow.* Euan Lloyd, who produced *Shalako*, was again the producer.

According to *Variety*, in 1970 Lloyd and actor Stephen Boyd formed the British company Frontier Films to make five Western movies based on L'Amour novels. Supposedly just two were made, *Catlow* and *The Man Called Noon* (1973).

The differences between the novel and the 1971 movie begin with the usual name changes. Abijah, shortened to Bijah, is Catlow's first name in the novel. It is Jedidiah in the movie. The film's two central females have their roles reversed from the novel. Rosita is the villainess in the movie and the heroine in the book, while Christina is the film's good gal and novel's bad gal. L'Amour's initial female character, Cordelia Burton, isn't featured in the film.

Miller is a hired gun in the movie and an army deserter and thief in the book. While Ben Cowan shoots him down in the book's climax, Catlow does the job in the film.

After Ben's first arrest of Catlow in the movie, the lawman is held at gunpoint by a little old lady, Mrs. Frost, so the outlaw can escape. She is not part of Louis's book. Corrupt rancher Parkman poses a threat to Catlow during the first half of each version. Louis's version, however, includes the rancher's alliance with gunman Matt Giles.

In the motion picture, Tonkawas menace the outlaws during the desert fight. The Seris are the Indians in the novel's battle. Featured in both versions is officer Diego Recalde. His commanding officer is Armijo in the book and Calderon in the film. Christina is Calderon's daughter in the film, while she is leather-maker Pesquiera's stepdaughter in the novel. Rosita's father for the movie, Pesquiera initially harbors Catlow's outlaw gang at his house.

Killed off by Louis is Rafael Vargas, who is in charge of the treasure train in each. The $2,000,000 treasure is all gold in the film but also includes silver in the book. In the novel, the silver and gold are returned to the Mexican Army. The movie concocts a tale of the treasure once being part of the Confederacy in the War Between the States.

For each version, there is a humorous finale with Catlow wearing Cowan's badge after the lawman is hurt by Miller. In the book, a postscript in a letter to Ben makes him aware that Catlow has escaped one more time. In the film it is somewhat up in the air whether the outlaw escaped or not. Yul Brynner's colorful performance in the title role was not hampered by L'Amour's making the character in the book an Irishman. The Irish Stephen Boyd was originally to play a role in *Catlow*, and it might just have been this one.

An exotic screen presence, Brynner often appeared bald and stoic, and he was usually quite good in Westerns. They included his best one, 1960's *The Magnificent Seven*, and 1964's underrated *Invitation to a Gunfighter*. He was unforgettable in his Oscar-winning performance in the 1956 musical *The King and I*.

Tall and lean was how Louis described his lawman and it certainly fit Richard Crenna's general appearance. He was in films and on television for quite some time before advancing as a leading man. Conveyed was a laid-back yet authoritative demeanor seen in *Catlow*, and in such films as *The Sand Pebbles* (1966) and the *Rambo* trilogy (1981–88).

Leonard Nimoy's claim to fame is his indelible Mr. Spock in the *Star Trek* TV series of the 1960s and the more recent follow-up movies. The 1987 hit *Three Men and a Baby* was one of his films as a director. While Nimoy's screen time as the villainous Miller was somewhat limited, he more than held his own. So did the lovely Daliah Lavi as the villainess. Lavi enjoyed some success in films; two of note were *Lord Jim* (1965) and *Casino Royale* (1967).

Spanish actor Julian Mateos was in both *Shalako* and *Catlow*. When Brynner reprised his earlier *Magnificent Seven* role of Chris in 1966's *Return of the Seven*, Mateos took over the role of Chico originally played in 1960 by Horst Buchholz.

Sam Wanamaker, who directed *Catlow*, appeared with Brynner in 1962's *Taras Bulba*. Of his work on the Western, *Variety* reported, "Wanamaker's direction is good, and helps maintain a nice-and-easy, no-sweat air of unpretentious, fun theatricality."

Rough-and-ready action was a plus for the film, along with some humor. Even so, *Catlow* came and went without much fuss at the box office. Like *Shalako*, it was filmed in Spain and its atmosphere was influenced by the Spaghetti Westerns.

Screenwriters J.J. Griffith and Scot Finch, who worked on *Shalako*, collaborated again. While this was Griffith's last film writing credit, Finch did others, including *The Man Called Noon* and a 1974 werewolf film, *The Beast Must Die*.

A reviewer for *The Encyclopedia of Western Movies*, not impressed by the script, remarked, "Little of the humor of the original Louis L'Amour novel ... remains."

Playing a small role in the novel is legendary gunman Wild Bill Hickok. He was the marshal of Abilene, Kansas, in 1871, when the cow town was still booming. Hickok actually started there on April 15, with his tenure lasting eight months as he was let go for carrying out his duties too forcefully.

Legend has it that Wild Bill even had an encounter with the gunman John Wesley Hardin at the time. According to Hardin, he left town when ordered to do so by Hickok, but not before showing the marshal just who was faster on the draw. This just might be true, for Hickok was known as a deliberate man who felt that accuracy meant more than speed.

Cancel My Reservation

1972. A NAHO Enterprises Production.
Released by Warner Brothers.
99 Minutes/Eastman Color.

Credits: Gordon Oliver (Producer), Paul Bogart (Director), Arthur Marx, Robert Fisher (Screenplay), Russell L. Metty (Photography), Michael A. Hoey (Editor), Rolland M. Brooks (Art Director), Anthony Mondell (Set Director), Mike Moschella, Thomas Tuttle (Makeup), Dominic Frontiere (Music). Based on a novel by Louis L'Amour.

Cast: Bob Hope (Dan Bartlett), Eva Marie Saint (Sheila Bartlett), Ralph Bellamy (John Ed), Forrest Tucker (Reese), Anne Archer (Crazy Hollister), Keenan Wynn (Sheriff Riley), Henry Darrow (Joe Little Cloud), Chief Dan George (Old Bear), Doodles Weaver (Cactus), Betty Ann Carr (Mary Little Cloud), Herb Vigran (Roscoe Snagby), Pat Morita (Yamamoto), Gordon Oliver (Mr. Sparker), Isabella Hoopes (Elderly Lady), Buster Schaefer (Doc Morton), Tracy Bogart, Trudy Bordoff (Teenage Girls), Richard Yniguez, Priscilla Garcia (Motorcyclists).

Synopsis: Dan Bartlett and his wife Sheila co-host a New York TV talk show. Stressed-out over her being on the show, Dan goes to their Arizona home for a vacation.

Landing at the airport, Dan meets an Indian woman who is apparently upset about something. He later finds her dead at his home, but the body soon disappears. Sheriff Riley and Deputy Cactus run Dan in after finding the dead woman, Mary Little Cloud, in his car.

However, Dan is soon released until the murder weapon, a .45 pistol, can be found. When he returns home, he finds another woman, Crazy Hollister, staying there after fighting with her stepfather John Ed, who owns a 50,000-acre spread called Strawberry Ranch.

Turning up with a search warrant, the sheriff arrests Dan again after the murder weapon is found at his place and is accidentally fired. But Dan is released thanks to the influence of John Ed. Worried about her husband, Sheila arrives and helps him search for the real killer. Joe Little Cloud, the dead woman's uncle, helps the Bartletts locate an ancient Indian mystic, Old Bear, who tells them about some rocks in a fireplace.

Crazy and Sheila stumble upon the rocks and surmise that they make up an Indian message involving Strawberry Ranch. John Ed and his underling, Reese, were responsible for the murders of Mary and county land recorder-extortionist Roscoe Snagby.

Snagby's body is found in Dan's car and once more he is arrested. This time Sheila helps him to escape and meet with Old Bear. Old Bear is mortally wounded by Reese. As the Bartletts are trapped in a cave by Reese, Crazy is abducted and nearly drowned. But John Ed, trying to not implicate himself, shoots down Reese as the others are rescued by the sheriff.

Recalling Old Bear's last words, Dan finds a hidden map in a rifle barrel. The map proves that the Strawberry Ranch land belongs to the Indians. Sheriff Riley goes to question John Ed. Dan and Sheila Bartlett return to New York. She has decided to give up her television work to become a mother.

Eva Marie Saint helps her husband, Bob Hope, clear his name in *Cancel My Reservation.*

1972 / *Cancel My Reservation*

Original Source: The novel *The Broken Gun.*

Plotline: In Arizona during the 1960s, writer Dan Sheridan is questioned by Detective Tom Riley about a murder. Dan learns about the recent killing of the murdered man's brother as well as two brothers, the Toomeys, killed nearly a century earlier.

Sheridan must fight for his own life against the owner of the Strawberry Ranch, Colin Wells, Wells' brother Jimbo and ranchhand Floyd Reese. Aiding Dan are Colin's sister-in-law, Belle Dawson, and Pio Alvarez, an old war pal and brother to the recently slain men.

Commentary: What could be odder than turning a L'Amour book into a Bob Hope comedy? Louis's 1966 Bantam publication *The Broken Gun* became the motion picture *Cancel My Reservation,* released by Warner Brothers in September 1972.

Both the novel and film are set in a contemporary West, and deal with murder and stolen land. The novel, however, is not a comedy by any stretch. And the movie, despite its comedy, has some serious moments.

L'Amour's writer-protagonist Dan Sheridan becomes TV personality Dan Bartlett for the film. Although each version relies on the narrative being told by its respective hero, the Hope film is punctuated by one-liners and visual gags. While Sheridan is unmarried, Bartlett has a wife, Sheila, and the film's plot revolves around the husband and wife becoming closer in the thick of danger. They then realize just how trivial their previous problems were by comparison.

Heroine Belle Dawson, unmarried in the book, is the romantic attraction for Sheridan. Their relationship also becomes stronger in the midst of the dangers they must face. Although there is a wife, Doris Wells, for Colin the book's leading villain, the movie's only living relation to dastardly John Ed is Crazy, the stepdaughter who knows his actions include her own mother's murder.

The book has a reference to Belle's sister meeting a tragic end due to Aukie, not only the sister's husband but Colin's brother as well. All the deaths in each version center around keeping the vast land on the Strawberry Ranch from its rightful owners.

Missing from the film are a number of characters from the novel. Two of the most pivotal are Pio Alvarez, Sheridan's Korean War comrade, and Jimbo Wells, Colin's bullying brother. The novel's murder victims, brothers Pete and Manuel Alvarez, have their screen counterparts being Mary Little Cloud and Roscoe Snagby. Mary's uncle Joe Little Cloud and Old Bear are other new characters for the film. Old Bear fills the role of the long-dead John Toomey from the book. The old Indian's words help to solve the mystery behind the murders, just as Toomey's diary pages aid in solving the nearly century-old mystery.

L'Amour's *The Broken Gun* quite touchingly concludes the tragedy of the Toomeys through Dan Sheridan's resolve to make sure they didn't die in vain. Sheridan's quest began when he found the diary pages in the barrel of a broken Bisley Colt. Dan Bartlett's quest, to clear himself of murder charges, ends when he discovers the map in the rifle barrel. Not exactly touching, but it shows respect for the Indians who were robbed and killed.

The *Cancel My Reservation* reviews were not exactly positive. *Variety* called it "a tame murder comedy," and both the *New York Times* and *Saturday Review* faulted Bob Hope, in his late 60s, for playing a man in his early 40s. The comedian apparently felt the same way for it was his last starring role in a film. While his comedy timing was not always as good as in the past, some of the old magic was still there. One of the most humorous sequences has Bob daydreaming that he is going to be hanged by a lynch mob. Seen briefly in solo shots poking fun at him are a few surprise stars, including John Wayne and Bing Crosby. Seven classic *Road* pictures teamed Crosby and Hope. Their first was 1940's *Road to Singapore*, and the last was 1962's *Road to Hong Kong*.

While director Paul Bogart made other films, like 1971's *Skin Game*, he was really known for his TV situation comedies. Two of his best were *All in the Family* (1971–78) and its sequel *Archie Bunker's Place* (1979–82).

"This sort of sniggering sitcom stuff belongs more properly on television," deemed *Time* magazine. It was a reference to the gag in *Cancel My Reservation* where Hope's character uses his wife's brassiere as a bow string to shoot an arrow.

Bob Hope and Eva Marie Saint are joined in this scene from *Cancel My Reservation* by a pair of friendly Indians played by Henry Darrow and Chief Dan George.

Eva Marie Saint's film debut in 1954's *On the Waterfront* earned her the Oscar for Best Supporting Actress. A starring role in the 1976 TV movie *The Macahans* led to a role in the 1977 follow-up series *How the West Was Won.*

Ralph Bellamy's film career encompassed a wide range of motion pictures. His best role was as Franklin D. Roosevelt in 1960's *Sunrise at Campobello.* He was also part of the fine ensemble of players in 1966's *The Professionals*, there portraying another conniving villain in the vein of his rancher.

In *Cancel My Reservation* and 1970's *Chisum*, Forrest Tucker made for a menacing bad guy with his awesome presence. Yet he was also heroic as Wild Bill Hickok in 1953's *Pony Express* and comical as Sgt. O'Rourke in the 1965–67 television series *F Troop.*

Cancel offered Anne Archer one of her first roles as the chic Crazy. Her more prominent roles included Harrison Ford's wife in 1992's *Patriot Games* and its follow-up, 1993's *Clear and Present Danger.* She was also the wife of Michael Douglas in the 1987 thriller *Fatal Attraction.* For that one, Archer's performance earned a Best Supporting Actress Oscar nomination.

Chief Dan George received a Best Supporting Actor Oscar nomination as Dustin Hoffman's Indian father in 1970's *Little Big Man.* He portrayed wise old Indians in other films as well, among them 1974's *Harry and Tonto* and 1976's *The Outlaw Josey Wales.*

Bob Hope, who was also *Cancel My Reservation*'s executive producer, was undoubtedly instrumental in securing the screenwriting team of Arthur Marx and Robert Fisher. They incorporated topical issues of the day, such as the pill and Women's Lib, to fit the comedy style of its star. *Cancel* was the first and only Hope picture to play New York City's prestigious Radio City Music Hall. Yet the movie's overall reception at the box office was disappointing.

Marx, the son of famous funnyman Groucho, and Fisher collaborated on three earlier films with Bob, *A Global Affair* (1964), *I'll Take Sweden* (1965) and *Eight on the Lam* (1967).

An interesting sidenote about the L'Amour novel: Louis and the novel's protagonist Dan Sheridan both were wartime veterans (Louis was in World War II and Dan saw action in Korea and Vietnam). Also they grew up in the West, and worked as lumbermen and in mining camps.

The Man Called Noon

1973. A Frontier Films Presentation.
A Euan Lloyd Production.
Released by National General Pictures.
94 Minutes/Technicolor.

Credits: Euan Lloyd (Producer), Peter Collinson (Director), Scot Finch (Screenplay), John Cabrera (Photography), Alan Pattillo (Editor), Jose Maria Tapiador (Art Director),

Augustin Jimenez (Costumes), Roman De Diego (Makeup), Luis Bacalov (Music). Based on a novel by Louis L'Amour.

Cast: Richard Crenna (Noon), Stephen Boyd (Rimes), Rosanna Schiaffino (Fan Davidge), Farley Granger (Judge Niland), Patty Shepard (Peg Cullane), Angel del Pozo (Janish), Howard Ross (Bayles), Aldo Sambrell (Kissling), Jose Jaspe (Henneker), Charley Bravo (Lang), Ricardo Palacios (Brakeman), Fernando Hilbeck (Ford), Jose Canalejas (Cherry), Cesar Burner (Charlie), Julian Ugarte (Cristobal).

Synopsis: In a western town, a man is shot; he falls through his hotel window and plummets to the street. Pursued, the injured man finds refuge on a moving train. Having lost his memory, he joins up with a man named Rimes. The two travel to a ghost town and hook up with Fan Davidge and a couple of others. Taken to Fan's ranch, the Rafter D, the injured man is cared for by Fan and there is a mutual attraction between them.

Calling himself Jonas, the man learns that the ranch is controlled by an outlaw gang led by Ben Janish. Fan's father has died of a heart attack and she is now a prisoner. Jonas also learns that it was Janish who shot at him. In a bunkhouse fight against two of the outlaws, Jonas wins.

In the hills, Jonas and Rimes find a hidden cabin apparently belonging to a gunman called Noon. Jonas discerns that he is Noon from an earlier message given him by Fan's foreman, Henneker. Disposing of some of the outlaws with the help of Rimes, Noon attempts to tie the message to lawyer Dean Cullane in El Paso. But Cullane is dead, supposedly murdered by Noon.

Cullane's sister, Peg, tries to capture Noon with the outlaws with whom Rimes seems to have joined. But Noon escapes to the safety of Judge Niland's home. With his memory still gone, Noon is informed by the judge that Tom Davidge, Fan's father, hired the gunman to force the outlaws off the ranch. They want Tom's savings which he converted to gold. When Cullane, who was helping Tom, told Peg, she informed Janish. And Peg killed her brother.

Returning to his cabin, Noon finds Rimes there with Fan. Although not part of the outlaw gang, Rimes is interested in a reward being offered for the whereabouts of Jonas Mandrin, Noon's true identity. Jonas became Noon following the murders of his wife and daughter back East.

The real leader of Peg and the outlaws is Judge Niland, and they have followed Jonas back to the cabin for the gold. Injured by Niland, Jonas finds his memory has returned and he reveals the gold to Fan and Rimes. Murdering Henneker, Niland and his gang are met with gunfire by Jonas, Rimes and Fan. Climbing out the chimney, Jonas battles with Janish and the outlaw is thrown off a cliff. When Jonas causes an avalanche, Niland is crushed by a boulder. Peg is shot down by Fan as the rest of the outlaws are defeated.

A grave marker is left by Rimes to deter others from looking for the man called Noon. Planning a life together, Jonas and Fan ride off in a wagon. Rimes has kept some of the gold for himself.

1973 / *The Man Called Noon*

Original Source: The novel *The Man Called Noon.*

Plotline: After his life is threatened, a man named Jonas loses his memory. Searching to learn his true identity, he believes he may be a gunfighter named Ruble Noon. Not only are things revolved around Noon but also to the hidden savings of the late Tom Davidge, who owned the Rafter D ranch.

Tom's daughter, Fan, foreman Arch Billing and ranchhand Henneker become allies with Noon in his quest, as do outlaw J.B. Rimes and a jailed man, Miguel Lebo. But looming all around are deadly enemies, the chief ones being Ben Janish, Judge Niland and Peg Cullane.

Commentary: Bantam Books originally published *The Man Called Noon* in 1970. The film version of the same title was released domestically by National General Pictures in September 1973.

Writing solo on this third L'Amour story, after collaborating on both *Catlow* and *Shalako,* Scot Finch followed the novel rather well. At the same time, there are surprising differences between the film and its source.

Richard Crenna protects Rosanna Schiaffino from the bad guys at the climax of *The Man Called Noon.*

Able to find common ground in ***The Man Called Noon*** are uneasy allies Richard Crenna and Stephen Boyd.

The story may not be L'Amour's *most* complicated, but it certainly is *one* of them. There is at least one mistake and a couple of omissions in the book. The mistake, a minor one, relates to the character Miguel Lebo, an ally of the title hero not found in the movie. In Chapter 17, Miguel claims that ranch hand Henneker told him how to find the so-called tree house. But then Lebo admits to not even seeing Henneker nor the book's actual foreman, Arch Billing, another character not in the film.

Incidentally, Henneker, the film's ranch foreman, survives in the book; he and Billing are able to defeat the outlaw element that remains on the Rafter D. Henneker's cold-blooded killing in the movie, as he's tied and blindfolded, prompts Noon, Rimes and Fan to aggressively confront their enemies.

While the motion picture has Judge Niland identifying Dean's murderer it becomes almost an afterthought in the novel. Noon finally assumes that outlaw Ben Janish, in cahoots with Peg and the judge, pulled the trigger. However, the novel's more revealing omission is not knowing if Noon's amnesia is completely gone by the conclusion.

Aside from Cagle, the assorted bad men in both versions include Bayles, Kissling, Lang, Ford, Cherry and Cristobal. In the main, their ultimate fates receive more attention in the book. Handled differently in each version are the fates of the villainous trio behind the bad men. Peg, Niland and Janish receive more melodramatic finishes in the movie.

J.B. Rimes is a major player only in the opening and closing passages of the L'Amour novel. The film features him more extensively throughout. In both versions, there is a $500 reward offered by Jonas Mandrin's arms company when he vanishes after losing his wife and child.

The hero's memory returns after he is shot at and falls a second time in the film.There is then a touching moment: He hears the voices of his late wife and daughter to help him gain consciousness.

But the most winning aspect of this rather neglected film is the friendship between Richard Crenna's Noon and Stephen Boyd's Rimes. Rimes good-naturedly ribs Noon; their amusing interplay was reminiscent of the gunmen played by Gary Cooper and Burt Lancaster in 1954's *Vera Cruz.*

Both Crenna and Boyd made only a limited number of Westerns between them, yet they were always good in them. During the late 1970s, Crenna did a villainous turn as one of the many stars of the TV miniseries *Centennial.* Boyd was Raquel Welch's protector in her 1971 Western *Hannie Caulder.*

The stunning Rosanna Schiaffino's other films of note included 1964's *The Long Ships*, which co-starred Richard Widmark and Sidney Poitier. Farley Granger played the main villain here with devilish charm. Perhaps best known for his early film work with Alfred Hitchcock, the actor also appeared in a 1967 episode of TV's *Hondo*, "Hondo and the Apache Kid."

In its review of *The Man Called Noon,* the *New York Times* conveyed its good points and bad: "Under Peter Collinson's brisk direction, the chases, fights and shootouts are serious and practically continuous. But the equally serious characterizations cry for fuller explanations." Collinson's other directorial film work included the mysteries *Ten Little Indians* and *The Spiral Staircase* (both 1975).

Like *Shalako* and *Catlow* before it, *The Man Called Noon* benefited from its action scenes, also supervised by Bob Simmons, and the Spanish locations. It too felt the weight of the Spaghetti Westerns, which were still reflective of a decadent and desolate West. Years after it was first seen, the film received a favorable comment by the *DVD & Video Guide*: "Great photography, direction and score make this one of the best." Unfortunately, Stephen Boyd and producer Euan Lloyd did not continue their involvement with Frontier Films and create an entire series of L'Amour's adaptations.

Crenna's interest in the work of Louis L'Amour did not end with *Catlow* and *The Man Called Noon*. In later years, he also read a number of Louis's stories on audio cassette presentations. Included was 1987's 180-minute, two-cassette reading of *Showdown Trail*.

In all of L'Amour's stories, the scenic backgrounds play a substantial part. Both his novel and the motion picture version of *The Man Called Noon* feature a secluded cabin for its hero. With the cabin's closet leading to an enormous cave, the rear entry is down an elevator shaft and out into a valley.

Not part of the movie is the tree house, actually a large sycamore which can be climbed to reach another cave. Camouflaged as musket balls in each version, Tom Davidge's gold, found in the film's cabin and the book's tree house, creates two rather amazing, violent climaxes.

While the cabin and its surrounding hills are featured in the film's climax, the novel's train station serves that purpose. Totally unexpected from L'Amour is his linking Rimes to the famous Pinkerton detectives. In the film he remains somewhat of a rascal keen on getting a share of the gold.

Allan Pinkerton's detective agency was founded in 1850. Not all adversaries were stopped as effectively as Peg and the judge. In January 1875, Pinkerton agents attacked the Missouri home of Zerelda Samuel, mistakenly believing her outlaw sons, Frank and Jesse James, were present. A bomb exploded, killing their eight-year-old stepbrother, Archie, and causing Zerelda's right arm to need amputation at the elbow.

The Sacketts

1979. A Douglas Netter–M.B. Scott Production.
In Association with Shalako Enterprises.
NBC Television.
Two Parts, 240 Minutes/Color

Credits: Douglas Netter (Producer), Robert Totten (Director), Jim Byrnes (Co-producer, teleplay), Jack A. Whitman, Jr. (Photography), Howard Smith (Editor), Johannes

Larson (Production Designer), Barton Kent James, Carole Brown-James (Wardrobe), Jerrod Immel (Music). Based on novels by Louis L'Amour.

Cast: Sam Elliott (Tell Sackett), Tom Selleck (Orrin Sackett), Jeff Osterhage (Tyrel Sackett), Glenn Ford (Tom Sunday), Ben Johnson (Cap Rountree), Gilbert Roland (Don Luis Alvarado), John Vernon (Jonathan Pritts), Ruth Roman (Rosie), Jack Elam (Ira Bigelow), Gene Evans (Benson Bigelow), L.Q. Jones (Belden), Paul Koslo (Kid Newton), Mercedes McCambridge (Ma Sackett), Slim Pickens (Jack Bigelow), Buck Taylor (Reed Carney), Pat Buttram (Tathill), Shug Fisher (Purgatorie Barkeep), Ana Alicia (Drusilla), Lee deBroux (Simpson), James Gammon (Wes Bigelow), Marcy Hanson (Laura Pritts), Frank Ramirez (Juan Torres), Wendy Rastatter (Ange Kerry), Henry Capps (Boyd), Ramon Chavez (Pete Romero), Don Collier (L.P. Seeker), Pam Earnhardt (Mary), Brian Libby (Durango), Kimo Owens (Fetterson), James O'Connell (Long Higgins), Louis L'Amour (Narrator).

Synopsis: A Higgins-Sackett feud in Tennessee continues with Long Higgins com-

The only entry in the L'Amour filmography to actually cover two of the author's books is *The Sacketts.* Brothers Tell, Orrin and Tyrel (Sam Elliott, Tom Selleck and Jeff Osterhage) unite for the climactic gunfight.

ing to kill Orrin Sackett on his wedding day. Protecting Orrin, his fiancée Mary is killed instead. Brother Tyrel Sackett is forced to kill Higgins. Bidding their mother goodbye, Tyrel (followed by Orrin) goes west. Older brother Tell Sackett is already working out west in a mining camp.

When cardsharp Wes Bigelow is caught cheating, he draws a gun on Tell and is shot dead. Tell heads into the mountains looking for gold. Tyrel and Orrin get jobs on a cattle drive ramrodded by Tom Sunday. The herd is owned by a man named Belden; Cap Rountree and Reed Carney are among the drovers. Carney, taking an immediate dislike to Tyrel, badgers him along the trail. When the herd reaches Abilene, Carney picks a gunfight with Tyrel. Sackett is faster, making his adversary drop his gun and holster into a water trough. Among the witnesses are Mexican landowner Don Luis Alvarado and his granddaughter, Drusilla. As Tyrel, Orrin, Tom and Cap set out after wild cattle, Don Luis wishes them to accompany him for protection against the Indians. Don Luis had initially turned down Tyrel's offer of such help as he is distrustful of Americans.

The ambitious Jonathan Pritts wants control of Mexican land in the New Mexico

After a long cattle drive in *The Sacketts,* Tom Selleck and Jeff Osterhage enjoy hot baths.

territory. While Orrin has taken a fancy to Laura, Jonathan's daughter, Drusilla and Tyrel fall in love. In the town of Purgatorie, Tell cashes in gold for $500. When a man named Boyd tries to steal it at knife point, Tell grabs him and cuts Boyd's mustache off with a Bowie knife. On Tell's trail for killing his brother earlier is Ira Bigelow.

All three Sackett brothers are reunited in town. Cap Rountree joins up with Tell to search for more gold. Tom Sunday sets out with Orrin and Tyrel to round up cattle. In another town, Cap is reunited with old friend Rosie. A drunken gunslinger, Kid Newton, starts a fight but Tell makes him back down.

As Tyrel, Orrin and Tom ride along, they find the ravages of an Indian attack. Tension builds with Tom when he wants to keep a dead couple's money; the Sacketts plan to send it to the couple's daughter. Sunday and the two brothers work hard rounding up their herd. In the mountains, Tell and Cap find a woman, Ange Kerry, who has lost her father to Indians.

Selling the herd in Santa Fe, the Sacketts and Tom learn that Jonathan Pritts owns the hotel. In his plan to oust the Mexicans, Pritts has hired gunmen. Joining up with Ira Bigelow to hunt down Tell is Kid Newton. Bigelow plans to meet his other brothers, Jack and Benson, in Purgatorie.

Offered jobs by Pritts, both Tyrel and Orrin turn him down. Instead, the Sacketts offer their help to Don Luis. To stop any possible warfare, Orrin suggests electing a sheriff for Santa Fe. Tom Sunday decides to oppose Orrin for the job of sheriff. But Pritts forces Tom to back off by bringing up his past as a disbarred lawyer and ex-convict (Tom killed a man in self-defense). Upset, Tom kills a gunman challenging him.

Kid Newton leads Ira and Jack Bigelow, along with others, into the mountains after Tell. Their brother Benson will arrive in town later on. After Orrin is elected sheriff, Tyrel offers the deputy's job to Tom. But the embittered Sunday refuses.

In the mountains, Cap Rountree is wounded by Jack Bigelow. Later, when the Bigelow gang is camped, Tell releases their horses. When Orrin refuses to oppose the Mexicans, Pritts threatens him. Orrin then realizes Laura Pritts is not the right woman for him.

An ill Don Luis passes away. Anticipating trouble with Pritts, Orrin makes Tyrel his deputy. After Pritts has a Mexican killed, he is arrested. Still bitter, Tom goes after Orrin with the intent to kill. A reluctant Tyrel shoots down Tom.

Despite Tell's concern for her safety, Ange Kerry goes to Purgatorie and sends a telegram to Tyrel and Orrin. Cap and Tell are soon confronted in town by the Bigelow gang, now including Benson. Orrin and Tyrel are there to help and the gang is wiped out in a gun battle The Sacketts are then joined by Cap as they proudly walk together.

Original Source: The novel *The Daybreakers.*

Plotline: After killing a man in a Tennessee feud, Tyrel Sackett follows his brother Orrin westward. They join a cattle drive, becoming friends with foreman Tom Sunday and old Cap Rountree. One of the other men, Reed Carney, proves a nuisance to Tye.

The Sacketts become embroiled in a land feud between Jonathan Pritts and Don

Luis Alvarado. Orrin marries Jonathan's daughter, Laura, while Tyrel romances Drusilla, Don Luis's granddaughter. Also vying for her affections are vaquero Antonio Baca and gunman Chico Cruz. Orrin's ambitions create an enemy in Tom Sunday.

Original Source: The novel *Sackett.*

Plotline: William Tell Sackett is forced to kill a card cheat, Wes Bigelow. After visiting his mother and brothers Orrin and Tyrel at their home in New Mexico, Tell then sets out with Cap Rountree looking for gold.

Founding a new town, Tell and Cap run into greedy, murderous men intent on ruining things. Among them are John Tuthill, Ben Hobes and Kid Newton. Out for vengeance over their brother's earlier killing are Tom and Ira, then Benson Bigelow. Tell's resolve is also tested over his love for homeless Ange Kerry.

Commentary: Louis L'Amour began his series of phenomenal Sackett novels beginning with *The Daybreakers*. Bantam Books published it in February 1960; 16 more novels, although not all in sequence, about various Sackett family members followed during the next 25 years. The last one was 1985's *Jubal Sackett.*

The Daybreakers, narrated by Tyrel Sackett, relates his going to the West for the first time along with older brother Orrin. Their oldest brother, William Tell, is mentioned during the story.

Sackett, the second novel in the series, came out in May 1961; narrated by Tell, it describes his adventures in the West with his two brothers figuring briefly into the story. In 1983, it ranked second to *Hondo* as L'Amour's biggest seller. *The Daybreakers* wasn't far behind at the time, as it was ranked fifth with *The Burning Hills.*

Of these three brothers, and all their kinfolk, Tell Sackett seemed to be the one favored by Louis. After *Sackett,* Tell appeared in a short story, "Booty for a Badman," initially seen in the July 30, 1961, issue of *The Saturday Evening Post.* The tale was compiled by Bantam with other L'Amour stories for 1975's *War Party.*

Five additional novels had Tell the narrator as well. Covering the years between 1875 and 1879, they were *Mojave Crossing* (1964), *The Sackett Brand* (1965), *The Lonely Men* (1969), *Treasure Mountain* (1972), and *Lonely on the Mountain* (1980). He also figured into three more Sackett novels, 1967's *The Sky-Liners,* 1970's *Galloway,* and 1972's *Ride the Dark Trail.*

Bantam's 1997 compilation of Louis's work, *End of the Drive,* included another short story featuring Tell, "The Courting of Griselda." Tell also figured in one of the author's non–Sackett novels, Bantam's *Dark Canyon* (1963).

Except for *Ride the Dark Trail* and "Booty for a Badman," Tyrel and Orrin are reflected in one capacity or another with the same Sackett titles as Tell. Unlike him, however, they are also included in the Sackett novels *Lando* (1962) and *Mustang Man* (1966).

Tye also appeared in the 1977 Bantam publication of Louis's *Borden Chantry.* Youngest sibling Joe Sackett is a murder victim in the novel, actually reflective of the Chantry family series. The only Sackett novel featuring Joe and brother Bob was *The Daybreakers.*

Sackett and *The Daybreakers* were the sources for the NBC miniseries *The Sacketts.* It was originally televised in two parts on consecutive nights, May 15 and 16, 1979. Jim Byrnes, who wrote the teleplay, combined elements from both novels. The first one takes place between 1867 and 1872, and the other between 1874 and 1875. Some things remained the same, yet a good many things were changed. While this fusion was not always smooth,

Seen in the advertisement for *The Sacketts* are Sam Elliott, Tom Selleck, Jeff Osterhage and long time Western star Glenn Ford. As Tom Sunday, Ford enjoyed one of his best roles.

it *was* always interesting and exciting. Especially captivating are those moments surrounding the final gunfight; prior to it, it appears that Tell might have to face off against the bad guys alone. Then his brothers show up (and Cap too), and afterwards all four men walk with pride side by side. None of this was part of L'Amour's stories.

The blazing gun battle which climaxes the miniseries is reminiscent of those seen in such films as 1952's *High Noon* and 1957's *Gunfight at the O.K. Corral.* Tyrel's showdown with Tom Sunday is the climactic highlight in *The Daybreakers*, as is Tell's shoot-out with Benson Bigelow in *Sackett.*

Of the Bigelow brothers, Benson is the worst in the novel, while it is Ira in *The Sacketts*. Ira is also the leader of the bad guys in the miniseries. John Tuthill, a minor character here, is the gang's leader in the book.

The novel's Tom Bigelow had his first name changed to Jack for the miniseries, possibly so he would not be confused with Tom Sunday. Tell shoots down Ira here, and Tyrel stops both Jack and Benson. In the novel, Ira and Tom succumb to the cold and snow with the rest of their gang.

Kid Newton, shot down by Cap in the climax of *The Sacketts*, is actually saved by Tell in the novel. While Tell's initial encounter with the Kid is disturbing, in the book it is handled amusingly. In the miniseries, it is handled with menace.

Reed Carney in the first novel, and Will Boyd in the second, are among the secondary villains included in the miniseries. Tye's making Carney remove his gun belt, and Tell's slicing-off of Boyd's mustache, proves more effective than killing them. It also shows that the Sacketts only kill when they have no other recourse.

Not part of the miniseries are villainous Mexicans Antonio Baca and Chico Cruz from *The Daybreakers*. The conflicts they generate create even more trouble for Don Luis Alvarado beyond that from head villain Jonathan Pritts. Pritts seems more formidable in the miniseries. Perhaps it is due in part to the fact that he is taken away in handcuffs by a U.S. marshal. In the book, he is simply run out of town.

The villainy from the novel's Laura Pritts is missing from *The Sacketts*. Unlike her merely charming counterpart here, who tries to sweet-talk Orrin into backing her ruthless father, she is shown in a hateful and cruel light by L'Amour.

Married to Orrin in the book, Laura returns to plague Tell in the novel *The Lonely Men*. Not knowing they are divorced, Tell is tricked by her into going after an imaginary son, Orry, she claims has been kidnapped by Apaches. Her reason is to try to have Tell killed just because he is Orrin's brother.

Both Drusilla and Ange are featured in several of the Sackett novels. Like Tye and Dru, Tell and Ange are also married. In *The Sackett Brand*, Tell finds his wife has been strangled.

Don Luis's death and the mistreatment of his people are sympathetically handled in both the miniseries and initial novel. There is a Mexican woman, Tina Fernandez, who is protected by Tyrel in *The Daybreakers*. She returns as a married woman in *Sackett*, and her husband, Esteban Mendoza, helps Tell.

Found at the opening of both novels are shootings — Tye of Long Higgins and Tell of Wes Bigelow — which act as the catalysts taking the Sackett brothers ever westward and to their destinies. The names of their folks, other than Ma and Pa Sackett, aren't disclosed in the miniseries. Louis has given them the names Mary Ann and Colborn (Colly for short). Having ventured to the West before his sons, their father is assumed dead. Searching for him in the novel *Treasure Mountain*, Orrin and Tell discover that he was shot to death.

Another close friend was Tom Sunday. In the miniseries, since he is older than his counterpart in *The Daybreakers*, Tom seems like a surrogate father to Tye and even Orrin. He teaches them to read and write, and he feels betrayed when they oppose his wishes and aspirations. Tom especially blames Orrin.

Although Sam Elliott, Tom Selleck and Jeff Osterhage have great chemistry as the Sackett brothers, Glenn Ford as Sunday contributed the most well-rounded performance. He deserved an Emmy nomination at the very least. Ford's versatility took him beyond the heroic roles he often played and into villainy as well. In 1946, his film stardom was assured with *Gilda*, as the gambler troubling Rita Hayworth. In the original *3:10 to Yuma* (1957), one of his best Westerns, he was the outlaw leader up against Van Heflin.

"Relatively gritty and realistic as TV Westerns go," remarked *Variety* about *The Sacketts*. "All three of the Sackett boys were effective, especially Elliott as the grimy and laconic Tell Sackett."

Sam Elliott began appearing in TV and movie Westerns in 1969. His initial TV appearances were on the series *The Guns of Will Sonnett* and *Lancer*. As a card player, he made his big screen debut in *Butch Cassidy and the Sundance Kid*. In later years, he starred in three more TV movies based on frontier tales by L'Amour. One of them, 1982's *The Shadow Riders,* co-starred Osterhage and Selleck. One *Lancer* episode, "Death Bait" (1969), had roles for both Selleck and Elliott.

Selleck's big-screen debut was playing a sexy stud in 1970's *Myra Breckenridge*. In 1978 and '79, he appeared as Lance White, trying to solve crimes and match wits with James Garner on the TV series *The Rockford Files*. Portraying the charming Orrin Sackett, Selleck proved, like Sam Elliott, that he had a natural flair for Westerns. He made two more from Louis's stories.

Prior to the miniseries, Jeff Osterhage showed his own fortitude in Westerns: He played in two for television: a 1978 film called *True Grit—A Further Adventure,* and a 1979 pilot, *The Legend of the Golden Gun*. As Tyrel, Jeff enjoyed the largest Sackett brother role. On the DVD of *The Sacketts,* he offers delightful insight about their winning the roles.

Poignantly portraying Ma Sackett was Mercedes McCambridge. She won a Best Supporting Actress Academy Award for 1949's *All the King's Men*. Another nomination was received for 1956's *Giant*. In '60, she was in *Cimarron* with Glenn Ford.

Of the many familiar supporting performers in the miniseries — including Gilbert Roland, Jack Elam and Slim Pickens — none came any better than Ben Johnson as loyal

Cap Rountree. John Ford's *Wagonmaster* (1950) gave Ben a starring role. He won a Best Supporting Actor Oscar for 1971's *The Last Picture Show.*

"The truth of our frontier mythology is explored in such familiar, simplistic and relaxed terms in *The Sacketts,*" said *TV Guide*, "that the two-part, four-hour adventure, written by Jim Byrnes and directed by Robert Totten, provides very pleasing entertainment."

It was by directing Westerns that Robert Totten first made his mark on television. His work included many episodes of *Gunsmoke* between 1966 and 1971. In '69, he directed a motion picture, *Death of a Gunfighter*, and a two-part Disney telecast, *Ride a Northbound Horse*, featuring Ben Johnson.

Some fine TV Western films were written by Jim Byrnes. They included two starring Jim Arness (*The Macahans* [1976] and *Gunsmoke: Return to Dodge* [1987]). He also worked on *The Shadow Riders.*

One of the nice surprises about *The Sacketts* was L'Amour's additional participation. His corporation, Shalako Enterprises, was involved with the production which included filming at Buckskin Joe's Frontier Town near Canon City, Colorado. Louis also narrated the introduction used for Parts 1 and 2. He mentions the Sacketts' Tennessee roots and that the country was settled first by the Indians and then white men—"Men like Davy Crockett and Andy Jackson, and a Welsh immigrant named Sackett."

The Cowboy Hall of Fame in Oklahoma City selected *The Sacketts* as the most authentic Western of the 1970s.

The 1980s

The Cherokee Trail

1981. A Walt Disney Production.
In Association with Douglas Netter Productions.
CBS Television.
60 Minutes/Color.

Credits: Douglas Netter (Executive Producer), Kieth Merrill (Director), Michael Terrance, Kieth Merrill (Teleplay), Jack A. Whitman, Jr. (Photography), Ernest Milano (Editor), Mark W. Mansbridge (Art Director), Norman Rockett (Set Director), Jack Sandeen (Costumes), Robert J. Schiffer (Makeup), Jerrold Immel (Music). Based on a novel by Louis L'Amour.

Cast: Cindy Pickett (Mary Breydon), Mary Larkin (Matty Maginnis), Richard Farnsworth (Ridge Fenton), Victor French (Scant Luther), Tina Yothers (Peg Breydon), David Hayward (Temple Boone), Tommy Petersen (Wat Tanner), Timothy Scott (Wilbur Pattishall), Buck Taylor (Laird), Murray McMurry (Cal Egan), Whitney Rydbeck (Bob Cochraine), Art Bradford (Charlie Bent).

Synopsis: After her husband's death, Mary Breydon takes on a job he was originally hired to do: With their young daughter Peg, Mary arrives in Cherokee, Colorado, to manage its stagecoach stop, Cherokee Station.

Claiming title to the run-down place is nasty Scant Luther. He is shown a letter attesting to Mary's authority to take over management. Angered, Scant tries to force mother and child to leave, but stagecoach drivers convince *him* to leave instead.

Cleaning up the station, the Breydons are assisted by immigrant Matty Maginnis, who stays on with them. They soon adapt to their new responsibilities. As Mary is unhitching some horses, they become spooked by gunfire. Cowboy Temple Boone settles the animals down. Peg comes across a little boy about her own age, an orphan named Wat Tanner.

In town, Mary is able to hire a man, Ridge Fenton, to help tend to the stock at the station. Ridge is a bit uneasy at first about working for a woman. When Wat bumps into Mary, she sees that he is being chased for stealing. She pays his debt and takes the boy home with her. Wat and Peg become good friends.

With a gang of men, Scant Luther comes to the station intending to hold up a stagecoach. Wat is able to run for Temple Boone, who gets there just as the stage pulls into the station. During the ensuing shoot-out, Mary is forced to wound Scant to protect Wat.

Original Source: The novel *The Cherokee Trail.*

Plotline: After her husband is killed following his military service in the Civil War, Mary Breydon and daughter Peg take on his intended job managing the stage stop at Cherokee Station. Ex-manager Scant Luther and wartime guerrilla leader Jason Flandrau prove to be dangerous adversaries.

The Breydons are aided in their duties at the station by Matty Maginnis, Temple Boone, Ridge Fenton and orphan Wat Tanner. Offering yet more support are stage agent Mark Stacy, rancher Preston Collier and Barry Owen, who was with her late husband in the war.

Commentary: L'Amour's novel *The Cherokee Trail* was first published by Bantam in August 1982. A TV pilot of the same title had already aired on CBS on November 28, 1981.

The pilot was derived from part of Louis's story, apparently as it was being written. Executive producer Douglas Netter also worked on *The Sacketts*, as did composer Jerrold Immel and photographer Jack A. Whitman, Jr.

By '81, the weekly Disney anthology series (a TV staple since 1954) had worked its way from ABC to NBC to CBS. Several title changes also occurred over the years which began with *Disneyland. Walt Disney* was the series' title at the time of *The Cherokee Trail.* One of the formats for CBS and Disney was to showcase pilot shows for possible series programming.

As the pilot was only 60 minutes, just one of L'Amour's villains, Scant Luther, made it to the screen. A notable number of the other characters he created were on hand, including Mary and Peg Breydon, Matty Maginnis, Wat Tanner, Ridge Fenton and Temple Boone.

Unlike Louis's conception, the pilot told its tale through the perspective of Mary's daughter, Peg. However Mary remains the central character in both versions.

Clearly shared by Louis is Mary's past which led to her current occupation as a stage manager. The Overland Stage Company, run by Ben Holladay, actually operated along the Cherokee Trail from Laramie, Wyoming to Denver, Colorado.

The novel, like the film, is set in 1864 Colorado, and the Civil War is still being fought back east. Mary's home state of Virginia certainly saw more than its share of the fighting and her plantation came under attack by guerrilla riders. Marshall, her husband, was a Yankee officer; among the men serving under him was Barry Owen.

After his wartime service ended, Marshall was en route to his new position at Cherokee Station when guerrillas, led by Jason Flandrau, made Mary a widow. Flandrau, like his cohorts gunmen Jordy Neff and Mody Mercer, undoubtedly would have played a major role had the pilot become a series. So too would have Mark Stacy and Preston Collier as other friends of Mary.

During the novel, Mary longs to return to Virginia, once the war is over, to rebuild her home. By novel's end, she refers to Cherokee Station as home and even has two prospective suitors, Boone and Stacy. These things seemed to lean toward a continuation of her frontier adventures as hinted at by Louis but which never came to pass.

L'Amour has his characters interested in books. Mary enjoys reading in the evenings to those who wish to listen. Temple is keen on reading stories by Sir Walter Scott. In both *The Daybreakers* and *Sackett,* respective heroes Tyrel and Tell want to improve their reading. One of the books Tye favors is James Fenimore Cooper's *The Deerslayer.*

For *The Cherokee Trail,* novel and film, Scant Luther remains a hateful cuss. Mary, forced to shoot and injure the man in each, is so upset by it that she needs to rest after the ordeal. Yet Mary understands all too well that such violence is sometimes necessary to protect the ones she loves. Mary Breydon's inner strength, as well as her vulnerable nature, make her one of L'Amour's most appealing heroines. Fearful yet courageous, she adapts to the West admirably.

TV Guide responded favorably: "New faces and a strong script by one of the most popular Western authors enhance *Louis L'Amour's The Cherokee Trail,* an unusual outing for *Walt Disney.*"

It was unusual in the sense of having females dominating the story the way a man would a conventional Western; *Variety* called it an "interesting concept." A similar path was explored by Disney in the 1957 frontier classic *Old Yeller*, with a mother coping alongside her two sons in the wilderness. In that instance, the father wasn't dead but just away on a cattle drive.

Like *Louis L'Amour's The Sacketts*, this 1981 entry also included the author's name as part of the title. Late in his career, Louis was being accorded the recognition he deserved.

Cindy Pickett and Tina Yothers were impressive as the mother and daughter. Pickett had appeared on the daytime soap opera *The Guiding Light* from 1976 until 1980. She was also in two TV movies, *The Ivory Ape* (1980) and *Margin for Murder* (1981).

This was the first television role for Yothers, an aspiring child actress. She played youngest sibling Jennifer Keaton on the popular sitcom *Family Ties* between 1982 and 1989. In '82, she also was in an episode of the *Father Murphy* series.

A relatively new face to the Western genre was David Hayward as the horse wrangler who befriends Peg and Mary. He appeared as Timothy Oates in the 1979 TV movie *The Chisholms* and had a recurring role during 1989 on the *Knots Landing* series.

Two fine Western actors, veterans Richard Farnsworth and Victor French, offered their customary solid support. Each had appeared earlier on episodes of *Bonanza* and an episode of *Cimarron Strip.* Farnsworth also enjoyed the title role in the 1983 film *The Grey Fox.* As the cantankerous yet endearing Isaiah Edwards, French appeared on both *Little House on the Prairie* (1974–77) and *Little House: A New Beginning* (1982–83).

Praise was given to *The Cherokee Trail* by *Variety* which said, "[T]he pilot's potential, *a la Little House on the Prairie,* was considerable."

This, of course, was a comparison to that beloved television series about the Ingalls family and their adventures on the frontier. While *The Cherokee Trail* never became a series, Disney did later rework its format for television as *Five Mile Creek.* Michael Terrance and Kieth Merrill collaborated on the teleplay for the 1981 pilot; Merrill also directed.

His other credits as a director included the 1980 TV special *Mr. Krueger's Christmas* (starring Jimmy Stewart) and the 1988 IMAX presentation *Alamo: The Price of Freedom.*

The Shadow Riders

1982. A Pegasus Group Ltd. Production.
In Association with Columbia Pictures Television.
CBS Television.
120 Minutes/Color.

Credits: Dennis Durney, Verne Nobles (Producers), Andrew V. McLaglen (Director), Jim Byrnes (Executive Producer, Teleplay), Jack Whitman (Photography), Bud Friedgen (Editor), Jack DeShields (Production Designer), Lon Bentley, Fred Williams (Makeup), Jerrold Immel (Music). Based on a novel by Louis L'Amour.

Cast: Tom Selleck (Mac Traven), Sam Elliott (Dal Traven), Ben Johnson (Black Jack Traven), Geoffrey Lewis (Major Ashbury), Jeffrey Osterhage (Jesse Traven), Gene Evans (Holiday Hammond), Katharine Ross (Kate Connery), R.G. Armstrong (Miles Gillette), Marshall Teague (Lt. Butler), Robert B. Craig (Laird), Ben Fuhrman (Devol), Jane Greer (Ma Traven), Harry Carey, Jr. (Pa Traven), Dominique Dunne (Sissy Traven), Natalie May (Heather Traven).

Synopsis: Yankee captain Mac Traven is charming a Southern belle when he learns the Civil War is over. Other Yankees are planning on executing his brother Dal, a Rebel soldier. But Dal is rescued by a Rebel force led by Major Ashbury. The major is interested in Dal joining in a personal war against the Union. But Dal wants to return home to Texas.

En route, Dal gets into more trouble and is rescued from a hanging by Mac. When the brothers get home, they find their father and mother have been plagued by Rebel renegades who have made prisoners of sisters Sissy and Heather, brother Jesse and Dal's former love, Kate Connery, who became engaged to another man when Dal was reported killed in the war.

Also held captive on the Gulf Coast are other men and women. They are all to be sold into slavery in Mexico by the renegade leader Ashbury and his followers in order to get money to buy munitions. With Kate's help, Jesse Traven escapes and is found by Mac and Dal.

Ashbury's connection, Holiday Hammond, arrives by ship and chooses the prisoners he wants. He buys Kate but has her remain behind under guard when he sails down the coast with the others, including Ashbury and the Traven sisters. Kate is rescued by the Traven brothers. Not familiar with Mexico, they break their scoundrel uncle, Black Jack Traven, out of jail as he does know the country. On Jack's trail is a posse led by Sheriff Miles Gillette.

In Mexico, Ashbury realizes he has been double-crossed by Hammond, who wants

In this publicity pose for *The Shadow Riders,* Tom Selleck, Katharine Ross and Sam Elliott appear to be quite contented.

Instead of *The Sacketts*, Tom Selleck, Jeffrey Osterhage and Sam Elliott are the Traven brothers in *The Shadow Riders.*

the prisoners without paying. An associate of Ashbury's is then shot and he is locked up. Kate is also captured by Hammond.

With guns and dynamite, all the Traven men defeat Hammond's gang. Dal reluctantly lets Ashbury escape to repay him for earlier saving his life. Although Jess frees the other prisoners, Kate and his sisters are taken on a train by Hammond. But Mac and Dal chase it down, capturing Hammond and saving them.

When the posse finally catches up to their uncle, the Travens exchange Hammond for him. It seems the sheriff's main gripe all along was that his wife and Jack were fooling around. With Dal riding beside Kate to propose to her, Mac smiles and leads all the Travens and others back to Texas.

Original Source: The novel *The Shadow Riders.*

Plotline: Having fought on opposite sides in the Civil War, brothers Mac and Dal Traven return home to discover renegades have taken their siblings, friends and neighbors. Led by Colonel Ashford, the worst of the renegades turns out to be one called Frank.

Dal and Mac's brother and sister, Jesse and Gretchen, and Dal's love Kate Connery are among the prisoners. While Ashford plans on selling them to Hammond, a ship's captain, much-needed aid for the Travens comes from their uncle Happy Jack Traven and Kate's uncle Martin Connery.

Commentary: L'Amour wrote *The Shadow Riders* even as the CBS version of the story was being made. In fact, he dedicated the novel to its "cast and crew." Bantam published it in October 1982, which followed the September 28 telecast.

Verne Nobles and Dennis Durney, the producers, worked initially with an outline from Louis. In each version, Mac and Dal Traven return home to find renegades have made off with captives. Neither brother harbors any animosity against the other for having fought on the opposite side in the Civil War.

For the TV movie, their brother Jesse also fought in the war yet it isn't specified which side. To Dal and Mac it really doesn't matter for they are thankful it is over. The film mentions that Mac was a captain; in the novel he was a major.

But the war is not over for the Confederate renegade officer in both. His full name in the book is Colonel Henry T. Ashford, while in the film it is Major Cooper Ashbury. The officer is allotted some form of redemption in each account. In the novel, it comes late when he arms Kate Connery so she can protect herself from his own men. And it is seen early in the film when he saves Dal from a firing squad.

A major villain in the TV movie, Holiday Hammond is actually more dastardly than the renegade officer. His role in the book, as Captain Hammond (without the fancy first name), is brief as he is seen only long enough to refuse his shady services to the movement to allow the South to fight again.

Only the vilest aspects of this intended venture are left to the film's Hammond and to the book's renegade Frank. While Hammond is very willing to show Kate some courtesies, even relish her companionship, he is also willing to turn the female captives into prostitutes in Mexico. And Frank is one of the men lusting after Kate.

Frank proves to be the most contemptible of all the villains. His only motivation is to kill and plunder for his own gain. Mac Traven will ultimately prove more than a match for him, however.

Another of the novel's plotlines revolves around Captain Martin Connery, a strong secondary character, and (like Frank) not featured in the film. While his current role is that of a rancher, Connery's most striking feature remains his past as a tough seafaring man. Yet in a nearby bay he still maintains an armed ship which undoubtedly would have been used against Hammond's own vessel had the need arose.

While he is called Happy Jack Traven in the novel, trouble seems to be the natural order of things. His counterpart in the film, Black Jack, is given more substance as a likable rascal with the law on his tail. Miles Gillette, the film's sheriff, is not part of the book.

The scenes with Black Jack give the film a grand dose of humor not found with the book. Especially exasperated with his uncle is Mac, who is continually surprised by his past criminal actions even though they are minor offenses. Jack's biggest problem is his womanizing.

Kate Connery is a strong figure in both novel and film. In the book she is especially resourceful. Renegades Hayden and Cutler find out the hard way after chasing her.

Another strong female presence in L'Amour's novel is captive Cordelia Atherton, who even comes to Mac's side against Frank. Neither Cordelia or her child Susan are part of the film. At eight years old, Susan is the same age as Peg Breydon in Louis's *The Cherokee Trail.*

Other characters not in the TV movie included Dulcie, Kate's sister, and Gretchen, the sister of the Traven brothers. The book's Dulcie and Gretchen are substituted in the film with sisters Heather and Sissy Traven.

Ma and Pa Traven figure in each version. They are seen in the film when sons Dal and Mac ride up to their home after the renegade attack. However, in the novel the parents are not actually seen. The brothers learn from a neighbor caring for Susan Atherton that their father was injured by the renegades.

When Mac and Dal stampede the renegades' cattle in the film, they seem to wipe out those men left behind with the herd and Kate when Ashbury goes to Mexico with Hammond. Kate is less fortunate during the novel's stampede, which also involves Happy Jack.

There are also other male captives in the film, unlike the novel. Kate gives Jesse a pen knife to cut his bonds during the film and he escapes by running out into the Gulf of Mexico. In the book, she cuts his ropes herself with broken glass and he runs off into the forest.

The movie's exciting climactic train chase, not at all part of the book, has Mac and Dal riding after the iron horse on horseback, then clambering up the caboose and jumping across other cars to rescue their sisters and Kate.

"Good, old-fashioned cowboy fun," was how the *DVD & Video Guide* sized up *The*

Never were there two better performers to portray L'Amour heroes than Tom Selleck and Sam Elliott, seen here pondering their next move for ***The Shadow Riders.***

Shadow Riders. While visiting the set during filming, L'Amour was approached to play one of Hammond's comancheros. In an interview at the end of his own novel, Louis reflected on not being prepared for it: "It was very hot and the costumes were hot, and I preferred not to."

Unusual for any Western is the use of the sea; Louis makes splendid use of the Gulf Coast of Texas. The filmmakers utilized locations in Santa Cruz, California, and Sonora, Mexico, which were equally captivating.

By the time he starred in *The Shadow Riders,* Tom Selleck had become a big television star courtesy of CBS's *Magnum, P.I.* series (1980–88). Found in both the show and *Shadow Riders* was his trademark smile while looking directly at the camera.

Orrin Sackett and Tom's Mac Traven bore similar characteristics. His charm with the ladies was evident. While Orrin ran for sheriff in *The Sacketts*, Mac plans on running for the job against Miles Gillett.

Between *The Sacketts* and their respective roles as Dal Traven and his uncle Jack, Sam Elliott and Ben Johnson appeared in another Western telemovie, 1980's *Wild Times.* Sam's deep, grumbling voice and laconic manner always made his Westerns something special. During Ben's younger days, he was a rodeo rider. In his early Westerns for John Ford, like 1949's *She Wore a Yellow Ribbon*, his fine riding ability was apparent.

In 1981 Elliott appeared with Katharine Ross as a bad guy in the TV movie *Murder in Texas*. For *The Shadow Riders*, the frustrated yet charming romance between his Dal and her warm but feisty Kate Connery even amuses his brothers.

Ross became a star with 1967's *The Graduate*, for which she received an Oscar nomination as Best Supporting Actress. She was Etta Place in 1969's *Butch Cassidy and the Sundance Kid.* In 1984, she and Sam were married.

Also returning from *The Sacketts* were Jeffrey Osterhage as Jesse Traven and Gene Evans as Holiday Hammond. Western regular Evans played Butch Cassidy in a 1955 movie called *Wyoming Renegades*, but he may be best remembered as the father on the 1955–56 series *My Friend Flicka.*

While Osterhage never reached the same level of stardom as his television brothers, he did have a starring role in his first feature film, *Sky Bandits* (1986). Included among his other TV appearances were two episodes of the Angela Lansbury mystery series *Murder, She Wrote*, in 1985 and 1986.

Seen as Major Ashbury, Geoffrey Lewis made a number of films with Clint Eastwood, including the Western *High Plains Drifter* (1972) and the contemporary cowboy tale *Bronco Billy* (1980).

This Western was the second teleplay written by Jim Byrnes, and the third TV entry in a row for composer Jerrold Immel and photographer Jack Whitman, based on a L'Amour story. Between his work on *The Shadow Riders*, Byrnes was involved on two TV movies starring Kenny Rogers, 1980's *The Gambler* and '83's *The Gambler, Part II—The Adventure Continues.*

Director Andrew V. McLaglen made four Westerns each with John Wayne and James

Stewart; and 1967's *The Way West* had Robert Mitchum, Richard Widmark and Kirk Douglas together. For television, McLaglen directed James Arness and Richard Boone in many episodes of their respective shows *Gunsmoke* and *Have Gun, Will Travel.*

When the first TV Movie Awards were held at the 1983 Locarno Film Festival in Switzerland, *Louis L'Amour's The Shadow Riders,* as it was also known, was cited for special recognition. Of the ten television entries in this filmography between *The Sacketts* and 2001's *The Diamond of Jeru,* only *Five Mile Creek* failed to include the author's name as part of the title.

Five Mile Creek

1983–85. A Valstar Pty. Ltd. Production.
In Association with the Disney Channel and the Seven Network Australia.
39 Episodes/Color.

Credits: Henry Crawford (Producer), Kevin James Dobson, Frank Arnold, Gary Conway, Di Drew, Michael Jenkins, Brendan Maher, George Miller, David Stevens, Rob Stewart, Chris Thomson, Brian Trenchard-Smith (Directors), David Boutland, Sarah Crawford, Graham Foreman, Tom Hegarty, Michael Joshua, Peter Kinloch, Gwenda Marsh, Greg Millin, Denise Morgan, Keith Thompson (Writers), Kevan Lind (Photography), Tim Wellburn (Editor), George Liddle (Production Designer), Lisa Elvy, Igor Nay (Art Directors), Jeny Arnott (Costumes), Jose Perez (Makeup), Bruce Smeaton (Music). Inspired by a Louis L'Amour novel.

Cast: Louise Caire Clark (Maggie Scott), Rod Mullinar (Jack Taylor), Jay Kerr (Con Madigan), Liz Burch (Kate Wallace), Michael Caton (Paddy Malone), Priscilla Weems (Hannah Scott), Martin Lewis (Sam Sawyer), Gus Mercurio (Ben Jones), Peter Carroll (Charles Withers), Tony Blackett (Backer Bowman), Nicole Kidman (Annie).

Episodes-Airdates: *Season 1*—"Making Tracks" 11/4/83; "Horses for Courses" 11/11/83; "Love Before a Fall" 12/7/83; "A Few Surprises" 12/21/83; "The Scrub Bulls" 1/4/84; "Bang the Big Drum" 1/18/84; "Gold Fever" 2/1/84; "Annie" 2/15/84; "Home and Away" 3/7/84; "The Awakening" 3/21/84; "The Prize" 4/4/84; "Tricks of the Trade" 4/18/84; "Thanksgiving" 5/2/84. *Season 2*—"Hangman's Noose" 5/16/84; "The Challenge" 6/6/84; "Blood, Sweat, and Faith" 6/20/84; "Mail Order Brides" 7/4/84; "Maggie" 7/18/84; "When the Kookaburra Cries" 8/1/84; "Walk Like a Man" 8/15/84; "Across the Great Divide" 9/5/84; "Missing, Presumed Lost" 9/19/84; "Matchmaker" 10/3/84; "Good Old Reliable Me" 10/17/84; "Women of Means" 11/7/84; "The Last Round Up" 12/5/84. *Season 3*—"Travellers Tales" 1/2/85; "The Gauntlet" 2/6/85; "Real Cowboys Play Fair" 3/6/85; "Possum" 3/20/85; "The Best of Mates" 4/3/85; "The Gold Cup" 4/17/85; "A Dog Called Johnson" 5/1/85; "Fish Out of Water" 5/15/85; "The Great Coach Race" 6/5/85; "A Death in the Family" 6/19/85; "A Lot of Hot Air" 7/3/85; "One Fine Day" 7/17/85; "America" 8/7/85.

Commentary: Just as Walt Disney Productions was winding up its two-year anthology series on CBS-TV, broadcasting started on its very own network: The Disney Channel debuted in April 1983.

Initially material from the Disney library was shown, but soon unveiled was brand new series programming. Included was the series *Five Mile Creek*, whose 39 episodes ran in a 60-minute slot from November 4, 1983, to August 7, 1985. It was reworked from the earlier pilot on CBS, *The Cherokee Trail,* and inspired by Louis's novel of the same title.

While the pilot had been filmed on the Golden Oak Ranch in Newhall, California, the new series was made in Australia. Doug Netter, who was involved with the pilot and also *The Sacketts,* served as executive producer.

"Making Tracks," the first episode, unfolded in the same period as the pilot, the 1860s, but the setting has moved from Colorado to Australia during its own gold rush. Both outlaws in the wild (bushrangers) and decent folks are trying to profit from the situation.

Traveling from San Francisco, Texan Con Madigan plans to set up a stage line called the Australian Express with Jack Taylor. The banker is Charles Withers in the town of Wilga. Fellow travelers are the Scotts, Maggie and daughter Hannah, who are soon helping Kate Wallace operate the stage station at Five Mile Creek, 40 miles north of Sydney. Paddy Malone is Kate's handyman.

The premiere episode was directed by George Miller; Peter Kinloch and story editor Graham Foreman collaborated on the teleplay. Miller also helmed the acclaimed 1982 feature *The Man from Snowy River.*

Maggie and Hannah are clearly drawn from the pilot's Mary and Peg Breydon, and Kate from Matty Maginnis. In this newer version, their roles at the station are somewhat reversed. Paddy's earlier counterpart was Ridge Fenton.

Recalling the pilot's Scant Luther in this episode is original station manager Eddie Wallace, Kate's brother. Skipping town, Eddie initially puts the full burden of running the station on Kate. Also seen in the episode is a character named Backer Bowman. When he tries to persuade the new Five Mile Creek team to leave in the next episode, Bowman brings to mind Luther's shenanigans.

Introduced in the second episode, "Horses for Courses" are other characters derived from the pilot. Wrangler Ben Jones brings horses to the stage line for Con; both men actually appear as composites for cowboy Temple Boone. The troubled juvenile cared for by Maggie, Sam Sawyer, is patterned after Wat Tanner.

In L'Amour's *The Cherokee Trail,* Mary's husband Marshall is already dead. Adam Scott, Maggie's spouse, turns up alive in *Five Mile Creek.* Having run off to the gold field, Adam was the reason she came to Australia with their child.

"Gold Fever," episode 7, has Adam showing up with a bounty out on him as a bushranger. Maggie refuses to go off with him until he can improve his life. In the thirteenth episode, "Thanksgiving," it is discovered that Adam was killed.

Hannah reveals her interest in boarding school in episode 23, "Matchmaker." She then tries to interest her mother in either Jack Taylor or Charles Withers for companionship. In Louis's novel, both Temple and stage agent Mark Stacy seem interested in Mary.

By episode 28, "The Gauntlet," the Five Mile Creek family has moved to the Emu Plains after a fire destroyed Wilga. Introduced in this episode is an orphaned shepherd girl named Annie. Kate and Maggie take her under their wing.

In episode 39, "America," Maggie is distraught when Charles dies as he had become her best friend. With the opportunity to go to New Mexico to run stage lines, Con proposes to Kate. Tom Hegarty wrote this final show and Kevin James Dobson was the director. Of the various directors involved on the series, Dobson directed the most episodes with (15). Sarah Crawford led the writers with ten episodes.

Television fans will recall Kevin Dobson's Mack MacKenzie on the series *Knots Landing* from 1982 to 1993. When Priscilla Weems began playing Hannah, she was eleven years old. Between 1986 and 1990, she had a recurring role on the series *Designing Women.* Like his character Con, Jay Kerr was also a Texan. In 1989, he appeared on an episode of the *Dynasty* series. Jonathan Frakes guest-starred in episode 7 as Maggie's husband Adam. He went on to a regular role in a series: He was Commander Riker on *Star Trek: The Next Generation* (1987–94).

A regular on the last twelve episodes of *Five Mile Creek* was 17-year-old Nicole Kidman as Annie. Although born in Hawaii, she grew up in Australia and became a major film star. *The Hours* (2002) won her an Oscar as Best Actress.

Down the Long Hills

1986. A Finnegan Company Production.
A Disney Channel Premiere Film.
89 Minutes/Color.

Credits: Bill Finnegan (Producer), Burt Kennedy (Director), Jon Povare, Ruth Povare (Teleplay), Reet Smoot (Photography), Warner E. Leighton (Editor), Roger S. Crandall (Art Director), Nina Padovana (Costumes), Karl E. Wessen (Makeup), Mark Snow (Music). Based on a novel by Louis L'Amour.

Cast: Bruce Boxleitner (Scott Collins), Bo Hopkins (Jud), Michael Wren (Cal), Don Shanks (Ashawakie), Ed Bruce (Bregman), Buck Taylor (Grey), Thomas Wilson Brown (Hardy Collins), Lisa MacFarlane (Betty Sue Powell), Jack Elam (Bill Squires), David Cass (Mr. Andy), Peggy Matheson (Mrs. Andy), Beverly Rowland (Mrs. Bregman), Michael Ruud (Wagonmaster), Roy J. Cohoe (Indian Chief), Richard J. Martin (War Chief).

Synopsis: Two children, Hardy Collins and Betty Sue Powell, are the sole surviving members of a wagon train attacked by Comanches. Hardy was traveling to Fort Bridger to join his father Scott Collins, a horse wrangler for the army. Betty Sue, going further west with her family to make a new home, is now orphaned. With the help of his horse Red, Hardy uses the skills taught him by his father, enabling the children to move on in the wilderness.

Scott learns about the wagon train attack from scout Bill Squires and realizes that the children may still be alive. Searching for them, the men discover that the attack was provoked when thieves Jud and Cal killed some Indians and stole their horses, then sold them to the unsuspecting wagonmaster.

An Indian named Ashawakie is following the children to get Red, as are Cal and Jud. On the trail of the pair of murderous thieves are the vengeful Comanches. Creating another dilemma for the children is a grizzly bear.

Scott and Bill do meet up with the children. Jud and Cal are stopped, and the band of Indians is driven away. Asawakie makes off with Red, then changes his mind. Understanding the boy's bond with the horse, he allows Red to return to Hardy.

Original Source: The novel *Down the Long Hills.*

Plotline: After an Indian attack on a wagon train, Hardy Collins, age 7, and Betty Sue, 3, are left alone in the wilderness with Big Red, the boy's horse. Searching for the children are Hardy's father Scott and mountain men Bill Squires and Frank Darrow.

Danger surrounds the children. Following them are Cheyenne Indians, including Ashawakie, and two men called Jud and Cal. Wolves and a grizzly also threaten.

Commentary: The L'Amour novel *Down the Long Hills* was published by Bantam Books in January 1968. The Western Writers of America honored it with that year's Golden Spur Award as the best Western novel. This particular novel is a bit unusual for a L'Amour tale in that the hero and heroine are children, and rather young ones at that. Aside from the animals which play a pivotal role, only eight characters are focused on.

The Disney Channel premiered the film version as *Louis L'Amour's Down the Long Hills* on November 15, 1986. The author's name was not part of the title on May 24, 1987, for the *Disney Movie* ABC telecast.

The thrust of the L'Amour plot, to rescue the pair of children after a series of harrowing adventures, was very unified in structure — one of his best in this regard. Its depiction of the survival skills of little Hardy Collins is nothing short of amazing.

Faulting the TV film, however, *Variety* said "the kid actors were somewhat limited in their ranges.... [T]he story wandered aimlessly from one conflict to the next."

Expanded for the film were characters mentioned in the book mainly in the past tense, like Mr. and Mrs. Andy Powell, the parents of toddler Betty Sue. There were also new characters added to the film, like Mr. and Mrs. Bregman.

There is no mountain man named Frank Darrow in the film, only Bill Squires to ride with Scott Collins to the children's rescue. While Jud and Cal are the core villains in both film and novel, Ashawakie is seen in a better light in the movie. Also seen in a somewhat better light are the Indians who attacked the wagon train. Even in 1986 there was a sense of political correctness as the teleplay's writers, Ruth and Jon Povare, concocted a reason for the attack. Cal and Jud take violent action against the Comanche Indians and then deceive the wagonmaster, thus involving the entire wagon train as unknowing co-conspirators; this triggers the violence that wipes out those pioneers traveling to California. Of course, such reasoning should not excuse the killing and raiding by the Indians any less than Louis's own direct narrative as being an attack by renegades. The Indians here are actually outnumbered but have the element of surprise and ferocity on their side.

Among the best things about the TV movie were its stunning Utah backgrounds and the remarkable use of animals. Filming took place in the Wasatch and Unita mountain ranges. The animal trainers included Rex Peterson for Big Red the stallion and Doug Seus for Three-Paws the bear.

Thomas Wilson Brown, at age 13, was much older than the novel's counterpart, Hardy. (For that matter, so was Lisa MacFarlane as Betty Sue.) Brown's first Western was 1985's *Silverado*; he was one of the young fliers in 2001's *Pearl Harbor*. MacFarlane's brief acting career also included the film drama *Promised Land* (1988). Always at home in a Western with his tall, rangy and heroic-looking appearance was Bruce Boxleitner. But *Variety* felt he "didn't quite pull off the role of macho cowboy hero" Scott Collins in *Down the Long Hills*.

Boxleitner's numerous appearances in TV Westerns included starring roles in 1983's *I Married Wyatt Earp* (as Earp), and the 1988 remake of *Red River* (as Matthew Garth). He was also in Sam Elliott's *Wild Times* (1980).

With a knack for playing bad guys and good guys, Jack Elam's many Western film roles included the crazed escaped convict in 1951's *Rawhide* and John Wayne's feisty sidekick in 1970's *Rio Lobo*. His TV work included the 1967 *Hondo* episode "Hondo and the Rebel Hat."

Making his Western film debut as Crazy Lee in 1969's classic *The Wild Bunch* was Bo Hopkins. Among his other impressive Westerns were 1970's *Monte Walsh* and 1973's *The Man Who Loved Cat Dancing*. Don Shanks had a flair for portraying strong Indians and was in several 1978–79 episodes of the series *The Life and Times of Grizzly Adams* as Nakomas. In the 1977 TV movie *Last of the Mohicans*, he was Uncas.

Like Andrew V. McLaglen, Burt Kennedy was highly regarded as a director of Western films beginning in the 1960s. His work included *Return of the Seven* (1966) and a pair with John Wayne, 1967's *The War Wagon* and 1973's *The Train Robbers*.

In the film version of *Down the Long Hills*, widower Scott Collins breaks horses at Fort Bridger. L'Amour made carpentry his trade in the novel. But in both instances, his son is journeying westward with the Powell family to be with him. Their previous home, mentioned by Louis in the novel, was in Wisconsin.

Also mentioned by Louis is the intent of that deadly duo of Cal and Jud to plunder travelers bound for California gold fields. The novel is set in 1848 following that historic gold rush to John Sutter's land grant in the Sacramento Valley. While building a sawmill there on the American River for Sutter, carpenter James Marshall discovered the first gold nuggets.

In the novel, Bill Squires recalls coming from "Sutter's place" to another called Dry Diggin's searching for gold with others. One of the men also there was Cal, who even then was suspected of being a thief.

The Quick and the Dead

1987. A HBO Pictures Presentation.
A Joe Cates Production.
120 Minutes/Color.

Credits: Phillip Cates (Producer), Robert Day (Director), James Lee Barrett (Teleplay), Dick Bush (Photography), Jay Freund (Editor), Chester Kaczenski (Production Designer), Doug Leonard (Art Director), Barbara Weiss (Costume Designer), Kenny Meyers, Marilyn Poucher (Makeup), Steve Dorff (Music). Based on a novel by Louis L'Amour.

Cast: Sam Elliott (Con Vallian), Kate Capshaw (Susanna McKaskel), Tom Conti (Duncan McKaskel), Kenny Morrison (Tom McKaskel), Matt Clark (Doc Shabitt), Patrick Kilpatrick (The Ute), Jerry Potter (Red Hayle), Billy Streater (Ike Mantle), Del Shores (Purdy Mantle), R.L. Tolbert (Johnny Dobbs), Jeffrey M. Meyer (Butcher McCloud), Kurt D. Lott (Lenny Shabitt), Hardy Rawls (Joy), Larry Sellers (Running Wolf), Bill Stedman (Bartender).

Synopsis: In 1876 Wyoming, Susanna and Duncan McKaskel and son Tom are traveling in a covered wagon. Passing through a town, they meet Doc Shabitt, an unsavory character bent on attacking the family with his gang. A stranger alerts the McKaskels when Doc steals their horses. While retrieving them, Duncan is nearly shot in the back by Lenny Shabitt, Doc's son; the stranger has stepped in, unbeknownst to the others. Both Lenny and another member of the gang, Butcher McCloud, are then cut down.

Shabitt and his gang follow after the McKaskels. When another of the gang, Johnny Dobbs, goes for his gun against the stranger, he too is killed. Introducing himself as Con Vallian to the McKaskel family, the heroic stranger is especially outspoken about Susanna's beauty. This very much annoys her husband. Susanna is attracted to Con which soon leads to a lingering kiss. It comes after she uses a stick to beat another of Doc's men, Red Hayle, who lusts for her.

Con learns that the family is planning to meet Susanna's brother, an officer in Custer's Seventh Cavalry. But after crossing trails with a band of Sioux Indians, Con is told that Custer's entire regiment was killed at the Little Big Horn. Nonetheless, the McKaskels, originally from Pennsylvania, are determined to begin a new life in the West.

Feeling that Con is making his father look bad in front of his mother, Tom McKaskel shows his irritation. Liking the boy's spunk, Con takes him hunting only to be shot by the Ute, a half-breed riding with the Shabitt gang. Duncan and Susanna care for the injured Con.

The family's wagon load of furniture is abandoned due to its excessive weight slowing things down. As the Ute looks over the furniture, he is surprised by Con and shot down. But Doc and three other men are still after the McKaskels. Along with Red, there are brothers Ike and Purdy Mantle. The brothers had hoped to give up the chase but Doc and Red want revenge. Purdy finally does ride away.

Finding an abandoned cabin she likes, Susanna's desire to live there is accepted by Duncan. Despite her attraction for Con, she realizes she loves her husband.

When Doc and his partners ride up to the cabin, Susanna is forced to shoot Red. Ike is wounded by Duncan. Facing off against Doc, Duncan shoots him down. Con then saves Duncan from another backshooting when he finishes off Ike.

Sam Elliott and Kate Capshaw in a publicity pose for *The Quick and the Dead,* Sam's third Western based on a L'Amour novel.

As Con is ready to move on, he is surprised when Duncan hits him for the aggravation he caused at times. But Duncan, like Susanna, will always be grateful for his kindness. Biding farewell to the family, Con rides off to the high country.

Original Source: The novel *The Quick and the Dead.*

Plotline: Westward-bound are the McKaskels: Duncan, wife Susanna and 12-year-old son Tom. Helping them when Doc Shabbitt and his gang threaten is a stranger named Con Vallian.

Doc's men include Red Hyle, brothers Purdy and Ike Mantle and an especially

This television ad for *The Quick and the Dead* highlights its three stars.

resourceful Huron Indian. When the Huron injures Con, Arapahoe Indians come to his aid during the series of mishaps which befall the McKaskel family.

Commentary: In 1973, Bantam published L'Amour's novel *The Quick and the Dead*. As in *Down the Long Hills*, villains chase after a family through the wilderness.

The film version was initially telecast as *Louis L'Amour's The Quick and the Dead* by the HBO cable network on February 23, 1987. Joseph Cates, whose production company worked with HBO on the project, served as executive producer.

The family's struggle was the strong point of both film and novel. Many characters were involved and thus many character changes. The Ute in the TV movie and his counterpart the Huron in Louis's book are both deadly trackers, wounding hero Con Vallian, but their fates leave vastly different impressions of each Indian. The Ute is shot down without mercy by Vallian in a moment quite unexpected; *Variety* referred to it as "a grim, striking event." The half-breed had been tracked by Con for 300 miles to open the film. The reason is because the Ute led a raid which killed Con's mother, a Blackfoot Indian. (Vallian is a half-breed in this version.) L'Amour makes the Huron a better woodsman than even the skilled Vallian. In the course of the story, the Indian comes to respect the stranger and the family. Thus is revealed a change of heart for L'Amour's Huron which undoubtedly proves his own salvation.

In the TV movie, Shabitt's name has only one "b" in it, unlike the novel's two. Doc is finally stopped in the film by Duncan McKaskel, while Louis has Susanna, his equally resourceful spouse, deciding the gang leader's fate. Con has no choice in the film but to shoot gang member Johnny Dobbs; the same character survives in the book.

The only gang member to survive the film's action, Purdy Mantle, becomes a target for fellow member Red Hyle in the novel. (Red's last name in the movie is Hayle.) L'Amour creates tension between Purdy and Red in his novel over just who is better with a gun.

Gang member Booker McCutcheon, hit with a stick by Susanna in the novel and later eliminated, is not part of the film. Instead the situation with the stick, or club, is between Susanna and Red. Red dies at Susanna's hand in the movie; Con gets the job done in the book. An additional bad guy faces elimination at different times in novel and movie. In the novel he is Boston Pangman and in the film he is Butcher McCloud.

Con refers to the Indians as Sioux when their trails cross in the TV movie; Louis has them being Arapahoe and they also play a larger part in the story. Injured badly in the thigh by the Huron in Louis's story, Con's recovery is due to the care he receives from the Arapahoe Indians. After he is shot in the chest by the Ute in the film, Con is saved when Duncan removes the bullet with the help of Tom and Susanna.

In each version, Con Vallian is a bit of a rascal, although an amiable one, regarding his attraction to Susanna. In the TV movie a kiss is involved, as well as a wonderfully sly grin when they say farewell.

The terrific chemistry between Kate Capshaw's Susanna and Sam Elliott's Con is one of *The Quick and the Dead*'s highlights. Although Louis wrote his story over 14 years earlier, it seemed tailor-made for Sam, whose performance was called "marvelous" by *DVD & Video Guide*. Another highlight was his fine horsemanship, with rider and horse seeming as one. "Mr. Elliott has developed into the niftiest cowboy this side of John Wayne and Walter Brennan," beamed the *New York Times* in its review of the Western.

Following his previous L'Amour adventure, *The Shadow Riders*, the actor co-starred with Cher in *Mask* (1985). Elliott also played Sam Houston in the 1986 TV movie *Houston: The Legend of Texas* (and later retitled *Gone to Texas*).

Both motion pictures and television offered starring roles for the stunning Kate Capshaw. The actress was in *Missing Children: A Mother's Story* for CBS-TV in '82, and one of her most memorable roles was as Willie Scott in 1984's *Indiana Jones and the Temple of Doom*. She later married that film's director, Steven Spielberg.

Her TV husband in *The Quick and The Dead*, Scottish-born actor Tom Conti, gave acclaimed performances in 1982's *Merry Christmas, Mr. Lawrence* and 1984's *Reuben, Reuben*. For the latter, Conti received an Oscar nomination as Best Actor.

Kenny Morrison, who played the young son quite well, later (1988–90) had a recurring role on the TV series *Growing Pains.* He was also Atreyu in 1990's *The Neverending Story II: The Next Chapter.*

A familiar actor to Western fans, and a good one, was Matt Clark. His movie roles included one of the vile Quints in 1968's *Will Penny* and Bob Younger in 1972's *The Great Northfield Minnesota Raid.* Clark played Buffalo Bill in a 1974 TV film called *This Is the West That Was.*

While Clark was the sly leader of the bad guys in this Western, the meanest of the bunch was played by Jerry Potter. A couple of his other TV Western films were with James Arness: *The Alamo, 13 Days to Glory* (1987) and *Red River* (1988).

Flavorful commentary can be found on *The Quick and the Dead*'s DVD from director Robert Day. He errs when saying that Larry Sellers played the Ute, who was actually played by Patrick Kilpatrick. Sellers was seen, however, as Running Wolf, the Sioux leader. Day's past directorial work included several Tarzan films, including one of the very best, 1960's *Tarzan the Magnificent* starring Gordon Scott. He also worked on the script for that movie. His television work included 1983's *Cook and Peary: The Race to the Pole.*

One of the better-known Western film writers, James Lee Barrett, wrote the teleplay. Barrett's screenplays included 1968's *Bandelero* for Dean Martin and Jimmy Stewart and 1969's *The Undefeated* for John Wayne and Rock Hudson. He also wrote the teleplay for the 1986 remake of *Stagecoach.*

Interesting background information was added by Barrett although initiated somewhat by L'Amour's original story. Louis's capture of Duncan by the gang results in a few lies to prevent his death, including one about a brother of his in the U.S. Army who will ride against the gang with troopers. Barrett has Susanna's brother, John, as a lieutenant serving with Custer in information shared with Con by the family.

The McKaskel family was reflective of the influx of settlers converging on the Indian lands, and which resulted in the confrontations between the Indians and soldiers protecting the settlers. Among the army officers planning action against both Sioux and Cheyenne forces was Lt. Colonel George Armstrong Custer. Apparently disobeying orders, Custer divided his troops of some 600 men and was attacked on June 25, 1876, near Montana's Little Bighorn River. Reports varied on the number of men killed with Custer and the number of Indians involved. *The Almanac of American History* relates that 250 soldiers died and between 2,000 to 4,000 Indians were united.

Striking Arizona locations filled in for the Wyoming setting on *The Quick and the Dead.* According to its director, the opening scenes set in the town of Bender's Flat were filmed outside Flagstaff, Arizona, and the colorful mountains were filmed in Sedona.

Another Western film with the same title came out in 1995. The players included Sharon Stone and Gene Hackman. But it was not based on the L'Amour novel.

The 1990s

Conagher

1991. A Turner Pictures–Imagine Entertainment Presentation.
On TNT Television.
150 Minutes/Color.

Credits: John Kuri (Producer), Reynaldo Villalobos (Director), Jeffrey M. Meyer, Sam Elliott, Katharine Ross (Teleplay), James H. Bagdonas (Photography), Zach Staenberg (Editor), Robert P. Benton (Production Designer), Joseph C. Fama, John A. Frick (Art Directors), Luster Bayless (Costume Designer), Melanie Hughes (Makeup), J.A.C. Redford (Music). Based on a novel by Louis L'Amour.

Cast: Sam Elliott (Conn Conagher), Katharine Ross (Evie Teale), Barry Corbin (Charlie McCloud), Billy Green Bush (Jacob Teale), Ken Curtis (Seaborn Tay), Paul Koslo (Kiowa Staples), Gavan O'Herlihy (Chris Mahler), James Parks (Curly), Daniel Quinn (Johnny McGivern), Pepe Serna (Pete Casuse), Buck Taylor (Tile Coker), Dub Taylor (Station Agent), Cody Braun (Laban Teale), Anndi McAfee (Ruthie Teale), James Gammon (Smoke Parnell), Richard Jury (Tom Webb), Jeffrey M. Meyer (Beaver Sampson), R.L. Tolbert (Ben Logan), Angelique L'Amour (Stage Passenger).

Synopsis: Traveling west from Missouri are the Teales: Jacob, wife Evie and their children, Laban and Ruthie. Leaving his family at a cabin, Jacob sets out to buy cattle. But along the trail he has an accident and dies, with the family unaware of it.

A stagecoach pulls up to the cabin driven by Charlie McCloud. Offered work to run a station stop from her place while another one is being built, Evie accepts. Laban will be the hostler. When McCloud and the stage come again with supplies for Evie, riding shotgun is Kiowa Staples. Sporting a black eye from a fistfight with a cowboy named Conn Conagher, Staples plans to kill him. Also wearing a shiner, Conagher and two other cowpokes, Chris Mahler and Johnny McGivern, later bring horses for the stage line to Evie's corral. Evie is attracted to Conn, and Laban is taken with his kind advice.

Moving on after a meal, the three cowboys take more horses to another station stop. When stage passengers arrive at her place, Evie admits her concern that Jacob is probably dead, which upsets Ruthie. After a band of Apaches attack the Teale home, Evie and Laban hold them off until another stage arrives. Everyone helps and the Indians are driven away by morning.

Stopping at yet another stage stop, Conagher trades rifles taken from fighting Apaches. After he leaves, Kiowa Staples appears, riding with outlaw leader Smoke Par-

Watching Sam Elliott on horseback was always a pleasure. He is pictured here in the title role in *Conagher.*

nell. Both Laban and Ruthie work hard with their mother and are a great comfort to her. Yet Evie is lonesome for a man and ties notes to tumbleweeds blowing by.

Riding onto the ranch of Seaborn Tay, Conagher finds a winter job. Also working there are Chris and Johnny. Conagher later rounds up some of the rancher's cattle being driven along by Tile Coker, who is part of Parnell's Ladder Five outfit. Apparently Chris, and even Johnny, are aware of it.

Charlie McCloud brings word to Evie that she will soon be out of a job with the new station set to open. Concerned for the family's welfare, he plans to stop by to help whenever he can. Meantime, Conagher begins finding Evie's notes on tumbleweeds but he is unaware that she is the writer.

Although he admits to Conagher that he is too old to hunt down rustlers, Tay also says he will fight them if they come after him. Conn and Chris argue over the rustling by the Ladder Five and it almost leads to a gunfight. Chris opts to leave the ranch, with Johnny staying.

After finding another of Evie's notes on a tumbleweed, Conagher stirs things up with Parnell by spooking him with gunfire. The outlaw retaliates by having men attack Tay's ranch, and two are shot down by Seaborn and Conagher.

When Tile Coker and others rustle more of the cattle, they are trailed by Conagher. During a rainy night, Conagher stops by Evie's place for food and rest. Catching up to the rustlers, Conagher recovers the herd. With Laban's help, he drives it into town and sells it for Tay. Witnessing it is a drunken Chris Mahler.

After Laban returns home, Conagher is nearly killed by Kiowa Staples. Conagher rushes into Smoke Parnell's camp and shoots Staples when he again threatens. When an exhausted and hurt Conagher falls from his horse, Parnell might have killed him. Instead he respects his adversary and decides to clear out with his gang.

Seaborn wants Conagher to stay on the ranch, but he rides on. With Charlie McCloud's encouragement, Conagher visits Evie and the children to see how they made out over the winter. Chris later rides up and quarrels with Conagher.

Pushing on, Conagher stops in town and beats Chris in a fistfight. Standing there is Evie, wanting Conagher to return home to her and the children. Now knowing she put the notes on the tumbleweeds, Conagher walks off with her.

Original Source: The novel *Conagher.*

Plotline: Jacob Teale was a widower with young children, Laban and Ruth, when he married Evie and took them westward. An unforeseen tragedy for the family results in Evie and the youngsters struggling to survive. Helping them are stage driver Charlie McCloud and cowboy Conn Conagher.

Conagher has his hands full siding with rancher Seaborn Tay against Smoke Parnell's rustlers. Fellow cowboy Kris Mahler also causes trouble. Yet Conagher still finds time to daydream about mysterious notes found on passing tumbleweeds.

Commentary: Bantam Books first published this story about the life of an honest and hardworking cowboy in September 1969. *Conagher* was presented as a television movie, airing July 1, 1991, on the TNT cable network. It quite possibly was the best treatment of a Louis L'Amour novel.

There were differences between the two versions. Children Laban and Ruth Teale are not Evie's by blood in the novel; but she loves them as dearly as the film's heroine who is assumed to be their natural mother.

Unlike the film, book hero Conn Connagher finds the remains of Jacob Teale as well as the savings he was carrying. Conn's nemesis Kiowa Staples is a presence in both film and novel. For the film only, Staples rides with Smoke Parnell and his gang of rustlers. Seen in a flash, it appears that Staples is shot down rushing at Conagher in the night. L'Amour ends Kiowa's threat earlier in his story with a thorough beating.

Another of Parnell's riders, Curly, is in both versions. More aspects of his life are revealed by Louis. He has Curly's sister, Lucy, and their aunt stopping at Evie's stage station. Two ladies seen stopping together in the movie remain anonymous. Curly's fate is nonetheless changed for the better in both versions when he helps an injured Conagher. The book goes even further by showing him taking on honest work.

L'Amour has Tay in his forties, but the rancher says in the film that he's in his seventies. One of Tay's men in the book, Leggett, is in his sixties and has some of the dialogue given to the movie's Seaborn (alluding to being too old to chase after rustlers). Besides Leggett, another pivotal secondary character who was only part of the L'Amour novel, Chip Euston, is there to help after the fight is brought by the rustlers onto Tay's ranch.

Other than Conagher, Johnny McGivern is the only Tay hand in the film to aid the rancher. The novel's Kris Mahler (Chris for the movie) remains embittered in each for selling out not only Tay but his saddle pards, Johnny and Conn, to the rustling element. Rustler Tile Coker initially opens Conagher's eyes to Mahler's involvement.

One of the most enjoyable sequences of the TV movie comes when Conagher, Mahler, McGivern and the Teale family share a meal. Yet this is only one of the numerous occasions which pull at the heartstrings for genuine warmth and goodwill.

While she is seen tying a note to a tumbleweed in the film, Louis never actually shows Evie doing so. In both versions of *Conagher*, it is stage driver Charlie McCloud who informs Conagher that other cowboys are finding notes too. This reinforces the romantic image of the American cowboy whose loneliness equals that of the widow.

Not seen in the film are the book's cattlemen, Sam Catlin and his nephew John, who give calves to Evie in exchange for donuts. Also omitted is the last encounter with the Apaches where Conagher prevents trouble.

Other entries in the L'Amour filmography are reminiscent of *Conagher*, especially *Hondo*, with its own touching relationship between the title hero and Angie. *The Cherokee Trail*'s widow Mary also runs a stage stop.

"Clearly the Elliotts have taken pains to preserve the spirit of the novel," reflected the *New York Times*, "and they succeed splendidly in this handsome production." Sam Elliott and his wife, Katharine Ross, starred in the Western and helped write the teleplay with Jeffrey M. Meyer. Sam also served as executive producer.

A grand ad for TV's *Conagher,* highlighting both Sam Elliott and Katharine Ross. They not only starred together but worked on the script too.

Tenacity and tenderness have never been better conveyed in a Western than by Sam Elliott. *DVD & Video Guide* said, "Elliott seems to have been born to play cowboys." He was nominated for a Golden Globe as best actor in a miniseries. Golden Globe and Emmy nominations were given to Sam in the supporting actor category, for his Wild Bill Hickok in the 1995 miniseries *Buffalo Girls.* In 1993's *Tombstone,* he was seen as Wyatt Earp's brother, Virgil.

For 1976's *Voyage of the Damned,* Katharine Ross received a Golden Globe nomination as Best Actress in a Supporting Role. *The Legacy* (1979) marked the first time she actually co-starred with Sam on a film. Katharine's frontier widow in *Conagher* shows great inner resolve which never masks the gentleness within her. Yet she is quite capable of defending her family when needed.

Particularly solid support came from Barry Corbin, Ken Curtis and Gavan O'Herlihy. Corbin and O'Herlihy had roles in 1989's grand Western miniseries, *Lonesome Dove.* During '93 and '94, Corbin received Emmy nominations as supporting actor for the TV drama series *Northern Exposure.* Television fans may recall O'Herlihy as Ron Howard's big brother in the *Happy Days* comedy series during 1974.

The impressive list of Western film credits for Ken Curtis include 1956's *The Searchers* and 1960's *The Alamo.* At one time a singer with the Sons of the Pioneers, Ken had a fine voice which was also heard in those Westerns. He will be remembered best of all for the *Gunsmoke* series. Also on *Gunsmoke* was Buck Taylor as Newly O'Brien. Always a tremendous asset in Western roles, Buck played supporting parts in three earlier L'Amour stories: *The Sacketts, The Cherokee Trail* and *Down the Long Hills.* His father, Dub Taylor, was also seen in *Conagher*, manning one of the stage stations. During the 1940s, he played sidekick to such B Western stars as Russell Hayden and Wild Bill Elliott.

Others seen in earlier L'Amour entries were Paul Koslo from *The Sacketts* and Jeffrey M. Meyer and R.L. Tolbert from *The Quick and the Dead.* Koslo's past Westerns included Clint Eastwood's *Joe Kidd* (1972) and John Wayne's *Rooster Cogburn* (1975). In addition to playing a stage driver, Tolbert played a big part in the making of *Louis L'Amour's Conagher*: He was its second unit director and stunt coordinator.

Jeffrey M. Meyer, seen as one of the stage line's shotgun riders, must be commended too for his participation on the writing. He was probably better known as a director during the 1990s for the shows *Coach* and *Everybody Loves Raymond.* Director Reynaldo Villalobos, whose skill on *Conagher* was evident, was actually better known as a film and TV cinematographer. For TV he did the miniseries *Sinatra* in 1992; and for films, he did 1980's *Urban Cowboy* starring John Travolta.

New Mexico was the setting of the story, yet Colorado locations were utilized for the film. Both Roberts Cordova Ranch and Buckeye Joe's Park and Railway received screen credit.

At 1992's Western Heritage Awards, held at Oklahoma's National Cowboy and Western Heritage Museum, *Conagher* won the Bronze Wrangler award. And at the 2007 awards,

Elliott was honored with the Wrangler Award as one of the inductees for Great Western Performer.

The film *Conagher* was dedicated to the memory of Louis L'Amour. His daughter Angelique portrayed one of the stage passengers.

Shaughnessy: The Iron Marshal

1996. An Allumination Filmworks and Hill/Fields Entertainment Presentation.
In Association with Aces & Eights Productions.
95 Minutes/Color.

Credits: Beau L'Amour, Verne Nobles, Bernadette Caulfield, Ardythe Goergens (Producers), Michael Rhodes (Director), William Blinn (Executive Producer, Teleplay), Michael Fash (Photography), Geoffrey Rowland (Editor), Jonathan Carlson (Production Designer), John Roberts Zachary (Art Director), Richard E. Lamotte (Costume Designer), Ann Montesanto (Makeup), Joseph Conlan (Music). Based on a novel by Louis L'Amour.

Cast: Matthew Settle (Tom Shaughnessy), Linda Kozlowski (Marla), Sarah Paulson (Dorrie), Bo Hopkins (Rig Barrett), Tom Bower (Marshall), Michael Jai White (George Carpenter), John Carroll Lynch (Reverend), O'Neal Compton (Castle), Cari Shayne (Megan), Daragh O'Malley (Morrissey), Stuart Whitman (Vince Patterson), Velina Brown (Genelva Carpenter), Christopher Shaw (Danny Moran), Tim Grimm, John Hawkes, Michael Ray Wisely (Drako Brothers).

Synopsis: In 1870 New York City, Irish immigrant Tom Shaughnessy is supposed to throw an illegal prize fight for pub owner Morrissey. Instead, beating his opponent, he is shot at by Morrissey. The injured Shaughnessy is carried away by friends and put aboard a freight train.

Ending up in Kansas, Shaughnessy receives medical attention and then meets a supposedly dying patient, Rig Barrett. A lawman, Barrett has Shaughnessy travel to the town of Haven with the intention of turning his horse, weapons and gear over to George Carpenter.

After meeting saloon and brothel owner Marla, Shaughnessy is accused by the town of killing Barrett. With a note from the man, Shaughnessy manages to fool the townsfolk into believing he is Barrett's partner. Shaughnessy's initial duty when made town marshal is to take the badge away from Hank Drako. This Shaughnessy does in a fistfight with nearly the whole town looking on. To handle the paperwork which comes with the job, Shaughnessy has Dorrie, the assistant to schoolteacher Castle, teach him to read. She takes a liking to the Irishman. Drako's two brothers come to town after the new marshal. Shaughnessy outsmarts them and runs them off.

Admiring Shaughnessy's derby hat, Genelva Carpenter is trying it on when she is mistaken for him and killed by an assassin. Two small children are now without a mother. Discerning that Shaughnessy is an imposter, Marla informs the Drako boys. Back in New

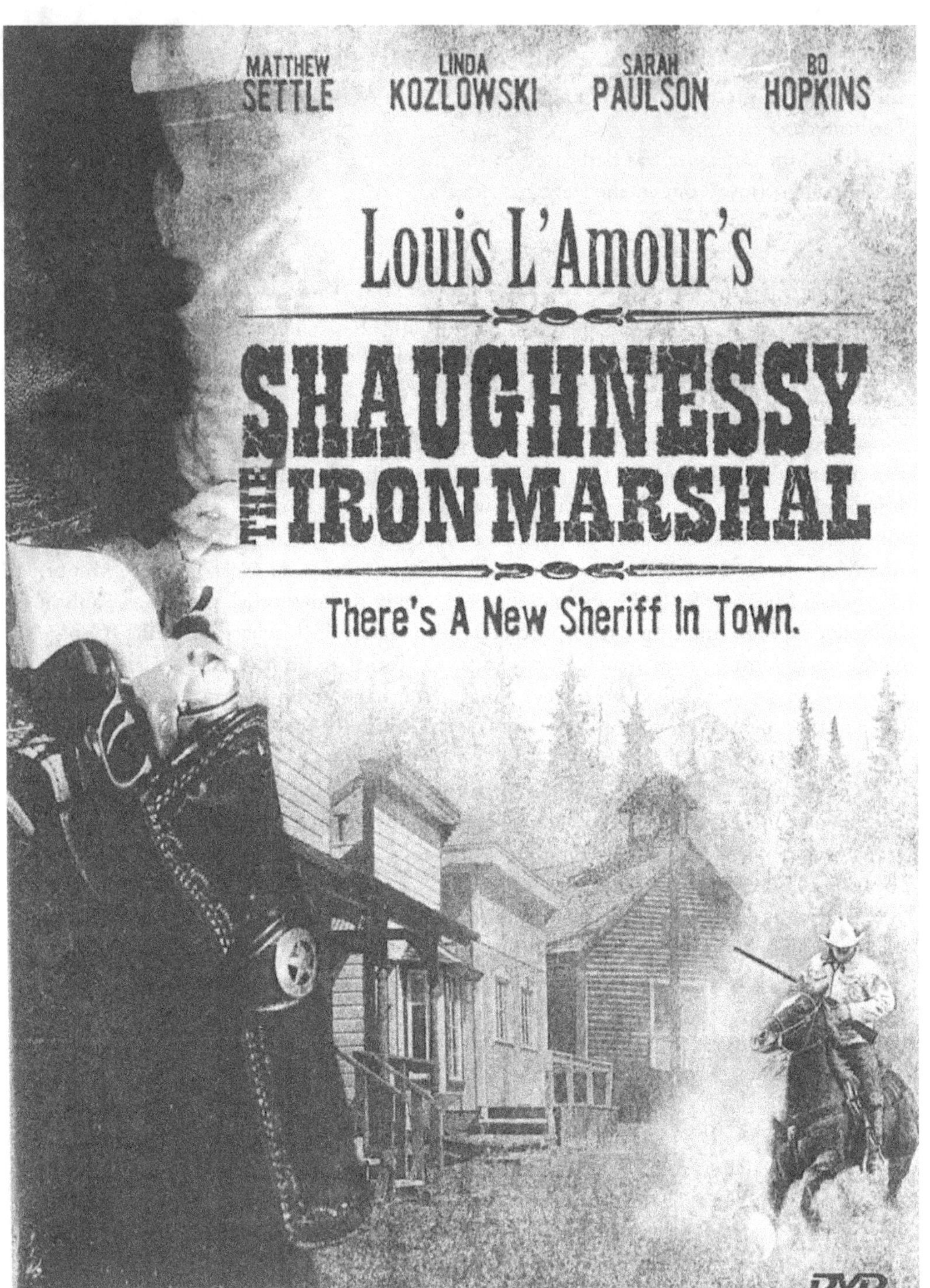

DVD advertisement for *Shaughnessy: The Iron Marshall.* Like *The Cherokee Trail* before it, the film was intended as a pilot for a television series.

York, Shaughnessy's friends Danny and Megan receive a letter from him written with Dorrie's help. Now aware Shaughnessy is still alive, Morrissey is determined to find out where he is.

With the town of Haven worried that cattleman Vince Patterson will want revenge for his son's death the year before, Shaughnessy pays him a visit out on the trail. But Vince is not hunting trouble and feels his no-good son got what he deserved. When Shaughnessy returns to town, all the folks know he is an imposter. The Drakos run him out of Haven. But Marla's bartender, Marshall, helps Shaughnessy. He also informs Shaughnessy about a train carrying $20,000 of the town's money for a new stockyard to entice the railroad to build a spur.

Suspecting the money could be stolen, Shaughnessy investigates. Sure enough, trying to steal it is none other than Rig Barrett. Stopping him, Shaughnessy also discovers that Barrett's partner killed Genelva Carpenter.

Taking his badge back from Hank Drako, Shaughnessy captures the killer: Castle the teacher. Not knowing that Morrissey has discovered his whereabouts, Shaughnessy seems to have found a new home in Haven.

Original Source: The novel *The Iron Marshal.*

Plotline: Involved in a war against the Childers gang, Tom Shanaghy is forced to flee New York City. Ending up in a small Kansas town, he becomes marshal, investigating the disappearance of Marshal Rig Barrett and trying to stop a robbery. Shanaghy also is accused of murder.

Among the shady locals are a mysterious blonde woman, the Drako gang, Helen Carpenter and Pin McBride. Allies are plentiful, however, and include Josh Lundy, Vince Patterson, Jan Pendleton and her brother Dick, who first helped Shanaghy when they were boys.

Commentary: The title of the film is *Louis L'Amour's Shaughnessy* but the DVD box cover has it subtitled *The Iron Marshal.* The latter was the title of Louis's 1979 novel for Bantam.

The hero's name was changed from Tom Shanaghy to Tom Shaughnessy for the film. In both novel and film, he immigrated to America from Ireland — with his mother at age 11 for the book, and age five for the movie with both parents and a sister.

Louis doesn't have Tom's mother survive the ship voyage over, and his father was earlier missing in action in British-occupied India. In the film, Shaughnessy mentions his folks dying of consumption some years ago and his sister then living with friends.

Fellow Irishman Morrissey is part of Tom's life in each version, in a good way in the novel and a bad way in the movie. Writer William Blinn (who was also the film's executive producer) created a good many variations between Louis's story and the film. Perhaps the most stunning to L'Amour fans is the movie's revelation that both Morrissey and Rig Barrett end up as enemies of the hero. In the novel, it is the Childers gang who try to kill, at the least maim, Tom rather than the film's Morrissey. The Childers are not part of the movie; and the book's upstanding Rig, whose presence is greatly felt, is never seen.

The New York City scenario, with its underworld atmosphere, was a nice surprise and perhaps even more so for those not acquainted with L'Amour's early pulp crime stories. Louis wrote detailed introductory scenes revolving around this aspect of the tale, but in the film they seem like mere filler to incite interest under the opening credits.

The problems between Shanaghy and the Childers begin in the book when his winning a horse race means that they lose heavily. For the film, the situation explodes with Morrissey when Shaughnessy wins the bare-knuckle fight, resulting in the loss of a substantial bet.

Shaughnessy, in the film is put on the freight train going west by pal Danny Moran, who is not part of the novel; neither is Shaughnessy's love in the city, Megan. In the book, Shanaghy is made to jump off the train by Pin McBride.

The great irony of the novel is, had Shanaghy not been forced from the train, he would not have been around to expose the gang of robbers that includes McBride. (L'Amour errs when first referring to him as Pin Brodie. Pin is not part of the film.)

While Mr. Carpenter is a blacksmith in both, he is a murder victim in the novel. L'Amour makes Helen, his wife, one of the story's most despicable figures. It is George Carpenter's wife Genelva who is the film's victim. One of the movie's most endearing figures, she is also its most tragic.

With the Carpenters having a little boy and girl in the film, the mother's death is totally unexpected. In *Shaughnessy*'s most touching sequence, the townsfolk speak warmly of her at the funeral. Incidentally, the family in the film is black.

Vince Patterson is not looking to avenge his son's death in the movie. In the book, he does initially want to punish the town for his brother's death. And in each instance, the deaths were caused by the marshal Hank Drako.

The Drakos, while troublesome in the film, are downright deadly in the book. Louis also errs when he introduces Drako with the first name Bert. Unlike in the film, the other members of the family are sons and not brothers.

A number of important supporting characters from the film are not part of L'Amour's story and vice versa. Missing from the novel are Marla, Dorrie, Marshall and Castle. Missing from the film are ranchhand Josh Lundy, townsmen Holstrum and Greenwood, and siblings Dick and Jan, who live on their father Alfred's ranch.

There is also an unnamed blonde in each. She appears to be one of Marla's working girls in the film. The blonde is given a far more substantial role in the book, as Shanaghy's icy nemesis.

Where Tom is not particularly adept with a gun in the film, he is very proficient with one in the book. Time and again he shows just *how* proficient, having been taught by a sharpshooter while running a shooting gallery in New York.

In both versions, Tom wears a derby. He is not an especially large man, but he does have incredible punching power. In the book, his fighting skills were enhanced by sparring with his mentor Morrissey, whose powerful influence in the city was due in no small part to being a bare-knuckle fighting champion.

While not having the same rugged qualities as L'Amour's creation, Matthew Settle gave a charming performance as the film's title hero; it was his first starring role. He was part of the stellar cast of 2005's miniseries *Into the West*; and in a 2004 TV entry, *The Mystery of Natalie Wood*, Settle portrayed actor Warren Beatty.

Linda Kozlowski, who played the sexy Marla, was the heroine in the three *Crocodile Dundee* movies made between 1986 and 2001. She also married their hero, Paul Hogan. The two were also together as well in 1990's *Almost an Angel.*

Listed as guest star for this Western was Bo Hopkins, playing another shifty character as he did in *Down the Long Hills*. In 1994, he was seen in yet another TV Western film, *Wyatt Earp: Return to Tombstone*, which brought back Hugh O'Brian as that legendary lawman.

A former Western star, Stuart Whitman lent great presence in his brief yet strong appearance as the decent cattleman. In 1961, he co-starred with John Wayne in *The Comancheros,* and also received an Oscar nomination as Best Actor for the drama *The Mark.*

Director Michael Rhodes directed and produced television's *Christy* series during the 1990s. In 1988, he directed an episode of *Star Trek: The Next Generation* as well as an episode of the Western series *Paradise.*

For Disney's *Davy Crockett* miniseries in the 1980s, William Blinn served the same double duty as he did on *Shaughnessy: The Iron Marshal.* Between 1967 and 1971, he wrote three episodes of *Gunsmoke.* Blinn was a story consultant in 1966 for the short-lived TV series version of *Shane.*

One of the producers of this 1996 Western was Beau L'Amour, Louis's son. Filming in California included the State Railroad Museum in Sacramento and the Red Hills Ranch in Sonora.

Although the movie was made as a pilot for a possible CBS series, it was not picked up. An original air date was not even determined for American viewers; the movie may have been shown initially in Australia. Eventually it surfaced on cable television. Comments then offered by viewers over the Internet included "an OK movie" and expected "a better story" due to its source.

Overall, while the film was enjoyable in part, it proved disappointing as a whole. Its aura of mystery involving conspirators Rig Barrett and Castle was rather tame except for Mrs. Carpenter's needless death. While L'Amour's story was really complicated, the red herrings he included, and the ruthless gang of conspirators going after an even greater sum of money aboard a train, bristled with his high level of energy.

Both versions highlighted the instances where the title hero is accused of wrongdoing in the fate of Rig Barrett. The suspense is generated when Tom is seen carrying one of the man's weapons. The witness is Holstrum in the novel and Marla in the film; she also happens to be Rig's sister in the film.

2001

Crossfire Trail

2001. A TNT Presentation.
A Michael Brandman Production in Association with TWS Productions II.
120 Minutes/Color.

Credits: Thomas Kane, Steven Brandman (Producers), Simon Wincer (Director), Charles Robert Carner (Teleplay), David Eggby (Photography), Terry Blythe (Editor), Roy Forge Smith (Production Designer), Janice Blackie-Goodine (Set Director), Elsa Zamparelli (Costume Designer), Gail Kennedy (Makeup), Eric Colvin (Music). Based on a novel by Louis L'Amour.

Cast: Tom Selleck (Rafe Covington), Virginia Madsen (Ann Rodney), Wilford Brimley (Joe Gill), David O'Hara (Rock Mullaney), Christian Kane (J.T. Langston), Barry Corbin (Sheriff Moncrieff), Brad Johnson (Bo Dorn), Mark Harmon (Bruce Barkow), Joanna Miles (Melissa Thompson), Ken Pogue (Gene Thompson), Patrick Kilpatrick (Mike Taggart), Rex Linn (Luke Taggart), William Sanderson (Pee Wee), Daniel Parker (Wylie), Marshall Teague (Snake Corville), James Nicholas (Red Cloud), Carmen Moore (Dancing Flower), Mark Acheson (Captain Gorgan), Michael O'Shea (Charles Rodney).

Synopsis: In 1880, aboard a ship off the coast of California, Rafe Covington makes a promise to the dying Charles Rodney. After beating up the captain responsible for Charles' death, Rafe and shipmates Rock Mullaney and J.T. Langston jump ship.

While Rock ventures on to Montana, Rafe and J.T. go to Charles' ranch in Wyoming and stay in the abandoned ranch house. Charles' widow Ann, now living in town, learns that Rafe was sent by him. When gunman Snake Corville claims that Charles was killed by a Sioux raiding party, Rafe calls him a liar. Saloon owner Bruce Barkow restrains Snake to prevent gunplay.

Rafe is joined by Joe Gill, who used to work for Charles. Finding an injured Indian woman, Rafe helps her, thereby incurring the wrath of the brothers Mike and Luke Taggart. But they are run off by Rafe and Joe.

Barkow wants Ann to marry him. Unbeknownst to her, Snake and the Taggarts work for him. Rafe surmises that Bruce wants both Ann and her ranch. Rejoining his friends on the ranch is Rock Mullaney.

Rafe tells Ann that her husband died only six weeks earlier and not the year before as attested to by Barkow. Bruce tries to convince Ann that Rafe is the liar. Visiting the ranch, Ann is told that Charles wanted Rafe to look out for her and the place, but she is still reluctant to believe him. Later, Rafe states that Charles was shanghaied by a freighter's captain and fatally beaten trying to escape. This was after Charles had sold holdings in San Francisco to pay off the ranch's mortgage.

Challenged to a gunfight by Mike Taggart, Rafe is forced to kill him. Attempting to ambush Rafe, Snake is shot down too. Barkow sends for professional gunfighter Bo Dorn.

Oil under the ranch is the reason Barkow wants it. Holding the mortgage, and lying

Crossfire Trail was Tom Selleck's third Western based on L'Amour's work.

about it not being paid, he tells Rafe to vacate the premises. When he arrives in town, Dorn makes himself an equal partner in sharing the spoils with a reluctant Barkow. Dorn knows Barkow had Charles shanghaied. While Ann and Rafe realize they have fallen in love, Dorn murders J.T. Langston. In his desperation to keep all her land, Barkow forces Ann to marry him. Pee Wee, his bartender, tries to stop him, but he is murdered by Barkow.

Rafe, Joe and Rock ride into town to confront their enemies. Walter Moncrieff, the worthless sheriff, wants no part of the fighting and leaves town. During the raging gun battle, storekeeper Gene Thompson stands with Gill and Mullaney to help defeat the enemy forces. Rock shoots down Luke Taggart.

After killing Dorn, Rafe is nearly killed by Barkow, but Ann saves his life by shooting the man. Rafe and Ann join their friends.

Original Source: The novel *Crossfire Trail.*

Plotline: A shanghaied Rafe Caradec promises a dying shipmate, Charles Rodney, to aid his (Charles') wife and daughter on their ranch. Fellow shipmates Tex Brisco, Roy Penn and Rock Mullaney offer support, as do cowboys Johnny Gill and Bo Marsh.

There is trouble on the ranch when Rafe is caught between ranchers Dan Shute and Bruce Barkow, who is engaged to Rodney's daughter Ann. Backing them are quick-on-the-draw men like Gee Bonero, Trigger Boyne and the Blazer brothers.

Commentary: The L'Amour novel *Crossfire Trail* was published by Ace Books in 1954 and republished by Bantam in 1983. But the story actually first appeared as a magazine novel (in the July 1948 issue of *West*) under the title "The Trail to Crazy Man." In 1986, Bantam published this yarn in a book of the same name which included two other L'Amour stories.

"It was 'Crazy Woman' in the original story I turned in," said Louis, "but the editor decided he preferred to call it 'Crazy Man.'" In *Crossfire Trail,* both novel and film, the Rodney cabin and range are again referred to as the Crazy Woman Ranch. L'Amour depicts it at the head of a canyon and along a creek, both bearing the same name.

While the book doesn't expand the magazine story, there are slight differences between Louis's stories (some of the wording; also, the initial magazine tale had more chapters compared to the later novel's fewer but longer ones). There are *substantial* differences between the L'Amour story and the 2001 film's teleplay by Charles Robert Carner. They begin with the name of the central hero Rafe Covington; in the novel he is called Rafe Caradec. Ann is Charles Rodney's wife in the film while Louis makes the heroine his daughter. Carol is the name of the wife in Louis's story.

Unlike the novel, Rafe is not shanghaied in the film but working his way down the Pacific coast. The mutiny in each version takes place following Rodney's fatal beating; the ship's captain is called Gorgan in the film and Bully Borger in the novel.

Rafe's shipmates Tex Brisco and Roy Penn are not part of the TV movie and J.T. Langston is not in the book. Rock Mullaney is in both. Langston seems to be the counterpart for L'Amour's cowboy Bo Marsh, simply because they end up being shot on the ranch by their enemies. Bo survives. The book's other cowboy, Johnny Gill, becomes the much older ranch hand Joe Gill for the movie.

The book's pivotal characters Dan Shute and Pod Gomer are not included in the film. Their screen counterparts are Bo Dorn and Sheriff Moncrieff. While hired killer Dorn and rancher Shute challenge associate Bruce Barkow's authority, the rancher's actions against him bear far greater weight. Moncrieff, finally having a bellyful of everything, leaves town on his own unlike Gomer's lawman who needs more persuasion.

There is no wild slugfest between Dorn and Covington like the brutal encounter in the town of Painted Rock with Shute and Caradec. For the film, hero and villain stalk each other in a shootout around a corral.

Another big difference is Barkow's fate. He is stopped sooner than expected in the novel, and by one of his own ilk, which comes as a real surprise. Less surprising is Ann's shooting him in the film which seems reminiscent of Grace Kelly using a gun to save the life of Gary Cooper at the climax of 1952's *High Noon.*

All of the secondary villains get different names in the movie. The novel's Blazer brothers function somewhat as the Taggart boys in the film; the movie's Mike Taggart and Snake Corville stand in for the novel's Trigger Boyne and Gee Bonero when going against Rafe. A fear of Rafe by both Bonero and Boyne heightens the novel's tension; their screen counterparts are unafraid. The bartenders in each version meet unfortunate fates — good guy Pee Wee is killed by his boss Barkow in the movie, and Shute supporter Joe Benson is slain by the book's rancher.

The Indians have a more substantial role to play during the course of the novel; they are only seen in the first part of the film. The injured Indian maiden Dancing Flower is Sioux leader Red Cloud's daughter in the TV movie. In the book, she remains unnamed and her father is Man Afraid of His Hoss (or Horse in "Trail to Crazy Man").

The Oglala Sioux did historically have prominent leaders named Red Cloud and Old-Man-Afraid-of-His-Horses. As related in L'Amour's story, there were Indian attacks over trespassing on land and atrocities to Indians. They occur here prior to the film's 1880 setting. Both the aforementioned leaders were present for the 1868 Fort Laramie peace treaty. Despite the disbanding of some military forts, a lasting peace was not maintained. Other Sioux leaders like Crazy Horse and Sitting Bull retaliated against military and civilian encroachment.

TV Guide called *Crossfire Trail* a "predictable cable Western." *Variety* felt it was "beautifully adapted," and "capitalizes on a restrained performance from Tom Selleck." The actor, also an executive producer on the film, gave rewarding performances in all his Western roles. As Rafe Covington, he certainly stands tall in size and values, and rides in a way that makes him seem born to the saddle.

Along with his three L'Amour entries, Tom starred in the television Westerns *Last Stand at Saber River* (1997) and *Monte Walsh* (2003).

Director Simon Wincer also directed him in 1990's Australia-set frontier adventure *Quigley Down Under.* Wincer, also a co-executive producer on *Crossfire Trail,* helmed

1989's wonderfully received *Lonesome Dove* miniseries and its 2008 prequel *Comanche Moon*. For the big screen he directed the 1996 adventure, *The Phantom*.

This Western's strong yet vulnerable heroine, Ann Rodney, was played by the elegant Virginia Madsen. She portrayed movie star Marion Davies in her very first TV movie, *The Hearst and Davies Affair* (1985). The actress, known for her diversity, co-hosted (with Robert Stack) the *Unsolved Mysteries* series during the 1998–99 TV season. The Academy of Science Fiction, Fantasy & Horror Films voted her best actress for the film *Candyman* (1992).

Despite his heroic persona on the *NCIS* television series, Mark Harmon's diversity as an actor also made him believable as a charming yet chilling villain. Along with his role as the scoundrel in *Crossfire Trail*, he was Kevin Costner's nemesis Johnny Behan in 1994's *Wyatt Earp*. Harmon received an Emmy nomination in the supporting actor category for his performance as Robert Dunlap in *Eleanor and Franklin: The White House Years* (1977).

Wilford Brimley began his film career riding horses as an extra and doing stunt work in the 1960s. Here he gives an engaging performance as Tom Selleck's sidekick; they also both appeared in 1983's *High Road to China*. Brimley's other roles included Governor Lew Wallace in the TNT Western *Gore Vidal's Billy the Kid* (1989) starring Val Kilmer.

Playing a professional gunman, Brad Johnson displayed both panache and menace. The former rodeo cowboy's other television jobs included the title role in 1994's *Siringo*. He was also with Sam Elliott in the 1997 TNT miniseries *Rough Riders*.

Seen to better advantage in their earlier L'Amour outing were *Conagher*'s Barry Corbin and *The Quick and the Dead*'s Patrick Kilpatrick. Here, their characters offer almost a comic respite from a serious situation: Corbin's sheriff (during the climactic gun battle) has whiskey bottles shot up around him; Kilpatrick is a troublemaker whose drunken rage leaves him dead and missing a boot.

In addition to these quirky touches, the Western benefited most vividly from the use of Calgary locations. Both a writer and director, Charles Robert Carner's TV credits included the Jon Voight film *The Fixer* (1998), and the 1990–91 series *Midnight Caller*. He also wrote the screenplay for a 1986 motion picture featuring Mark Harmon, *Let's Get Harry*.

When *Crossfire Trail* premiered on the TNT channel on January 21, 2001, the *New York Times* reported that it "was watched in 7.7 million homes," at the time "the largest audience ever for an original movie shown on cable." Like *Conagher* before it, the television film received a Bronze Wrangler at the 2002 Western Heritage Awards. Although the better film, *Conagher* only touched on a romantic triangle developing between widow Evie and cowboys Conn and Mahler. Far more intense, since it plays a major role, is the triangle with Ann, Rafe and Barkow.

The most intricate aspect of both film and novel is the way Ann's relationship with Barkow is played out. The movie's forced marriage substitutes for her willingly going away with him initially in the book.

The Diamond of Jeru

2001. A Michael R. Joyce Production.
Distributed by USA Cable Entertainment.
120 Minutes/Color.

Credits: Beau L'Amour, Michael R. Joyce (Executive Producers), Dick Lowry, Ian Barry (Directors), Beau L'Amour (Teleplay), Stephen F. Windon (Photography), Tod Feuerman (Editor), Nicholas McCallum (Production Designer), Jennifer O'Connell (Art Director), Sally Campbell (Costume Designer), Tess Natoli (Makeup & Hair Supervisor), Christopher Tyng (Music). Based on a story by Louis L'Amour.

Cast: Billy Zane (Mike Kardec), Paris Jefferson (Helen Lacklan), Keith Carradine (John Lacklan), Jackson Raine (Raj), Khoa Do (Dyak Boy), Peter Carroll (Clifton Vandover), Wi Kuki Ka (Inghai), Piripi Waretini (Jeru), David Webb (Fairchild), Stefan Abeydeera (Ishan Patel), Christopher Stevenson (Maddox), Ken Radley (Dozer Driver), Lorna Lesley (Jenny Vandover), Tae Allison (Raj's Girlfriend).

Synopsis: In the wilds of Borneo, adventurer Mike Kardec attempts to fight off enemies trying to rob and kill him. Swept over a waterfall, he is rescued by friendly Penan tribesmen.

Later working on a construction site, Kardec and pal Raj are fired after fighting with another worker. Local official Clifton Vandover approaches Kardec about a job helping a scientist on a diamond search.

When Kardec meets fellow American John Lacklan and his wife Helen, he learns they are looking for a diamond to fit her wedding ring to rekindle their marriage. The scientist, rigid in his ways, acts put back by Kardec having been upriver before and losing diamonds. Nonetheless, Kardec introduces the couple to a jeweler who shows them samples of what can be found. Preparations are then set in motion for an expedition.

John's jealousy soon gets the better of him over an innocent attraction shared between his wife and Kardec. Firing Kardec, he then hires a Dyak native boy to take them upriver.

Concerned about a headhunter named Jeru enticing tourists to their deaths with a big diamond, Kardec is convinced by Vandover to follow the expedition. Raj and his grandfather Inghai accompany Kardec.

Several Dyaks, including the native boy, are with the Lacklans. John becomes upset with them when personal belongings are searched. Aware of Kardec's presence, and fearful of the natives, Helen shares her concerns with her husband. Not caring about the diamonds, she had only wanted the trip to bring them closer together.

Inghai is killed by the Dyak boy and the natives take the Lacklans captive. Following them to Jeru's compound, Kardec and Raj see that the grandfather was beheaded. John will be the next victim despite Helen's protests.

Destroying the compound, Kardec and Raj rescue the Lacklans. But Jeru, the Dyak boy, and other natives chase after them.

Using the natives' superstitions against them, the rescuers detonate a fiery explosion

The stars are highlighted on the DVD cover for ***The Diamond of Jeru.*** Billy Zane particularly captured the spirit of Louis L'Amour's early short story adventurers like Ponga Jim Mayo and Turk Madden.

in a cave with bats flying out. Only Jeru and the Dyak boy remain as the rest flee in fear. Although wounded, Kardec beats Jeru in their ensuing fight. To save Kardec's life, Raj kills the Dyak boy.

Reaching the coast, the four survivors are picked up by a passing boat. Helen and Kardec share a parting kiss when she leaves with her husband. Yet Kardec plans to return to America as well, having taken from Jeru the big diamond.

Original Source: The short story "The Diamond of Jeru."

Plotline: Kardec is a down-on-his-luck American living in Borneo. His prospects get worse when Americans John and Helen Lacklan replace him with local natives to search for diamonds. Worried about the couple, Kardec and Raj, his houseboy, follow them. Natives and their leader, Jeru, pose a deadly threat.

Commentary: After Louis's passing, son Beau found in a box of papers the unpublished "The Diamond of Jeru." In a 2000 Bantam compilation of L'Amour short stories, *Off the Mangrove Coast,* this tale was included.

On November 6 of the following year, this film was televised on the USA Network as *Louis L'Amour's The Diamond of Jeru.* Beau L'Amour wrote the teleplay and was also an executive producer. While the gist of his father's story made it to the screen, there were interesting alterations. The film takes place in 1955 Borneo while the actual short story does not specify a year. Neither Kardec or official Vandover are given first names by Louis, unlike the film's Mike and Clifton. Coming to Borneo for diamonds, Kardec in the short story recalls losing them in the river. He also loses the gems in the film's river fight. Both versions show that the hero has an interest in literature, particularly a novel by Norman Douglas titled *South Wind.*

While a physicist in the film, John is a government administrator (at least according to Kardec) in the L'Amour tale; John also mentions having built weapons capable of destroying the island. Involvement with the atom bomb is mentioned in each account. A young man in the TV movie, Kardec's sidekick Raj is only sixteen in the short story. Only his mother is a Penan in the story while he is a Sea Dyak.

Also a Sea Dyak native in the short story is Jeru, described as an old, thin man with a scar on his face. The movie depicts him as a younger man, and huge in size. In both he is most formidable with the parang, the blade he uses in his headhunting rituals.

A native belief discussed in both versions, even felt to some extent by Raj, is the fear of the mountain and forest spirits known as the Toh. A highlight of film and short story is the use of bats from these places to create that fear.

While there is only a brief nod to an islander called Inghai by Louis, he is a key character in the film. As Raj's doomed grandfather, he is its most sympathetic figure. His severed head is the only one depicted here. (A number of heads hang in Jeru's longhouse in the short story; they belong to poor souls not part of the lives of the couple or their rescuers.)

The most riveting action in each version is the battle at the longhouse. The mayhem as Kardec and Raj risk their lives to save the Lacklans may move at too furious a pace for viewers to absorb it all.

In the movie, other Dyak natives have joined Jeru; L'Amour has outcasts of various tribes as his followers. The Dyak boy in the film is revealed to be Jeru's nephew; his counterpart in the story has a somewhat smaller role to play but is still a dangerous threat. While Raj slays the movie's Dyak boy with a parang, in the story a little roughing-up by Kardec proves sufficient. As for Jeru, in both versions he takes a sound beating from the hero. A particularly touching moment occurs in the movie when Helen reveals to John that their time with each other is what matters to her and not any diamonds.

Farewell kisses are shared in both versions by Kardec and Helen. And in the short story, Kardec reveals a deeper feeling when he openly admits that she was the reason he followed the couple upriver. While the film concludes with him displaying the diamond of Jeru to Vandover, the moment is shared with Helen in the L'Amour tale. In both instances, Kardec reveals that the diamond was taken after defeating Jeru.

There is a real romantic chemistry in the TV film between Billy Zane's Kardec and Paris Jefferson's Helen that comes not from anything said but simply from exchanging glances. Still, its finest asset is an old-fashioned sense of adventure. This old-fashioned quality, however, was not as appreciated as it should have been. *TV Guide* said the movie "doesn't aim high," and *Variety* found it "surprisingly flat." "If Kardec became a franchise character," *Variety* added, "Zane's rogue attitude and good looks would make for a potentially watchable small-screen hero." (*The Diamond of Jeru* wasn't intended as a pilot for any series.)

Intended as the start of a film franchise had it clicked at the box office was Zane's *The Phantom* in 1996. In the title role, he seemed the perfect embodiment of the comic strip hero. Movie fans may remember Zane best as one of the great screen villains in 1997's blockbuster *Titanic.*

During 2000, a stunning actress Paris Jefferson had a recurring role as the goddess Athena on the series *Xena: Warrior Princess.* In a 1993 TV movie, *Tales from a Darkened Room: Ball and Chain,* she played Janis Joplin.

A member of that versatile family of performers, Keith Carradine managed to make his edgy character into a vulnerable human being. His song "I'm Easy" from the 1975 movie *Nashville* won him an Academy Award. His many acting roles also include Bigfoot Wallace in *Dead Man's Walk,* the 1996 miniseries and prequel to *Lonesome Dove*'s adventures. Carradine wasn't the only family member to be part of a film based on material from Louis L'Amour. His father John was in *Stranger on Horseback* and his brother David in *Taggart.*

As Raj, Jackson Raine sported short pants on the journey with Kardec. Yet in Louis's story, Kardec made it clear, at least to the Lacklans, not to wear short pants because of the leeches found in Borneo.

Queensland, Australia, substituted in the film for the island of Borneo, which is part of both Malaysia and Indonesia. In fact, the Indonesians refer to the island as Kalimantan, which means River of Diamonds. Whereas story and film utilized the name Dyak for a contingent of the natives, the majority of the islanders are called Dayaks.

Having two directors (Ian Barry and Dick Lowry) on *The Diamond of Jeru* undoubtedly made things easier on the rugged Gold Coast locations. Barry's other work in Australia during 2001 included a series called *Farscape*. He also helmed a television movie, *Flight of the Reindeer*, in 2000. The miniseries *Attila*, also on the USA Network in 2001, was another directorial achievement for Lowry.

The Diamond of Jeru was only the second feature-length film of L'Amour's work that isn't a Western. The first, *East of Sumatra*, also took advantage of an exotic setting that was part of the author's own early adventures. Beau L'Amour deserves a great deal of credit for adapting his father's story and helping to produce the film when Western stories had been the norm. As vice-president of Louis L'Amour Enterprises, Beau worked diligently with Bantam Books to bring forth other previously unpublished stories for Louis's fans.

In the twenty years following his passing, over 100 million of his books have been sold. And some 300 million since about 1955. About four million audio cassettes have sold since 1988 through Random House Audio Publishing. Some of the stories in this filmography are on audio cassette, including *The Daybreakers* and *Sackett* (the basis for *The Sacketts*). There are even selected stories on cassette (read by Keith Carradine) from Bantam's initial publication of *With These Hands*.

Epilogue

In a 2004 poll by the Western Writers of America, Louis L'Amour was ranked #4 of the 25 names on the list of best authors. (Although Elmer Kelton, Willa Cather and A.B. Guthrie, Jr., were certainly not as commercially successful as Louis had been, their names headed the list in that order.) The Western Writers, however, did not make the selections based on popularity, or else Louis would have topped the list. While the top three choices may be a bit surprising to readers, the Western Writers are highly respected.

Louis's *Down the Long Hills* had been voted the best novel for 1968 by the Western Writers. The story's structure and characterization assuredly outweighed any popularity due to its author's name. Elmer Kelton was initially honored, like L'Amour, with this same Spur Award by the Writers for 1957's *Buffalo Wagons*. In later years, Kelton again won the award for his novels.

Kelton's Spur Award novels in respectively '71 and '73 were *The Day the Cowboys Quit* and *The Time It Never Rained.* In the Western Writers' 2004 listing of best novels, the latter title was #4 and the former #20. L'Amour's *Hondo* was #11 on this list.

Also on the list were A.B. Guthrie, Jr.'s novel *The Big Sky* (#3) and Willa Cather's *Death Comes for the Archbishop* (#7). Jack Schaefer's *Shane* was chosen as the best Western novel; he was #12 on the poll of authors.

The Western writer best-known by younger readers today is perhaps Larry McMurtry, #9 on the 2004 list of authors; his *Lonesome Dove* was ranked #2 on the poll of novels. Like L'Amour, he was not incapable of including Western clichés in his stories; despite not having the same massive body of work, however, McMurtry's work was given better overall treatment when turned into films. One effective non–Western was *Terms of Endearment*; the movie version won the Oscar for Best Picture of 1983.

Critics also tended to favor McMurtry partly because his novels were published in hardcover before becoming paperbacks. (L'Amour, who began his writing career with pulp magazine stories, made his mark later through the paperback market.) This is not to say that Louis never had his work published in hardcover; before Bantam, his very first novel *Westward the Tide* and *Guns of the Timberlands* were among those in hardcover. Bantam Books began publishing his work in hardcover rather late in Louis's career, starting in 1983 with the epic *The Lonesome Gods.*

L'Amour had previously felt that critics were labeling him as simply a Western writer because his stories were mainly printed in paperback. He once commented, "If you write a book about a bygone period that lies east of the Mississippi River, then it's a historical novel. If it's west of the Mississippi, it's a Western, a different category."

In his later years L'Amour was more popular with his readers, and eventually the critics began appreciating his abilities a little more despite the repetition still found in his stories. "The critics back east were finally reviewing his work," wrote Charles Leeshsen in *Newsweek,* "and praising his unpretentious, lean-as-a-grass-fed-steer style." "His attention to authenticity and detail," wrote *Esquire's* Ben Yagoda, "[was] probably the biggest reason for L'Amour's success."

While the historical and geographical reflections in his writing also found favor with the literary establishment, Louis simply never rested on his laurels. In the few years before his death, he stretched himself with several hardcover epic novels. Along with *The Lonesome Gods* and its frontier theme set in pre–Civil War California, they included *The Walking Drum* (1984), a twelfth century tale set in Europe and the Middle East, and a pair of modern-day adventures, *Last of the Breed* (1986) and *The Haunted Mesa* (1987). While the latter is set in Utah, its tale also dealt with the supernatural in an earlier century. It was Louis's final novel. *Last of the Breed* sold some 3.5 million copies in the ten years after Louis's passing, making it then his most successful book with Bantam.

Ideas for books kept coming to L'Amour. There were plans to expand on his family sagas — the seventeen novels about the Sacketts, as well as on the five about the Chantrys and three about the Talons. One novel would have elaborated on the Civil War experiences of his most famous Sackett of all, William Tell. In all some fifty books were planned about these families.

Among his greatest characteristics were his fortitude and humility. On the day he died in 1988, Louis was proofreading his autobiography. Despite his great fortune and the popularity of his writings, he felt there was always room for improvement.

Bibliography

Books

Aaker, Everett. *Television Western Players of the Fifties: A Biographical Encyclopedia of All Regular Cast Members in Western Series 1949–1959.* Jefferson NC: McFarland, 1997.

Anderson, Christopher. *Hollywood TV: The Studio System in the Fifties.* Austin: University of Texas, 1994.

Blottner, Gene. *Universal-International Westerns 1947–1963: The Complete Filmography.* Jefferson, NC: McFarland, 2000.

Brooks, Tim, and Earle Marsh. *The Complete Directory to Prime Time Network and Cable TV Shows, 1946–Present.* New York: Ballantine, 1999.

Buscombe, Edward (ed.). *The BFI Companion to the Western.* New York: Atheneum, 1988.

Caesar, Gene. *King of the Mountain Men: The Life of Jim Bridger.* New York: E.P. Dutton, 1961.

Calder, Jenni. *There Must Be a Lone Ranger: The American West in Film and in Reality.* New York: Taplinger, 1974.

Callan, Michael Feeney. *Sean Connery.* New York: Stein and Day, 1983.

Capua, Michelangelo. *Yul Brynner: A Biography.* Jefferson, NC: McFarland, 2006.

Collins, James L. *Lawmen of the Old West.* New York: Franklin Watts, 1990.

Cotter, Bill. *The Wonderful World of Disney Television: A Complete History.* New York: Hyperion, 1997.

Davis, Ronald L. *Duke: The Life and Image of John Wayne.* Norman: University of Oklahoma, 1998.

Eliot, Marc. *Jimmy Stewart: A Biography.* New York: Harmony, 2006.

Evory, Ann (ed.). *Contemporary Authors: New Revision Series Volume 3.* Detroit: Gale Research, 1981.

Eyles, Allen. *The Western.* New York: A.S. Barnes, 1975.

Finstad, Suzanne. *Natasha: The Biography of Natalie Wood.* New York: Harmony, 2001.

Fujiwara, Chris. *Jacques Tourneur: The Cinema of Nightfall.* Jefferson, NC: McFarland, 1998.

Gale, Robert. *Louis L'Amour: Revised Edition.* New York: Twayne, 1992.

Garfield, Brian. *Western Films.* New York: Rawson, 1982.

Griggs, John. *The Films of Gregory Peck.* Secaucus, N.J.: Citadel, 1984.

Hall, Hal W. *The Work of Louis L'Amour: An Annotated Bibliography.* San Bernardino, CA: Borgo, 1991.

Harris, Warren G. *Sophia Loren: A Bibliography.* New York: Simon & Schuster, 1998.

Henry, Marilyn, and Ron DeSourdis. *The Films of Alan Ladd.* Secaucus, NJ: Citadel, 1981.

Hitt, Jim. *The American West from Fiction (1823–1976) into Film (1909–1986).* Jefferson, NC: McFarland, 1990.

Hunter, Tab, with Eddie Muller. *Tab Hunter Confidential: The Making of a Movie Star.* Chapel Hill, NC: Algonquin, 2005.

International Dictionary of Films and Filmmakers. Vol. 2: Directors. 1984. *Vol. 3: Actors and Actresses.* 1986. *Vol. 4: Writers and Production Artists.* 1987. Detroit: St. James/Gale.

Jackson, Carlton. *Zane Grey: Revised Edition.* Boston: Twayne, 1989.

Jackson, Ronald. *Classic TV Westerns.* Secaucus, NJ: Citadel, 1994.

Krafsur, Richard P. (executive ed.). *The American Film Institute Catalog: Feature Films, 1961–70.* New York: R.R. Bowker, 1976.

Lamar, Howard R. (ed.). *The New Encyclopedia of the American West.* New Haven, CT: Yale University, 1998.

L'Amour, Angelique (compiler). *A Trail of Mem-*

ories: The Quotations of Louis L'Amour. New York: Bantam, 1988.

L'Amour, Louis. *The Broken Gun.* New York: Bantam, 1966.

_____. *The Burning Hills.* New York: Bantam, 1956.

_____. *Catlow.* New York: Bantam, 1963.

_____. *The Cherokee Trail.* New York: Bantam, 1982.

_____. *The Collected Short Stories of Louis L'Amour: The Frontier Stories, Vol. 1.* New York: Bantam, 2003.

_____. *The Collected Short Stories of Louis L'Amour: The Frontier Stories, Vol. 2.* New York: Bantam, 2004.

_____. *The Collected Short Stories of Louis L'Amour: The Frontier Stories, Vol. 3.* New York: Bantam, 2005.

_____. *Conagher.* New York: Bantam, 1969.

_____. *Crossfire Trail.* New York: Bantam, 1983.

_____. *The Daybreakers.* New York: Bantam, 1960.

_____. *Down the Long Hills.* New York: Bantam, 1968.

_____. *Education of a Wondering Man.* New York: Bantam, 1989.

_____. *End of the Drive.* New York: Bantam, 1997.

_____. *Frontier.* New York: Bantam, 1984.

_____. *Guns of the Timberlands.* New York: Bantam, 1955.

_____. *Heller with a Gun.* New York: Bantam, 1962.

_____. *The Iron Marshal.* New York: Bantam, 1979.

_____. *Kid Rodelo.* New York: Bantam, 1966.

_____. *Kilkenny.* New York: Bantam, 1983.

_____. *Last Stand at Papago Wells.* New York: Bantam, 1986.

_____. *The Lonely Men.* New York: Bantam, 1969.

_____. *The Man Called Noon.* New York: Bantam, 1970.

_____. *May There Be a Road.* New York: Bantam, 2001.

_____. *Off the Mangrove Coast.* New York: Bantam, 2000.

_____. *The Outlaws of Mesquite.* New York: Bantam, 1990.

_____. *The Quick and the Dead.* New York: Bantam, 1973.

_____. *The Rider of the Ruby Hills.* New York: Bantam, 1986.

_____. *Sackett.* New York: Bantam, 1961.

_____. *The Sackett Brand.* New York: 1965.

_____. *The Sackett Companion: A Personal Guide to the Sackett Novels.* New York: Bantam, 1988.

_____. *The Shadow Riders.* New York: Bantam, 1982.

_____. *Shalako.* New York: Bantam, 1962.

_____. *The Sixth Shotgun.* New York: Leisure, 2005.

_____. *Taggart.* New York: Bantam, 1959.

_____. *The Tall Stranger.* New York: Bantam, 1986.

_____. *The Trail to Crazy Man.* New York: Bantam, 1986.

_____. *Treasure Mountain.* New York: Bantam, 1972.

_____. *Utah Blaine.* New York: Bantam, 1983.

_____. *Valley of the Sun.* New York: Bantam, 1995.

_____. *West of Dodge.* New York: Bantam, 1996.

_____. *Where the Long Grass Blows.* New York: Bantam, 1976.

Lentz, Harris M., III. *Television Western Episode Guide: All United States Series, 1949–1996.* Jefferson, NC: McFarland, 1997.

_____. *Western and Frontier Film and Television Credits, 1903–1995. Vol. 1: Actors and Actresses; Directors, Producers and Writers. Vol. 2: Film Index; Television Index.* Jefferson, N.C.: McFarland, 1996.

Linet, Beverly. *Ladd: The Life, the Legend, the Legacy of Alan Ladd.* New York: Arbor House, 1979.

Marill, Alvin H. *The Films of Anthony Quinn.* Secaucus, NJ: Citadel, 1975.

_____. *Movies Made for Television, 1964–2004. Vol. 1, 1964–1979. Vol. 2, 1980–1989. Vol. 3, 1990–1999. Vol. 4, 2000–2004. Vol. 5, Index.* Lanham, MD: Scarecrow, 2005.

Mart, John. *Read the High Country: A Guide to Western Books and Films.* Englewood, CT: Libraries Unlimited, 2006.

Marx, Arthur. *The Secret Life of Bob Hope.* New York: Barricade, 1993.

McCaffrey, Donald W. *The Road to Comedy: The Films of Bob Hope.* CT: Praeger, 2005.

Moritz, Charles (ed.). *Current Biography 1980*. New York: H.W. Wilson, 1980.
Murdoch, David Hamilton. *The American West: The Invention of a Myth*. Reno: University of Nevada, 2001.
Murray, Aaron R. (ed.). *Civil War Battles and Leaders*. New York: DK Publishing, 2006.
Nash, Jay Robert. *Encyclopedia of Western Lawmen & Outlaws*. New York: Paragon House, 1992.
_____, and Stanley Ralph Ross (eds.). *The Motion Picture Guide. A–B, C–D*. 1985. *E–G, H–K, L–M, N–R*. 1986. *S, T–V, W–Z*. 1987. Detroit: St. James/Gale.
Nott, Robert. *Last of the Cowboy Heroes: The Westerns of Randolph Scott, Joel McCrea and Audie Murphy*. Jefferson, NC: McFarland, 2000.
O'Neal, Bill. *Encyclopedia of Western Gunfighters*. Norman: University of Oklahoma, 1979.
Parkinson, Michael, and Clyde Jeavons. *A Pictorial History of Westerns*. London: Homlyn, 1972.
Pfeiffer, Lee. *The John Wayne Scrapbook*. Secaucus, NJ: Citadel, 1991.
_____, and Philip Lisa. *The Films of Sean Connery*. Secaucus, NJ: Citadel, 1993.
Phillips, Gene D. *George Cukor*. Boston: Twayne, 1982.
Phillips, Robert. *Louis L'Amour: His Life and Trails*. New York: Knightsbridge, 1990.
Quinlan, David. *Quinlan's Character Stars*. London: Reynolds & Hearn, 2004.
Robbins, Jhan. *Yul Brynner: The Inscrutable King*. New York: Dodd, Mead, 1983.
Roud, Karen L., Jean W. Ross and Richard Ziegfield. *Dictionary of Literary Biography Yearbook 1980*. Detroit: Gale Research, 1981.
Server, Lee. *Encyclopedia of Pulp Fiction Writers*. New York: Facts on File, 2002.
Sharp, Michael D. (ed.). *Popular Contemporary Writers, Vol. 8*. New York: Marshall Cavendish, 2006.
Smith, Dave. *Disney A to Z: The Updated Official Encyclopedia*. New York: Hyperion, 1998.
Terrace, Vincent. *Encyclopedia of Television Series, Pilots and Specials: 1937–1973*. New York: New York Zoetrope, 1986.
Thomas, Tony. *Joel McCrea: Riding the High Country*. Burbank, CA: Riverwood, 1991.
Tibballs, Geoff. *The Boxtree Encyclopedia of TV Detectives*. London: Boxtree Limited, 1992.
Tuska, Jon, and Vicki Piekarski. *The Frontier Experience: A Reader's Guide to the Life and Literature of the American West*. Jefferson, NC: McFarland, 1984.
Tweton, D. Jerome, and Theodore B. Jelliff. *North Dakota: The Heritage of a People*. Fargo: North Dakota Institute for Regional Studies, 1976.
Utley, Robert M. *The Indian Frontier: 1846–1890*. Albuquerque: University of New Mexico, 2003.
Weinberg, Robert. *The Louis L'Amour Companion*. New York: Bantam, 1992.
Wexler, Bruce. *The Wild, Wild West of Louis L'Amour*. Philadelphia: Courage, 2005.
Wiley, Mason, and Damien Bona. *Inside Oscar: 10th Anniversary Edition*. New York: Ballantine, 1996.
Woolley, Lynn, Robert W. Malsbary and Robert G. Strange, Jr. *Warner Bros. Television*. Jefferson, NC: McFarland, 1985.

Selected Magazine and Newspaper Profiles

Brennan, Richard J. "Louis L'Amour: Prolific Teller of Western Tales." *Christian Science Monitor*, November 18, 1982.
Hubbell, John G. "Louis L'Amour — Storyteller of the Wild West." *Reader's Digest*, July 1980.
L'Amour, Louis. "How Wild Was the Old West?" *TV Guide*, February 28, 1987.
Weber, Bruce. "The Provost of the Prairie Gallops On." *New York Times*, June 10, 1998.
Yagoda, Ben. "L'Amour Rides the Range." *Esquire*, March 13, 1979.

Selected Internet Sources

Afi.chadwyck.com
Galenet.galegroup.com
www.amazon.com
www.bumscorner.com
www.dvdtalk.com
www.IMDb.com
www.louislamour.com
www.TV.com

Index

Index

Index

Index

Index

Index

www.ingramcontent.com/pod-product-compliance
Lightning Source LLC
Chambersburg PA
CBHW081332090726
47907CB00011B/2455
9780786433360